DEATH IS THE ONE THAT GOT AWAY

BY

RANDALL J. FUNK

Published in the United States by Ghost Light Press, LLC

www.randalljfunk.com

ISBN: 978-1-7351016-9-9

Cover design by Ann McMan

First edition

Special Thanks to:

Samantha Papke, for her help in preparing the manuscript and for inadvertently giving me the title of this book.

Ann McMan, for her usual awesome work on the cover.

Kris Snow, for listening when I first created Lisa Cleary.

Everyone who has bought the previous Joe Davis books and helped me along on this adventure.

For Michelle, who helped me believe again.

CHAPTER ONE

DECEMBER, JUNIOR YEAR

I don't remember the first time I actually saw Lisa Cleary. She doesn't burst into my memory all at once. Instead, she emerges, slowly, from the mist. And once I see her clearly, the image remains indelible.

The first time she spoke to me, we were in the offices of The Bay Breeze, *the Porter's Bay High School newspaper. (Hey, I didn't name it.) I had been given an assignment to write an article about a recently deceased teacher I never much cared for. I was at a table in the middle of the office, cursing my luck, as annoyed high school juniors will do, when I heard a voice nearby.*

"You don't like the work?"

I knew her name was Lisa Cleary and that her family moved to Porter's Bay the previous summer. I wasn't sure where the family had moved from, but the sight of a small town on the north shore of Minnesota couldn't have been inspiring. I knew, vaguely, that Lisa threw herself into a ton of activities: yearbook, speech, drama, the school newspaper, etc. The cumulative effect was she was already as popular as I was (not that the bar was set high there). Her bright blue eyes looked at me through a pair of wire frame glasses. Her dark wavy hair was corralled into something resembling a ponytail, with stray hairs dropping over her eyes. She wore a plaid shirt over a white, long sleeve tee, ripped and faded blue jeans, and a pair of white sneakers. Her voice was direct and businesslike. The whole effect was like a punch in my chest. Or maybe I just remember it that way.

"I don't mind the work," I said, "I'm just not sure what to write."

We chatted about the teacher, Mr. Jacobson, then Lisa said, "You realize you might be missing the biggest part of the story?"

She went on to tell me the suspicious circumstances surrounding Mr. Jacobson's death: he hadn't been dressed for work (despite being found in a classroom), he had no history of heart trouble (despite having supposedly died of a heart attack), a coffee cup he always kept on his desk had gone missing (even then, I knew you don't separate someone from their favorite coffee mug). When I asked how she knew all this, Lisa looked at her thumbnail and said, "Just did some research." Then she gathered up her stuff and said, "I know, I'm a freak."

My voice stopped her before she could walk away. "I'm just impressed you did all that."

A corner of Lisa's mouth went up, slightly. "You are?"

Maybe that's when she knew she could trust me. Maybe that's what she needed: a co-conspirator. Whatever it was, Lisa brought me into her suspicion: Mr. Jacobson had been murdered. That was the story I was missing, the story I should write. I wasn't sure if I should believe her. I certainly couldn't write that story alone. Maybe she knew that all along. Whatever the case, I agreed to work with her.

And Lisa was right. Mr. Jacobson had been murdered. Finding that out wasn't easy. We questioned suspicious teachers, almost got caught breaking into Mr. Jacobson's house, were almost shot by a gun-toting redneck, and had to blackmail a disreputable classmate in order to set a trap for the murderer. Along the way, I was amazed by Lisa's tenacity and intelligence. She was a born reporter. I was pulled along in her wake. Eventually, we set a trap for the person we suspected was the murderer. As we sat in a darkened classroom in the high school, she slipped me a look and said, "It's been fun."

It had to be acknowledged that Lisa had a funny sense of fun. But I agreed with her. It had been fun.

The murderer walked into our trap. (Although, it turned out to be a little more complicated than that.) A chase and a tense standoff ensued. We got some help from my best friends, Sam and Andy, and managed to corral the murderer. The only thing left was to call the police, which we did from the Bay Breeze *offices. After placing the call, Lisa looked at me, her eyes wild and her glasses askew.*

"We did it," she said.

"We did."

"We pulled it off. I mean, we actually got the story."

"We did."

Lisa threw her arms around me, and we both laughed. A few minutes earlier, we had been wondering if we were even going to be alive, and now here we were, ready to write this incredible story. It was crazy and absurd and wonderful all at the same time.

Then we realized we'd been hugging for nearly a minute.

Lisa broke away, her face slightly red. I stared at the floor. After a few seconds, Lisa regained her air of command and laid out a plan for talking to the police and writing the story that night. She suggested we go to the Hub Diner and grab some coffee to help fuel us. I dragged my feet a little.

"I, uh, I don't even like coffee," I said.

Lisa smiled. "I'll have to cure you of that." Then she led the way out the door.

My name is Joe Davis. That's how that story starts. This is how this one starts.

"Music be the food of love," my friend Lars says, his long fingers wrapped around a pint of coal black ale. "Paul McCartney said that."

"Shakespeare said that," I tell him.

Lars's head snaps back, his quasi-pompadour flapping in the breeze. "Are you sure?"

"As a fan of both The Beatles and Shakespeare," I say, "you can take my word on this."

His horse face tightens. He turns to Mike and Carol, as if to say *look at Mr. Big Shot here.* They can only roll their eyes and bury themselves in their own beverages.

The four of us are seated at a high-top table in the corner of our favorite watering hole, The Tav. It's been my go-to location since I first moved into the neighborhood seven years ago. It's on Selby Avenue, just down the street from the St. Paul Cathedral and a stone's throw from downtown St. Paul (if anyone hung out after hours in St. Paul to actually throw a stone). The Tav is a combination pub and sports bar, featuring a lot of quaint decorations, high-top tables and big screen TVs. It draws clientele from both the blue collar and artistic denizens of the Cathedral Hill neighborhood. Tonight, the place is busy. It's Saturday night and a Golden Gophers football game draws the attention of the patrons, particularly Freddie, the bouncer whose cheers register on the Richter Scale. My table, however, remains indifferent to the game.

Carol turns her piercing blue eyes on Lars. "I understand needing to save a buck on the movie," she says, "but you really can't score this thing yourself."

Lars props a pipe cleaner arm on the table. "And why not?"

"For starters," Carol says, "and please don't take this the wrong way: you have no musical talent. *None.*"

I sit back. "Prosecution rests, your honor."

Lars swings toward our friend Mike and waves a flipper-like hand at Carol and me. "Are you hearing this?"

Mike tries to hide his big bulldog head behind a pint of India Pale Ale (a fool's errand). "I'm trying not to."

Lars's arm drops to the table. He no doubt feels ganged up on, even if Mike and Carol are largely indifferent to our little argument. He drums his fingers on the table, unable to find a consistent rhythm.

"I don't think I have to explain this to you, Joe," Lars says, thus indicating he is about to explain this to me. "Music is the key to any film. It sets the tone. It guides the audience's emotions. Even the lack of it is a statement."

"I'm starting to like that *lack of it* idea," I say.

Lars slaps the table and returns to his adult beverage. I should probably explain what's going on. About six months ago, Lars managed to talk two wealthy (if more than slightly clueless) siblings into backing a film venture. He recruited me to write the script, and against my better judgment, I accepted on the condition I could be a producer and have a say in what was going on. Lars was agreeable to these terms. It was probably the last thing we've agreed on.

"Look, brother, I appreciate your concerns," Lars says, "But we have to find places to save money. Ever since Ollie was brought on board, the budget keeps growing."

Carol brushes back the dark hair flowing past her shoulders. "Who's Ollie?"

"The director," Lars says, practically spitting out the words.

Lars's bitterness is understandable, if misplaced. He harbored ambitions of actually directing the movie. So, you can understand his dismay when Frankie and Fabio (the trust fund babies who are bankrolling us) brought Ollie to our last meeting and announced he was the film's director. Lars taps the table in front of me.

"I'd be on the lookout, brother," he says. "I don't think Ollie is going to like the script."

"What makes you say that?" I ask.

"I talked to him on the phone. He didn't seem sold on our plot idea."

That gets my hackles up. I may be new to screenwriting, but I make my living as a writer. I'm a thrice-weekly columnist for *The Daily Bugle*, an independent newspaper that became an independent website when the hippies in charge realized they could save money by eliminating printing costs. My column, *Cup o' Joe*, covers all manner of things—entertainment, social mores, politics, sports, philosophy, what have you—all with the same depth and conviction one finds in an episode of *Tiny Toons*. But it (barely) pays my bills and affords me a weenie bit of local celebrity. Why, in the face of that, would Ollie be so bold as to criticize my work?

"It's a combination vampire and heist movie," I say. "Which part doesn't Ollie like, the vampires or the heist?"

"He doesn't sound thrilled with either," Lars says. "He thinks the heist plot is implausible and the vampire story lacks eroticism."

"Lacks eroticism?" I say, my face getting warm. "It's as erotic as shit."

Lars holds up his hands. "I'm just the messenger."

Carol twists her mouth to one side. "Maybe I can read it. Give you some suggestions."

It's not a bad idea. Carol makes her living as an ad writer, one of the better ones you'll find. But I'm too preoccupied with Ollie's objections to my script to give her my full attention.

"Does *Ollie* have any suggestions?" I ask.

"Not yet, but they're coming," Lars says. "Apparently, he's made a number of short films. All of them are high concept and visually spectacular. And cost an arm and a leg. Already he's asking for more spectacular action scenes and a larger crew. That's why I'm putting myself forward as the composer of the score."

Mike looks up from his Grand Brewing Oktoberfest. "You don't play any instruments."

Lars wags a long finger. "You stand corrected, mien Freund. I currently have a sideline business designing scores for the cinema."

That brings the conversation to a halt. Lars treats this information, as he tends to do, as if it's something we all should know. He believes he's more of a public figure than he actually is. As far as I know, the extent of his notoriety is being the superintendent of my building.

"What the hell are you talking about?" I ask.

Lars takes on a superior air. "Our friend The Wheeze got me involved. He has a sideline business running a website that dabbles in the entertainment industry."

The Wheeze is a longtime buddy of ours. He runs a comic book store that's still frequented by Mike and Lars. I haven't collected comics in years, so usually, I only see The Wheeze at his annual birthday party (which can be held anywhere between January and December, since no one— possibly including The Wheeze—knows the actual date of his birth). Beyond that, I know very little about him. It comes as a surprise, although it really shouldn't, that he has a sideline business.

"What kind of entertainment?" I ask.

"They are self-funded independent adult features for the discerning cinephile," Lars says.

Carol skates the verbiage faster than the rest. "The Wheeze is pedaling porno films?"

Lars flinches, as if stung. "Carol, please. *Porno* is such an outdated term. These are erotic films made by spirited amateurs from a variety of ages, backgrounds, and sexual kinks."

"Uh-huh," I say. "And where can we find these cinematic classics?"

"Bangshangalang.com," Lars says.

The reaction around the table varies. Carol puts a hand over her face. I take a larger-than-average sip of my Oktoberfest. Mike's brown eyes light up.

"Then you *are* a musician," Mike says.

Lars waggles his eyebrows (which always look as if they're about to leave his face and go into business for themselves). "Not a lot of musical skill needed, brother. As long as you have a bass guitar and a Casio keyboard, you're in business."

Ah. That solves *Nancy Drew and the Mystery of the Bass Guitar Coming through My Floorboards*. I'll have to thank The Wheeze the next time I see him (perhaps by urinating on the floor of his store).

"That's all well and good," I say, "but I don't think those skills are going to translate to the movie we're making."

Lars's face falls. "You mean the movie *Ollie* is making. As long as he's got Frankie's and Fabio's ears, he'll be running the show."

Well, that casts a bit of a pall over the evening (not that we weren't palled up already). We finish our drinks and call it a night. Carol huddles into her trench coat and flutters her fingers at us as she walks to her car. It's only about five blocks back to my building, so I walk. Lars, never ambitious when it comes to exercise, chooses to drive. He offers me a ride home, but I decline. Mike lingers, hoping to chat with me.

"You going anywhere now?" I ask, half considering asking Mike to back to my place for one more beer.

"Going to hook up with Gillian," he says.

That will certainly take priority over my offer. Gillian is Mike's latest girlfriend. I haven't met her, but so far the reviews are positive. She seems like a nice person. Why Gillian wants to date a man-child with no money and fewer prospects is, perhaps, more of a mystery.

"Things still going well there?" I ask.

"Absolutely," Mike says, a little too quickly. "Just great."

"You sure about that?"

He runs a hand through the brush of brown hair atop his Cro-Magnon forehead. "It's just… I don't know. I told you Gillian has a twin sister, right?"

"I do recall."

"I've only met Moira—that's the twin—a couple of times. But Gillian constantly talks about this twin bond they have, how she trusts Moira more than anybody else. We were hanging out with Moira the other night, and she wasn't all that friendly."

"Maybe she's shy."

"I don't think that's it," Mike says, chewing a corner of his goatee. "She was okay the first time I met her. This time, she was kind of standoffish. I don't think she likes me."

"So? You're dating Gillian, not Moira."

"But if Moira doesn't like me, she's going to say something to Gillian. Then the whole relationship will be fucked."

"Did you say something that might have set her off?" I ask.

"No. I was as friendly as fuck. I think Moira just gets a bad vibe from me."

"And the fact she is totally justified in getting a bad vibe from you...?"

Mike gives me the stink eye. I'm being hard on him, but I'm not wrong. Mike and I have been best friends since we met at student orientation at Adams College. He was a military brat, having grown up under the collective thumb of two controlling parents. When he got to college and discovered he was no longer under adult supervision, he went on the kind of rampage that would have resulted in Attila kicking him out of the Huns for being too toxic. He hasn't changed much since.

"I don't want to screw up anything with Gillian," Mike says. "She's awesome. Sweet, funny, sensitive, uninhibited in the sack. And it's gonna get ruined unless I figure out a way to cozy up to her twin sister. You got any suggestions?"

"I'd have to meet the ladies in question first."

Mike's eyes light up. "You might be on to something there. Maybe we can arrange a little get-together. Sort of like a quasi-double date. Did I use *quasi* right?"

"Your diploma will be in the mail."

"What do you think?"

"Let me think about it."

Mike frowns. "That means you're not going to do it, and you're just buying time."

Damn. My mom always used *Let me think about it* and it took me nearly thirty years to figure out that always meant *No*. Mike's known me for half that time and has already figured out the bullshit. Mental note: cultivate new, more ignorant friends.

"I will genuinely think about," I say. "That's all I can do for now."

Mike isn't satisfied, but he accepts it as an answer. We say our goodbyes, and I start walking home, huddling into my peacoat to fight the chilly breeze.

My parents regard the Twin Cities as one giant den of iniquity; this largely rooted in the provincialism of spending their entire lives in a small town in northern Minnesota. My neighborhood may be near downtown St. Paul, but with its tree-lined streets, old houses, and brown brick apartment buildings, it's positively cozy. The trees form a canopy of red, yellow, and orange visible above the streetlights. Leaves carpet the sidewalks and blow listlessly in the street. Minnesota autumn in full bloom.

I think about Mike's offer of a double date, even if it's a sham double date. Maybe I should take him up on it. It's not as if the last year or so has been the greatest time in my dating life. There have been a few excursions here and there: a disastrous encounter with a woman I knew in college (don't ask), a one-night stand with a contract killer (*really* don't ask), and recently, a weekend with a woman named Charley, who was largely using me to get back at her wastrel boyfriend. (I realized that was the case and was fine with it.) Still, nothing steady. What's more concerning: I haven't been all that interested. I'm thirty-five and might be descending into boring, celibate middle age. There's a pleasant thought.

I exit Oakland Avenue and jaywalk across Summit Avenue, a thoroughfare lined with spectacular homes, once dubbed by F. Scott Fitzgerald *a museum of architectural failures.* (And yet, here in Minnesota, we celebrate his bitter, drunken ass. Speaking of provincialism…) My apartment is on the third floor of a converted row house near the intersection of Summit and Dale. I can either go in through the front or stroll around the back and climb the erector set of stairs and decks that lead to my backdoor. The front is the shortest route. When I step into the foyer, someone is standing there. That's not an unusual sight. People frequently lurk about, either waiting for a tenant to join them or waiting for a tenant to come out so they can slip inside. (This is a security building in name only.) *Who* is waiting, though, is the unusual part.

I come to a halt. "Rick?"

He tosses up a hand by way of greeting. "Good to see you again, Joe."

Rick Michaels was a friend of mine in high school. Not a close friend, but a good dude to hang out with. Rick was an unusual case. He was a three-sport athlete who didn't much care to hang out with the jocks. He seemed more interested in the company of geeks like me who were into theatre, speech, and writing. He came back into my life again, briefly, last spring when he dated Carol for a few weeks. They made a handsome couple, but the relationship foundered when I accidentally relayed some sexual TMI about Carol. (Information I got from Mike, since Carol, to her everlasting regret, once dated him.) I won't say Rick is the last person I expected to find loitering in my foyer, but he's certainly in the running.

I tuck my hands into my jacket pockets, "What's going on?"

"Just wanted to visit," he says. "I tried buzzing, but you weren't home. Thought I'd wait."

Rick looks a lot like he did back in the day: brown hair, blue eyes, square jaw. He's put on a pound or two, but he wears it well. He still moves with an athlete's easy grace. Frankly, though, he's looked better than he does at this moment. The hair is a little shaggy, he could use a shave, and his clothes look as if they've been slept in. His eyes keep cutting past me, toward the street. I guess my parents aren't the only ones who get nervous in this neighborhood.

I unlock the front door. "Come on up. We can grab a beer."

"Sounds good," Rick says, relief in his voice.

We head up to the third floor. My apartment is a simple affair. The living room features my desk in one corner and three arch windows at the front. A breakfast bar serves as the dividing line between the living room and my sliver of a kitchen. A hallway at the back leads to the deck, passing the single bedroom and bathroom en route. I set my keys in an ashtray on the table next to the door. (The ashtray is used only for that purpose since I don't smoke.) My cats, Lenny and Squiggy, make their way out of the bedroom to greet us. They sniff Rick suspiciously. Since he isn't food and isn't likely to provide food, they turn their attention back to me. I toss some kibble in their bowls and grab a couple of Oktoberfests from the fridge. When I get back to the living room, Rick still hasn't removed his black coat. He takes the beer and thanks me with a nod.

"Nice place," he says. "You lived here long?"

"About seven years," I say. Geez, that's starting to sound like a long time.

"I've got a place downtown. Gives me easy access to the Senator's office."

That's right. When last I saw Rick, he was working for Senator Bill Longson, a guy whose political views lean just to the right of Genghis Khan. Longson is currently running for re-election, likely as a precursor to a presidential run. His brand of angry populism has drawn enough support from the rural areas and the suburbs that he is sadly leading in the polls. God help us all.

"How's that going?" I ask, mumbling into my beer.

"Good," Rick says, without much conviction. "Pay is good."

I grab a seat at my desk. "What is it you do for the Senator?"

"A little of this and that. Mostly I'm a glorified errand boy."

"But it's working out?"

"Kind of. Things don't always work out like we hope."

"How do you mean?"

"Nothing."

Rick keeps looking past me and out the arch windows. I glance over my shoulder, wondering if something is going on in the street. No sign of trouble (or even a person out there, to be honest). I turn back to my guest.

"What brings you by, Rick?" I ask.

He tears himself away from the window. "Do you know how to get ahold of Lisa?"

That hits me like a sucker-punch. I know Rick didn't intend it that way, but it's the effect, nonetheless. I'm tempted to ask *Lisa Cleary?* But there is no other Lisa he'd ask me about. It takes a second for the fog to clear.

"If you look up one of her articles on the Metro Communications site, it probably has her contact info," I say.

"No, sorry. I need to get ahold of her personally. It's…a business thing. I don't want anyone else knowing about it."

"Okay," I say, "but I'm not sure how to do that."

"You guys don't talk?"

"We chat on Facebook every now and again. I think the last time we did that was almost two years ago."

"You don't ever see her?"

"No. Last time was…about sixteen years ago." Geez, *that* is starting to sound like a long time ago.

Rick frowns. "Then I guess you don't have her number."

I start to answer in the negative, then stop. I spin the chair around to face the desk. Like the rest of the apartment, it's spotless and organized. I've acquired a reputation as a neat freak, and I can't help disagreeing. I don't do what I do out of compulsion. I do it because I need a neat area in which to write. (Orderly space, orderly mind.) The advantage in this case is that I find my address book in short order. I page through it.

"This is a number Lisa gave me," I say, showing it to Rick so he can put it in his phone. "It was around the time of that last Facebook chat. I don't know if it's still good or not."

"I guess I'll find out," Rick says. He slips his phone into his pocket. "Thanks, man. I appreciate it."

"I hope it works out." I try to be nonchalant. "What do you need to talk to Lisa about?"

"Nothing big. Nothing I want to get you involved in. I'm sorry, that's a really shitty explanation. Just…something I need to talk to her about."

I'll give him credit. It's the nicest *Mind your own damn business* I've ever gotten. I'm tempted to press him further, but I still feel guilty about his breakup with Carol. I let it go. Rick plunks down on the arm on the futon and takes a half-hearted sip of his beer.

"It's too bad you guys don't stay in touch," Rick says. "You made a nice couple."

"That's what I hear. You and Carol made a nice couple. I'm sorry that didn't work out."

He shrugs. "Shit happens, I guess."

"I was up in Porter's Bay last summer, for my dad's retirement. I gave Carol a tour of the high school. Showed her the trophy case."

Rick's body sags. "The picture."

Everyone in my hometown of Porter's Bay knows the name *Rick Michaels*. While his overall playing career for the Porter's Bay Cardinals might not have been the stuff of his legend, he had one moment that was. He scored the game-winning goal—in overtime, no less—to bring Porter's Bay the state hockey championship. And not just any goal. A goal that still gets hits on YouTube as one of the greatest ever scored. I half-expect the city fathers in Porter's Bay will eventually build a statue of the image in front of the Memorial Arena. Rick Michaels flying through the air, his body perpendicular to the ice, slapping a rebound past the goalie for St. Patrick's Academy. It would be based on the picture sitting next to the state championship trophy in the high school trophy case.

"She thought it was cool," I say, wondering if I'm on dangerous ground.

"That's nice." Rick picks at the label of his beer bottle. "I never talked to her about it."

"It was your choice," I say. "Sorry I outed you on it."

He flips a hand at that. "No big deal." Rick sets the beer bottle on the coffee table and stands. "I should probably get going. Sorry for barging in."

"Don't be. It was good to see you. We should get together soon. Go out for a beer."

"That would be nice." He looks down the hallway. "Can I go out that way? Through the backdoor?"

"Yeah. Just take the stairs down and cross the parking lot. The alley takes you to Dale."

We walk down the hallway to the backdoor. There are two steps up to the door itself. Rick rests a foot on the step. He faces at the door as he speaks.

"You know scoring that goal was the best thing I ever did in my life?" he says.

"It made you a legend."

"Funny thing about being a legend. It doesn't pay your rent. Doesn't give you a job you actually like doing. Doesn't come in handy for much of anything, really."

I'm not sure what to say. There was a time, however brief, when I would have loved to be in Rick Michaels's shoes.

I never dreamed they wouldn't fit him all that comfortably. I fumble for a response.

"It means a lot to a lot of people," I say.

"I guess. Problem is, you have to live up to it. Whatever *it* is. "

"But you seem successful now."

Rick scoffs. "*Seem*. That was all my old man ever wanted. He just wanted to seem successful to everyone. He wanted to show off. Maybe that's why he traded in me and my mom. Like buying a more stylish suit. He had to keep up appearances." Rick runs a hand over his coat. "Guess I'm not any better. You want people to think you made something of yourself. Gets easy to sell your soul for a thing like that." He sighs. "There's got to be more to it than that, right? You've got to do the right thing. No matter what." He must realize he's been rambling. "At any rate, thanks for the phone number. Take care."

He opens the door. I stop him before he can leave. "What's going on, Rick? Are you okay?"

Rick debates an answer. After a few moments, he claps me on the shoulder and says, "Thanks for the beer."

I sputter out a goodbye but deliver most of it to the door. I wonder if I should call Rick back and say something. Nothing comes to mind. I lock the door and walk back to the living room. I pick up Rick's half-empty beer bottle and put it in the trash.

***

It's three days later and I'm finishing my work. I give the article I've completed one more looksee, hit *Send*, and move it along to my editor, Lance, at *The Daily Bugle*. It's almost two o'clock and my workday is done. After starting at noon. Ah, the rat race.

I finish the last of the sandwich I made to help power me through my workday (turkey, whole wheat bread, a little mayo, a little spicy mustard, lettuce and tomato, pickle spear on the side). I carry the plate to the dishwasher. It's a gray and blustery day outside, which must be impacting my mood. (Unlike the sounds of Lars's bass guitar coming from downstairs, which just pisses me off.)

Rick's unannounced visit has been on my mind. I keep, perhaps illogically, expecting him to contact me. Yes, we said something about grabbing beers sometime and that would be nice. But moreover, I'm curious about what's going on with his day job. I can't help thinking that's what was on his mind when he stopped over the other night.

Why else would he want to contact Lisa? Sure, there are the usual reasons a straight male would wish to contact a straight female, but I don't think those apply here. Lisa lives in New York (when she lives anywhere at all). That's a long way to go for a date. If it's about some kind of publicity or photo op, Rick wouldn't be so secretive about it. What does he want with Lisa?

I go to the internet and gather some information about Rick's boss. Senator Bill Longson inherited money from his father, who started a lumber company, then expanded his interests into iron ore and real estate. Longson took this fortune and gambled on real estate, picking up large sums of money on increasingly dubious investments, always managing to get out with a good amount of cash before the whole enterprise went belly up. Somewhere along the way, he developed a love of publicity. He made appearances on radio shows and talk shows, promoting various get-rich-quick schemes. A guy who inherited enough money to make chancy investments was somehow a guru on fiscal management.

Somewhere along the way, Longson also developed an interest in politics. He cultivated friends from both major parties and described himself as politically independent. As he drifted closer to becoming an active candidate, he grew chummier with the Republican Party, frequently appearing at fundraisers for various local candidates. He began to espouse a form of populism that exploited the worst instincts of working-class people who were not evolving with the world around them. Free trade had given away America's greatness. Immigrants were pouring in, taking our jobs. Minorities were promoters of crime, destabilizing the country. Jewish bankers allowed all this to happen in order to maintain their control of the money supply. The LGBTQIA+ community was an affront to traditional values, weakening the fiber that built America. According to Longson, the press was complicit, painting special interest groups as victims while the real victims—hardworking Americans—found their cause ignored. They now had a savior in Bill Longson.

Longson caught a break, of sorts, when Senator Mark Gardner, a Democrat, was killed in a plane crash. The crash was later discovered to be an act of sabotage, caused by a bomb planted by a domestic terrorism group called Sons of the Soil. The leader of the group, Jeremiah Kincade, was arrested by the FBI and later executed. Gardner's widow was appointed to fill his seat until a special election could be held. Bill Longson was considered a long shot when he first entered the race. However, he had a solid base of support among far-right yahoos and as each of the front runners imploded, Longson became the man to beat. He managed to narrowly defeat the Democratic lieutenant governor to reach the Senate.

Many (nearly a majority) viewed Longson's political rise as an embarrassment and a harbinger of doom. Indeed, in four years in the U.S. Senate, Longson has shown more gift for demeaning invective than meaningful legislation. But his gift for self-promotion has helped him find audiences in other states. In fact, until the re-election campaign ramped up, it was rare to find Bill Longson *in* the state he represents in Congress. Still, the legitimacy of incumbency has helped him take a solid lead in the polls. The election is still a month off, but local Democrats are despairing about their chances of getting rid of Longson. Once he wins, it will only be a matter of time before he announces his presidential campaign. And then God knows what will happen.

Rick has been working for Longson for about a year-and-a-half, according to what he told me when he was dating Carol. While not being in sympathy with Longson's political views, Rick has been very well compensated. Beyond that, and his comment about being an errand boy, I don't really know what Rick does for the Senator. Maybe I need to ask him.

There's a knock at my front door. That's startling, but not unusual. As I've said, my building is secure unless someone can catch an open door or a trusting tenant (which is frequent). My friends get by the building's front door as often as not. I hop up from the desk and get the door, wondering who it could be.

I flip open the door. And when I see who's there, a thunderbolt goes through my chest.

Lisa gives me a shy smile. "Hi, Joe."

CHAPTER TWO

FEBRUARY, JUNIOR YEAR

The story of Mr. Jacobson's murder was written in early December and yet I didn't immediately ask Lisa out. I sometimes wondered if I was ever *going to ask her. Even with all we had been through in getting the story, I was still intimidated by her. How could I not be? Lisa was funny and composed and confident. She knew everything that was going on in the news and generally had a wisecrack about or an opinion on everything she read. At lunch, she was inclined to sit by herself and read a collection of Flannery O'Conner short stories. She could quote Monty Python sketches and lines from* The Simpsons *off the top of her head. She gave off an air that she didn't care what people thought of her. She wasn't confrontational. She just had the kind of self-awareness and self-esteem you don't generally find in someone who wasn't quite seventeen yet. Or really, most people at any age.*

Instead of asking Lisa out, I hung around the Bay Breeze *offices and chatted with her practically every afternoon. During one of these sessions, in the first week of February, Lisa looked up from a page she was proofreading and said, "Are you going to ask me out or what?"*

Well, since she put it that way…

Our first date was a late afternoon movie followed by dinner at Arthur's Diner, my favorite after school hangout. Looking back, it wasn't the fanciest first date, but we lived in a small town, and I had a limited budget. Lisa didn't have any complaints, though. We chatted easily before and after the movie. (But not during, I appreciated that about her). The conversation continued at Arthur's, and I tried to tamp down my excitement. ("This is going really well!" screamed an inner voice. Thank you, voice, just make sure that thought doesn't show up on my face.) While we ate, the topic of conversation turned to music.

"Anything you like right now?" Lisa asked.

"I like 'Broken China Doll.' Soul Driver. That's the band, right?"

A french fry stopped just short of Lisa's mouth. "You like that song?"

For the first time in my dating life—but certainly not the last—I wondered what I had said wrong. "I just…I think it's kind of catchy."

"You haven't really listened to Soul Driver, have you?"

Truthfully, I knew nothing about the band. If someone told me they were a Billy Joel cover band prior to recording "Broken China Doll," I would have believed them. I could have tried bluffing my way through it, but somehow, I knew Lisa wouldn't buy it.

"No, I haven't really listened to Soul Driver," I said. "Just 'Broken China Doll.'"

A grin slid across Lisa's face. She tossed down the french fry and said, "Grab a to-go box. We're going back to my house. You're going to school."

We paid for dinner and rushed out to my car. Ten minutes later, we were back at Lisa's house. It was a two-story number with a front porch and stone steps. Lisa took my hand and led me through the foyer and into the living room. Her parents were in the living room, watching TV. Her dad was a stocky guy with stubby black hair. Her mom had wavy hair and a slightly plump figure. They barely looked up from the TV when Lisa stopped in the entrance to the living room.

"Mom and Dad, this is Joe. We're going up to my room to listen to some music."

Before either of them could answer, Lisa tugged my hand and led me up the stairs. Her room was the first one on the right. Her bed was on the far side of the room, just below the window. A checked comforter covered it and a large stereo system loomed at the foot. Lisa took off her oversized gray coat and tossed it over her desk chair.

"Just set your coat anywhere," she said. "And keep the door open. That way, my mom and dad won't bother us."

I did as instructed. Lisa sat cross-legged on her bed and waved me into a nearby chair. The room was warm and cozy. Framed articles lined the walls. The curtains were a little lacey and the posters on the wall exclusively featured the male gender. A plethora of stuffed animals gathered at the head of the bed. A poster of Soul Driver was tacked to the wall. Seventeen years old and this was the first time I had been in a girl's bedroom. Having grown up with two brothers, I was in completely foreign territory.

If it was any big deal to Lisa, she didn't show it. She turned to a stack of Soul Driver CDs on the bookshelf. They were separate from the others, as if they held a place of honor. I was close enough to pick up one of the CDs. It was titled River of Doubt.

"This looks interesting," I said.

Lisa gently took the CD from me. "No, no. Not yet. You have to walk before you can run."

She returned River of Doubt to the stack and took out one called Front Street. She handled the CDs as if they were precious. She popped it into her CD player then sat on her bed and crossed her legs like a Buddha. I noticed she was looking at me rather than the CD player. I withered under the scrutiny and looked at the floor. Then the music started.

It was a seminal moment. All the hours I've spent listening to Soul Driver (as well as solo albums by Steve Jones, the lead singer, and Brian Douglas, the guitar player) and this was the moment I really truly discovered them. The music came right at you: wailing guitar, rumbling bass, cascading drums; all setting the stage for the macho growl of the singer. The lyrics were Dylan-esque images spit at you by someone both bemused by and invested in the swirl of emotions around him. The band effortlessly kept up with vocals, like a distance runner not breathing too terribly hard. I had difficulty wrapping my head around this music. It was simple and raw. Just guitar, bass, drums, and vocals. It was timeless but didn't belong to any particular time. It was too edgy to be pop, too weird to be rock, too spontaneous to be progressive, too calculated to be punk. The band seemed to delight in taking every expectation they created and flipping it on its ear.

Every now and again, I caught sight of Lisa watching me and grinning. When the final number, "Front Street Trash," faded out, I found myself mumbling, "Holy crap." Lisa leaned toward me.

"You realize you said that at least once during every song?" she asked.

"Did I? Sorry, it's just…it's all I could think."

"Now you know why I'm not that crazy about by 'Broken China Doll'?"

"I totally get it." (Though, to Lisa's everlasting chagrin, I never stopped liking "Broken China Doll.") I reached for another CD. "Let's listen to this one."

Lisa nodded toward the open door; an indication of her parents downstairs. "It's getting kind of late. We can listen to it next time."

I have to confess: I was so cluelessly disappointed that I was halfway down the stairs before realizing I had just secured a second date. Lisa walked me to the front door and stepped onto the front porch with me. She had left her coat in her room, so she hugged herself, bracing against the February cold. I slipped my hands in my jacket pocket.

"I had fun," I said.

Lisa slipped a hand behind my head and gave me a peck on the lips. I was so caught off guard, I'm not sure if I remembered to close my eyes. The surprise showed on my face when we parted.

"Thank you," was all I could think to say.

Lisa met that with an embarrassed little laugh. "It's okay. You scored points tonight."

She stepped back inside, looking at me until the door closed. I skipped through the snow to my car, then drove home thinking about Lisa and humming every Soul Driver tune I could remember.

And now she was standing outside my apartment.

For a few seconds, I don't say anything. My heart is pounding in my ears. It is and isn't the Lisa I remember. The dark hair still flows past her shoulders, but it's been trimmed slightly and tamed. The wire-rim glasses are still there. Her blue eyes are still direct and penetrating. Her clothing is still unpretentious, just a brown suede coat over a simple blouse and a pair of jeans. A slightly battered laptop bag hangs over one shoulder. She bites the corner of her lip, an age-old sign of uncertainty that maybe only I can spot. Maybe.

"Can I come in?" Lisa asks.

That snaps me out of my reverie. "Of course. I'm sorry."

I step aside and let her into the apartment. She looks around as I close the door behind her. There's another silent second, then Lisa opens her arms.

"It's good to see you," she says.

We have a brief hug. Its slight awkwardness sends a shudder of sadness through me. Lisa runs a hand along the strap of her bag.

"I'm sorry to just drop by," she says. "I tried calling, but there was no answer."

"I always turn the ringer off when I'm working. Sometimes I forget to turn it back on."

A corner of Lisa's mouth rises. "*Cup o' Joe.* I always thought you'd wind up with something like that. At least, I hoped so."

"Pays the bills."

Lisa does a one-eighty turn, giving the room a fuller look. "This is a nice place. It's cozy." Her gaze returns to me. "You do *live* here, right? I mean, it's so spic and span."

"A thing I learned once: orderly place, orderly mind. I keep it this way so I can write."

"Mission accomplished."

There's another moment of silence, which I can't stand. Maybe Lisa and I had awkward silences back in the day, but I don't remember any.

"What brings you by?" I ask.

She slides the bag off her shoulder and sets it on the futon. "Have you talked to Rick Michaels lately?"

That stirs a bit of worry. "I just saw him Saturday night. He was waiting for me when I got home. He wanted your number. I gave it to him. I hope that that was okay."

"You haven't heard from him since?"

"No, I haven't. Why? Is something wrong?"

Lisa debates what—if anything—to tell me. She adjusts her glasses. "Rick called me and said he had something on Senator Longson. He wanted to know if I would come to Minnesota and talk to him about it. He assured me it would be worth my time."

"You flew all the way from New York for that?"

"No. I was in Chicago, wrapping something up. I have the time to come here."

"He couldn't tell you over the phone?"

"I asked him the same thing. He said it was something he had to show me."

"So, what happened?"

"We arranged to meet at a McDonald's in Forest Lake. It was supposed to be last night at six. He never showed. I've been trying to get ahold of him. His phone goes straight to voicemail." She sits on the arm of the futon. "Rick *did* mention that he got my number from you. It seemed worth a shot to talk with you."

I pick up my phone from the desk and check it. No calls from Rick. (I didn't expect any, but it's worth looking.) Just for the hell of it, I try his number. It goes straight to voicemail. I set the phone on the desk.

"Any idea what Rick had to show you?" I ask.

"I was going to ask you the same thing," Lisa says. "Did he mention anything when you saw him?"

I run the conversation through my head. "He said he didn't want to get me involved. He seemed down and…a little paranoid, maybe? I don't know. I could be reading too much into it."

"Then again, maybe you're not. I've been keeping an eye on Longson since the idea of him running for president got serious. His business and finance people don't want anyone coming near him. Longson refuses to disclose his tax returns or open his company's books."

"You think he's corrupt?"

"I think he's suspicious. I won't know about corrupt until I have proof." Lisa tilts her head slightly as she thinks. "Maybe that's what Rick had for me. I don't know."

"Whatever it was, it sounded serious. He didn't want to get me involved. That's not the kind of thing you tell someone if you're looking to do a story on how the Senator likes duckies and bunnies."

A corner of Lisa's mouth goes up. "And if that's the story you want written, you aren't going to come to me."

Before we can speculate further, my cats make an appearance. Lenny rubs up against Lisa's leg. Squiggy stands just behind him, a model of reserve and decorum. Lisa reaches down to pet them.

"Who do we have here?" she asks.

"The lords of the manor," I say.

Two cats, littermates, run my household: Lenny, a butterscotch tabby who's more stomach than brains; and Squiggy, the nervous former runt of the litter whose black-and-white coloring and obsequious manner puts me in mind of a butler. Even as Lenny begs for affection, Squiggy looks at Lisa as if to say *Welcome, madam. May I offer you some tea? A hot towel, perhaps?* Lenny purrs loudly as Lisa scratches his ears.

"What are their names?" Lisa asks.

"The one you are petting is Lenny. His brother Squiggy right behind him."

"Lenny and Squiggy?"

"Don't tell me you're surprised."

"Not in the least."

Lisa pets the cats for several more moments. I offer her some coffee and she accepts. We step into the kitchen. She stands by the breakfast bar while I pour the java.

"If Rick's disappeared," I say, "somebody else has to have noticed, right?"

"Maybe," she says. "Rick doesn't really have friends outside of work. He has an ex-wife and they're in touch every now and again. But that's all. If anyone else has missed Rick, they have to be people he works with."

I hand Lisa her cup of coffee. "How do you know all that?"

She swings a finger toward herself. "Intrepid reporter. Remember?"

"How could I have forgotten?" We take seats on either side of the breakfast bar. "Have you talked to anyone with the Longson campaign?"

"Not yet. That might get tricky. Look, I'm not bragging, but I've got a reputation."

"It's well earned."

"Thank you," Lisa says, "If I show up at your campaign events and start asking questions, it's because I'm trying to get a story you probably don't want printed. And if I tell them I'm there because Rick Michaels missed a meeting he scheduled with me, people might get *really* nervous. You see what I mean by *tricky*?"

"I do. There's one more person I can try. But it's a long shot."

I grab my cellphone off the desk and punch in Carol's number. She picks up on the third ring, sounding—as she usually does—like she's in the middle of something.

"What's going on?" she asks. "Did Lars kill somebody?"

"No," I say, "but give it time. I'm wondering if you've heard from Rick Michaels."

There's a pause. I get the feeling Carol has dropped whatever she's doing. "No, I haven't. Why would I hear from Rick?"

"It's a long story. I just thought I'd take a chance."

"Is Rick in trouble?" Carol asks.

"That's an excellent question."

I ring off without giving her an explanation. (I'll pay for that later.) I return to the breakfast bar and explain Carol's relationship with Rick. And that she hasn't heard from him. Lisa takes another sip of her coffee.

"I wonder if his ex-wife has heard from him," she says. "That should be my next stop."

She goes to the futon to collect her bag. I grab my peacoat from the coat tree and beat Lisa to the front door.

"I'll go with you," I tell her.

Her eyes shift away from me. "I appreciate that, Joe. But this is my job."

"I know. I want to help."

Lisa straightens her glasses. "Look, you've had success with a few things: getting your friend out of jail, finding out who killed James Queen, taking down a police conspiracy in Brooklyn Point. But this could get dangerous."

"And those weren't?" I hold up a cautioning hand. "Look, Rick's a good guy. If he's in trouble, I want to help."

In all likelihood, Lisa prefers working alone. And it's been a hell of a long time since she and I had any kind of adventure together. Slowly, a corner of her mouth rises.

"I never could say no to you," Lisa says.

"I wouldn't go that far," I say.

Lisa's face freezes. I kick myself for saying that. First time I've been around Lisa in sixteen years and *that* is what I choose to bring up? We stand there for a few fraught moments. Finally, some light comes back into Lisa's eyes.

"This is your neck of the woods, not mine," she says. "Feel free to lead the way, sir."

"I'm parked out back. Do you have a rental car?"

"I do. It's a Mustang. What do you drive?"

"A Saturn Ion," I say.

"So, I'll drive."

"That's what I was thinking."

I flip open the door. Lisa leads the way out. As we descend the stairs, I can't help thinking how surreal this is. It's as if I'm going to wake up any moment and wonder why I was dreaming about seeing Lisa. I'm still not convinced that won't happen.

***

Lisa finds the address of Rick's ex-wife, Katie Silver. It's a house in South Minneapolis, in the Seward neighborhood, nestled between the light rail line and the Mississippi River. It's a decent area, if a bit rundown. Grain silos line Hiawatha Avenue and a few abandoned factories beg for gentrification. (They'll get to it sooner or later.) The house itself is a two-story number, probably built around the time the neighborhood came into existence. The front yard is roughly the size of a postage stamp and, even though it's hidden by a fence, the backyard doesn't look much bigger. A small A-frame garage sits at the end of a cracked cement driveway. The lady of the house has done what she can, adding a flower garden that rims the front and side of the house. The garden is fading with the advance of fall. Katie Silver herself is decorating for Halloween, placing pumpkins on a hay bale in the front yard as Lisa and I walk up. She's a short woman about our age. Her dark hair is pulled back into a ponytail, and she has large hazel eyes. She wears a plaid shirt, jeans, and a pair of gardening gloves. Her greeting is pleasant, but she's probably waiting for us to talk about sharing scripture with her.

"Katie Silver?" Lisa asks.

That throws Katie off. How did the Jehovah's Witnesses get her name? She must have accidently gotten on some mailing list. "Who are you?" she asks.

"My name is Lisa Cleary." She produces a business card and hands it over. "I'm with Metro Communications. This is my…this is Joe Davis."

Katie's eyes brighten. "You're friends of Rick's, right? From high school?"

Lisa seems thrown. "We are. I mean, we knew Rick back then."

"He's talked about you both."

Again, this surprises Lisa. I know where she's coming from. I liked Rick a lot in high school, and I knew he was a fan of my column (both in high school and in the present day). But I never knew we were tight enough to warrant his continued admiration. Lisa recovers quickly.

"That's really nice," she says. "I'm hoping we could have a minute of your time."

Katie studies the card. "About Rick?"

"Yes," Lisa says.

"Did he do something?"

"I don't know. He asked for a meeting with me, and he didn't show. We haven't been able to get ahold of him."

Katie steadies herself by putting a hand on the hay bale. "Would you like to come inside?"

"That would be great," Lisa says.

Katie leads us into the house. It's a fairly simple affair. None of the rooms are particularly large. A small arch separates the living room from the dining room. There's a small study to our right. The kitchen is situated to the right of the dining room. The floors are hardwood. Most of the furniture appears to be secondhand. A few prints adorn the walls and plants are scattered about. Katie offers us the sofa and goes into the kitchen to fetch some coffee. When she returns, she takes a seat in a glider chair near the couch.

"Your meeting with Rick," Katie says, her voice subdued, "was it about his work?"

"It was," Lisa says, "but he didn't go into details."

Katie flicks a look toward me. "Did he talk to you, too?"

I nod. "Rick got Lisa's contact info from me."

"He reads your column all the time."

"Did you talk to Rick much?" I ask. "After…y'know, the divorce?"

Katie doesn't seem bothered by my fumbling around that particular elephant in the room. "We'd talk every now and then. Just call or have coffee. Check in with each other."

"Did he tell you much about his work for Longson?" I ask.

"No," Katie says. "I don't like Longson very much. Sorry."

Lisa flips a hand. "No need to apologize for an opinion. Did Rick talk about what exactly he did for Longson?"

"No, he was kind of vague about it. He just said he was a glorified errand boy. Honestly, I was just happy he had a job. It was one of those things that…didn't work out for us."

My eyebrows go up. "I didn't realize that."

"He was working for NewCo Mutual when we first met," she says. "He lost that job after a few years. He didn't seem to miss it much. Then he went through a lot of jobs. He was never happy with anything. I had to handle the finances, making money and keeping track of it. When he did bring money in…I wasn't sure where it came from."

Lisa rests her chin in her hand. "How do you mean?"

"Rick would tell me he got money for helping a friend move. Then I'd see the friend a few months later and he'd be living in the same place he'd lived for a few years. Or Rick would tell me he had a temp job downtown and, after he'd supposedly been there for a few weeks, the temp agency would call and say they had an assignment for him. Things like that. And those were just the times I caught him. When I'd ask him about it, he'd say everything was fine. After a while, I realized I couldn't trust him. And when you can't trust somebody, you can't have a relationship. You certainly can't have a marriage."

I haven't been married, but trust has been fraught in a number of my relationships. So, I can agree with Katie on that much. "How did Rick handle the divorce?" I ask.

"Not well," Katie says. "He didn't fly into a rage or anything. He just seemed hurt. Lost, I guess. Then again, maybe he was always like that."

"How so?" I ask.

Katie gives us a rueful smile. "You're from Porter's Bay. You know. He's a legend up there. He's had to spend his life living up to it."

That I get. Sports are the coin of the realm in a small town like Porter's Bay. Sure, I had my column in the high school newspaper and people knew who I was. But I was forgotten five minutes after I left town. (Even these days, people back home seem unaware my brothers Kevin and Owen, both athletes, had another brother.) Rick did the greatest thing any Porter's Bay athlete has ever done. He brought us a state championship. I never realized that might strangle the rest of someone's life.

Lisa pushes up her glasses. "When was the last time you talked to Rick?"

"Last Friday," Katie says. "He stopped by to get some of his things. He has a few boxes of old mementos and stuff he hasn't gotten around to moving. I told him to go ahead. I had just gotten home from work, and all I wanted was to have dinner and watch TV. He didn't stay long."

"Did you notice anything unusual?" Lisa asks, her voice more casual than interrogating. "Did he say or do anything that seemed odd?"

Katie sits up. "I guess he did. I didn't think about it until you mentioned it. But he didn't take anything with him when he left. He stopped over here to get stuff, and he didn't do it."

Interesting. What was the point of stopping over then? Friday was the day before Rick showed up at my apartment. Apparently, he was in a cryptic and furtive mode. Lisa sneaks me a look. She's on my same wavelength.

"Would you mind if we look at Rick's stuff?" Lisa asks. "I know that sounds intrusive, but if it gives us an idea where he is…"

"Go ahead," Katie says. "I'll show you down there."

Katie leads us to the basement door, located in the kitchen. The steep steps go down to a basement with a half-bath and a couple storage areas. Boxes line most of the walls. Katie points us to a couple boxes in one corner.

"It's just those," she says. "I'm not sure why Rick didn't take anything. He could be kind of scatterbrained."

We thank Katie, who goes back upstairs. Rick's possessions are in a couple of hastily taped together cardboard boxes. Lisa takes one, and I take the other. I use my car keys to crack the packing tape.

"Any idea what we're looking for?" I ask.

"Nope," Lisa says. "Just hoping for something useful."

My box has a lot of keepsakes from Rick's past jobs. Between getting fired from his day job and holding several temp jobs afterwards, he and Mike have a lot in common. There are a few mementos of his marriage to Katie: events they attended, vacation souvenirs, stray pictures. I glance toward the corner. A hockey stick is propped against one of the storage shelves.

"I assume that belonged to Rick," I say. "I wasn't aware he still played."

"It looks like it's been repaired."

She's right. There are screws on each side, right around the middle of the stick. Why would Rick would keep that around rather than just buy a new one? If the last few days have taught me anything, it's that the man works in mysterious ways. We keep looking through the boxes, but I'm not coming up with much.

"You find anything?" I ask.

"Nothing interesting," Lisa says. She holds up a photo. "Hawaii looks beautiful. I guess they went there on their honeymoon."

"You've never been to Hawaii? A globetrotting reporter such as yourself?"

"Hawaii is a vacation spot. I don't take vacations."

We finish going through the boxes, but don't find anything worth noting. We go back upstairs. Katie is waiting for us in the dining room.

"Anything interesting?" she asks.

"Nothing that helps much," I say. "Thanks for letting us look.'

We return to the living room. Lisa picks up her coffee cup, but also doesn't take a sip. She turns to Katie.

"Did Rick ever talk about the people he worked with?" Lisa asks.

The look on Katie's face sours. "He mentioned a woman named Madeline. I think they were dating."

"What makes you say that?" Lisa asks.

"Rick mentioned her a few times and sort of went out of his way to be casual. Problem is, it has the exact opposite effect. When you know somebody, you know when they're keeping something from you. You get what I mean?"

"I'm afraid I do," Lisa says.

"That's how I know Rick never cheated on me. He couldn't hide something like that. Not from me. I know he had kind of a reputation before we got married. I shouldn't be surprised he went back to that sort of thing after we broke up."

Lisa and I exchange a look. Rick was a decent guy in high school, but he *did* have a reputation. Lisa faces Katie.

"Rick didn't directly say anything about dating this Madeline?" she asks.

"Not directly, no," Katie says.

"Did you get a last name for Madeline?"

"No. I don't think he ever mentioned it."

Lisa nods. She hasn't written anything down, but I can tell that the name *Madeline* is imprinted in her mind. Lisa steps toward the door, prompting me to follow.

"Thank you for the coffee," Lisa says. "You have my card. If you hear from Rick, please let me know."

"I will." Katie walks us to the front door. "Please let me know if *you* hear from Rick. I want to know if he's okay. We're divorced, but…you never stop caring for somebody, right?"

Lisa's eyes dip. "We'll let you know if we hear anything."

We step across the tiny front lawn and walk to Lisa's rented Mustang. Katie sits on the front steps. Maybe thinking about the past.

I know what that's like.

CHAPTER THREE

MARCH, JUNIOR YEAR

On one hand, things developed quickly with Lisa. We would see each other once a weekend, spend considerable time together in the Bay Breeze *offices after school, and eat lunch together almost every day (to the consternation of my best friends, Sam and Andy). We even talked on the phone, which was a big sacrifice on my part. (Lisa understood I regarded the telephone as the tool of the devil. Besides, we had one phone line in my house, and I couldn't use it without my parents being aware of what was going on.)*

On the other hand, things were also going a little slowly. For all the time we spent together, I was never sure where things were at with Lisa. Were we dating or were we just good friends? The sheer number of good night kisses (which were becoming more ardent each time out) certainly suggested we were more than the latter. But I had never formally dated a girl, so I wasn't sure how one went about it. (I assumed you had to get something notarized.) So, I danced around it, knowing what my heart's fondest wish was but being too afraid to voice it. Lisa and I stayed in this holding pattern for more than a month.

We were having lunch in the theater at Porter's Bay High School. Like the entirety of the school, the theater was built back in the Twenties. The place was cavernous, with ornate chandeliers hanging from the ceiling, a stage the size of an aircraft hangar, and plenty of gold and brass ornamentation. We were sitting near the back, plunked into two plush seats. Even though she'd been at Porter's Bay High for about six months, Lisa still gaped at the place.

"If you had told me a little town like Porter's Bay could afford a theater like this," she said, "I never would have believed you."

"It's all iron ore money," I say. "Porter's Bay was a major shipping center back in the day, taking the iron ore off the Iron Range and sending it east. They used to scoop it off the top of the soil. It was all over the place. The money afforded some pretty nice things in this town." I took a bite of my turkey sandwich. "Eventually, the original iron ore dried up. By that point, the North Shore Highway had been built and the tourist trade became big around here. Once the steel companies figured out how to turn taconite—which they thought was just a waste product before—into a useable raw material, the whole Iron Range had a renaissance." Yes, I used words like renaissance *when I was in high school. It's probably why I didn't date more often. That reason and no other. "But Porter's Bay was pretty comfortable with the tourist trade.* Everything *started shipping out of Duluth." I suddenly realized how boring all this must be to Lisa. "Sorry. I was kind of rambling."*

"Don't apologize," Lisa said, propping her feet up on the seat in front of her. "I like hearing you talk."

She laid her head on my shoulder. I hoped she couldn't detect my heart pounding. I kept talking about whatever Porter's Bay history I could think of. Lisa ignored her PB&J and snuggled into me. Then one of the side doors opened, the crash echoing around the theatre.

"What is this?" a voice jeered.

My heart sank into the vicinity of my shoes. I knew that voice. It was Beans Madden, a reprobate student who was more destructive force than human being. Beans wasn't a bully in the classic sense. He wouldn't pound you and take your lunch money. He'd mock you until you'd just give him the damn lunch money to make him go away. He stood inside the door, hands tucked into the pockets of the jean jacket that attempted to cover his bulbous body. His jeans were dirty and the rips in his shirt were not a fashion statement (unless the statement was, "I can't afford a decent shirt"). His malevolent bug eyes were trained on us.

"Oh, for the love of pound cake," I muttered.

Lisa's head came off my shoulder. She whispered, "For the love of pound cake? Did you really just say that?"

"Sorry," I said,

"Don't apologize," Lisa said. "It's cute."

While I appreciated the compliment, I was dearly hoping Beans didn't hear it. Thankfully, he did not. But there was still the matter of his odious presence. He walked toward Lisa and me.

"What's the story, Davis?" Beans said, brushing some of the greasy black hair out of his eyes. "You trying to finally pop your cherry?"

I stared ahead. "Beans, why don't you let that cut under your nose heal?"

Lisa snorted. Beans being Beans, he didn't catch the insult (not that it would have stopped him). He came to a halt at the end of our row, as if he was about to plop down and join us. He laid each hand on the back of a seat.

"I think you guys need some adult supervision," he said. "Can't have you playing sticky finger on school property."

I tried not to look at him. "We're fine. Thank you very much for your concern."

"No, no, Davis," Beans said. "I feel a moral obligation to stay here and make sure everything is on the up and up. Assuming you can get it up and up."

I let out a short, disgusted breath. I knew Beans well enough to know exactly where this was going. He would irritate Lisa and me until we finally got up and left. Having shown that much weakness, there was a good likelihood Beans would keep returning at lunch hour and renewing the torture. Lisa and I could pretty much say goodbye to lunches in the school theater. Lisa looked past me.

"Beans Madden," she said, a businesslike mask coming over her face, "you're the one who put the manure in Mr. Altavilla's Buick."

Here was the thing about Beans: yes, he was a destructive force, but he was tactical as well. There were things he wanted full credit for, and things he disavowed any knowledge of. He didn't mind if rumor connected him to some of those disavowed activities. But you'd never get him to admit it. He tried to smirk at Lisa's accusation, but he looked nervous.

"You got me confused with somebody else, sweetie," he said.

"No, I really don't," Lisa said. "You bragged about it to Jason Bergeson. And Jerome Raymond lives right across the street. He's pretty sure he saw you in Mr. Altavilla's driveway that night. And the clerk at the L&M Supply in Center City is positive you're the one he sold the manure to."

Beans's face appeared sickly. (He might have turned green, but the lighting was low, so I can't say for sure.) "That's bull," he said, weakly.

"Maybe," Lisa said. "We can always find out. It would make a nice article for The Bay Breeze. *Of course, I might not submit it if you go away and never bother us again."*

The shoe, as it were, was now firmly planted on the other foot. Beans hated being bested under any circumstances. But Lisa had him by the short hairs. Beans pushed off from the seats.

"That how it is, Davis?" he said. "Your girlfriend has to fight your battles for you?"

Lisa stood up and put a fist on each hip. "He doesn't need his girlfriend to fight his battles for him. I do it because I want to. Now, get out of here before I go over to the Bay Breeze *offices and file a story."*

Beans backed toward the side doors, trying not to look as if he was rushing to get the hell out of there. He pushed the door open and looked for a crusher to give him the last word.

"*Let that be a lesson to you, Davis,*" *Beans said. Then he disappeared out the side door.*

My head swung that direction. "Let that be a…what the hell did he mean by that?" Before I could go too far down the road of befuddlement, the significance of something Lisa said hit me. I turned toward her. "Did you…did you just say you were my girlfriend?"

Lisa adjusted her glasses. "Did I say the wrong thing?"

"No, you…you really *did not."*

She let out a relieved breath. I stood up and kissed her, for once acting without thinking about it. Lisa stroked my face. Then, naturally, the bell rang and shattered the moment. We parted, laughing.

"Our timing is flawless," Lisa said.

We got up and walked to the side door. Lisa slipped her hand into mine and our fingers interlaced. We stepped into the hallway, and I swung around to face her.

"Does a boyfriend walk his girlfriend to class?" I asked.

Lisa smiled. "You've got five minutes and it's a big school. I'll take a raincheck."

I was tempted to kiss her again, but people were milling about. Instead, I leaned close and asked, "Want to go to Arthur's after school? Get something to eat?"

"That sounds great. I'll see you then."

I lifted her hand to my face and kissed the back of it. She gave me a little finger wave as we parted. There was more bounce in my step as

I walked to class. I couldn't help wondering how the hell I was going to concentrate when all I could think about was my new girlfriend.

Right now, I would welcome a similar distraction. Any distraction, come to that.

"Spectacle is the thing," Ollie says, leaning so far over his pasta primavera he might do a faceplant in it. "If you don't have spectacle, what have you got?"

I stop a forkful of linguine just below my mouth. "Story? Dialogue? Characters?"

Ollie doesn't even look my direction. "You've got nothing. You've got a corpse with no lifeblood."

I'm envying the corpse. Any corpse, really. I wasn't thrilled about this meeting in the first place. With the distraction of Rick going missing, I'd rather not be here at all. But the production meeting for the film had been scheduled, and Lars insisted I couldn't beg it off. Now that I'm here, ensconced in a corner table in the restaurant section of The Tav, I'm like an animal willing to chew off its own leg to get out of a bear trap.

"We *are* doing a vampire film," I say. "Corpses are kind of our thing."

Ollie ignores me and digs into his pasta. I'm not sure if he's an artist, but he certainly strives to look the part. He has a thick hipster beard and his brown hair pulled back into a ponytail. The green eyes flick about with either unbridled enthusiasm or some variety of narcotic. (One likely fuels the other.) There's a hole in the armpit of his green sweater and his fingernails are dirty, though I get the feeling all that is affectation.

I look to Fabio, one of our backers for the film, wondering if he's buying any of this. Fabio, a good-looking guy with dark hair, brown eyes, and bright teeth, picks at his sea bass.

"What kind of spectacle are we talking about?" he asks.

"The scene where the boss dies," Ollie says. "I see a car going out the window of a skyscraper. Top floor. We got cameras mounted on helicopters, and we follow the flight all the way to the street."

Frankie is our other backer and Fabio's twin sister. She looks like a slightly more feminine version of her brother. Like her brother, she wears a white collared shirt, open to the chest, (though the difference is…noticeable.)

"Far out," Frankie says.

Yep. This whole thing is getting closer and closer to the brink. Fabio and Frankie are a couple of rich kids whose father, a prominent doctor, is providing the money for the film, in the (likely vain) hope his kids will find a purpose in life (and perhaps move out of the house). They seem enamored of this idiot. Speaking of idiots, Lars, resplendent in his Nehru jacket and gold chain, stares out the window, providing no help whatsoever. I guess this is up to me. (Oh joy.)

"Okay, I'll start small," I say, tugging at the collar of my black dress shirt. "The boss is killed by an attack from our main character. He gets bitten on the neck and dies when his blood is drained. What does a car going out a skyscraper window have to do with any of that?"

"The boss has a car in his office," Ollie says, as if it should be obvious. "It's a classic model. Something he's restored. He keeps it around as a symbol of his bourgeois vanity."

"How did he get it into the office?" I ask.

Ollie bats the air with his hand. "The audience isn't going to care."

"You're sure?" I ask. "It's not possible someone might wonder, 'How the fuck did that guy get a working car into his office?'"

"If they're worried about that," Ollie says, "we aren't doing our jobs with the story."

That's exactly my fear, but I need to take this one disaster at a time. I run my hands up the legs of my jeans. "The story aside, how are *we* going to get a working car into an office?"

"That's a technical problem," Ollie says. "The art director can worry about that."

I turn to Lars and ask, "We have an art director?" Lars doesn't seem inclined to answer. I pinch the bridge of my nose, fighting off the F-5 migraine that's developing. "Even if we get the car into the office, how are we going to get it out a window? What skyscraper are we going to use? How are we going to get the streets of either Minneapolis or St. Paul cleared for that? How are we going to get permits to even try it?"

Ollie turns his attention to his pasta. "The stunt coordinator can handle the first part. The rest of it, I leave to you guys. You're the producers, right?"

"Yes, but—" Then it hits me. "We have a stunt coordinator?"

"We have to have one," Ollie says. "If we're going to do the stunt." If gaslighting is a key to good directing, Ollie might be the second coming of Akira Kurosawa. He continues with his mouth full. "I know a guy who can do it, if that helps. He won't come cheap, though."

Frankie has been staring dreamily at Ollie through his entire artistic tirade. Fabio doesn't seem pleased with this development. However, something at the bar catches his attention. Carol is there, sipping a Cosmo. Fabio stares in her direction as he speaks.

"What about boobs?" he asks, absently, "We need some boobs in this thing. Do they come cheap?"

"I know a couple actresses I can ask," Ollie asks.

I drop my head into my hand. "I only have one potential nude scene. And no scenes with a car going out a skyscraper window."

"Not a problem," Ollie says, taking a piece of battered notebook paper from the pocket of his jeans. "I got a list of rewrites right here."

He offers me the paper and I hesitantly take it. The writing is largely illegible, so I'll wait until later to decipher it. Ollie slugs the rest of his white wine and dives back into his pasta, making sure to get some in his beard. Frankie smacks Fabio on the arm, breaking his concentration on Carol. They do a little sidebar. It doesn't look friendly. Lars starts eating his spaghetti and meatballs but adds nothing else. I hear a voice over my shoulder.

"How goes the meeting?" Carol asks.

She's addressing the table, but her focus is on Fabio. Carol rests a hand on the back of my chair while I introduce her to everyone. Ollie largely ignores her. Frankie digs into her steak sandwich. Fabio offers his hand.

"Nice to meet you," he says.

Carol takes it, lightly running her other hand down the collar of her blue blouse. "Are you talking about ideas for the movie?"

"We're trading some ideas," I say. "Most of them are coming from Ollie, our director."

Ollie looks slightly annoyed, as if the general public won't let a big star like him just eat a meal in peace. Carol, though, seems intrigued.

"What kind of ideas?" she asks.

I take a slug of my merlot. "The one we were discussing involves a car flying out the window of a skyscraper."

"A skyscraper?" Carol asks. "Isn't this a vampire movie?"

Before Ollie can respond, I keep rolling. "Then there was an earlier one involving a motorcycle chase through a Halloween parade."

"There are Halloween parades?" Carol asks. "Since when?"

Ollie starts to speak up, but again, I beat him to the humiliating punch. "And there's something about a ritual sacrifice involving a prostitute and a Catholic Church."

Carol covers her mouth, but her eyes betray her amusement. "You're making that up."

If Carol and I planned this in advance, we couldn't have done a better tag team beatdown of Ollie. The director's response, not surprisingly, is to toss his cloth napkin over his unfinished pasta and rise dramatically to his feet.

"I don't have to sit here and listen to this," he says, his voice going up an octave and further threatening Carol's composure. "These are the ideas of a genius and I don't want them quoted out of context by a hack writer and mocked by some woman who doesn't know a damn thing about the art of film. Good day!"

With that, Ollie storms out of the restaurant. Frankie follows him, giving Carol a dirty look as she passes. Lars serenely eats his spaghetti. Fabio glides over to Carol.

"I liked what you had to say," he tells her. "Can we talk a little more?"

Carol blushes slightly, "I just raised a few object—"

"How about I buy you a drink?" Fabio asks, gesturing toward the bar.

"I like Cosmos," Carol says, slipping her white coat over her shoulder.

The two of them walk to the bar. I'm not sure what the hell is going on there, but it's probably best that Frankie didn't witness it. I swivel toward Lars.

"Thanks a shit ton for the help back there," I say. "That was a wonderful impression of Johnny Tight Lips."

Lars finally snaps out of his reverie. "My apologies, mon Ami. It's all part of the plan."

"What plan?"

Lars brings two fingers to this mouth and gives me the *zipping the lips* gesture. I'm surprised, annoyed, and dismayed all at the same time. Lars is not one to play his cards close to the vest. His constant need for applause works against this (and every other plan in his life). He lowers his fork and speaks over the top of his meatball.

"By the way, if building management comes around," Lars says, "I'm going to need you to cover for me."

Oh, this just gets better and better. "Cover for you how?"

He flips a hand, as if the whole issue is a trifling thing. "They've been getting complaints from Mrs. Hanratty, one of my neighbors. She's been hearing the noises coming from my apartment when I'm…doing my work for the adult film industry."

"The bass guitar and the keyboard?"

"That and the screaming, panting, moaning, animal cries of ecstasy. The ambient noises that accompany such a venture. It's a beautiful thing, but Mrs. Hanratty doesn't see it that way."

I can understand. Since I know the true nature of Lars's enterprise, I can ignore the sounds coming from his apartment. Mrs. Hanratty, a widow of some years, doesn't have the same sanguinity on the subject.

"She's complaining to management?" I say.

"Indeed," Lars says. "She doesn't realize I'm scoring adult features. She thinks I'm *making* adult features."

Eep. "Where the hell did she get that idea?"

Lars strokes his beard. "I've been telling everyone I'm making a movie. Then Mrs. Hanratty heard the noises from my apartment, and she jumped to the wrong conclusion. And let management in on that wrong conclusion."

I can see why management would object to a thing like that; their perfectly lovely building being turned into a den of iniquity. If I didn't know any better, as a tenant I would object as well. No matter how many visits to the set I insisted upon.

"Wait a minute," I say. "I'm making the movie, too. Does management think I'm in on the porn thing?"

"No. I didn't tell any of the neighbors about your involvement. To be perfectly honest, they don't really care for you."

Not sure how to feel about that. It's the first time my general unpopularity with my neighbors has worked in my favor. I pick at what's left of my dinner.

"Can't you straighten out management on this stuff?" I ask.

"To be honest, I don't think they'd be any more thrilled with what I *am* doing. Scoring the porn, I mean. They're remarkably close-minded when it comes to the enjoyment of the flesh and the exploitation of same. I'm going to have to keep this on the downlow."

"How are you going to do that?"

"I'll figure something out," Lars says, slurping the last of his spaghetti. "This project has the potential to be lucrative. And helpful with our more…legitimate cinematic endeavors. For now, just remember to keep management in the dark."

"Fine by me," I say. When it comes to management, I prefer that our relations be kept strictly to my rent payments, certificate of rent paid, and lease renewals. Otherwise, I prefer to go through life anonymously.

The server arrives and leaves us the check we are apparently stuck paying. While Lars and I collect our funds, my cell phone rings. It's Lisa. I step away from the table, leaving Lars to handle the money. (A dangerous proposition, but I don't really have a choice.)

"Did you find anything?" I ask.

After talking to Katie, I had to come straight to this production meeting. Lisa went back to her hotel to do some research. I've been hoping she would call. Her timing is flawless.

"I think so," Lisa says. "I'm guessing Madeline is Madeline Hauser. She's the campaign manager for Senator Longson."

"Wow," I say. "Diddling the boss. Didn't know Rick rated that."

"*Allegedly* diddling the boss," Lisa says. "We only have Katie's thoughts on that."

"Have you tried calling this Madeline Hauser?"

"I did," Lisa says. "She hasn't returned my calls. Maybe I should pay them a visit."

A little jolt runs through me. "You're going to do it now?"

"No. They've closed down for the day. I'll go there first thing tomorrow."

"What time?" I ask. "I'll go with you."

Lisa sounds slightly annoyed. "Joe, I've been in a war zone. I don't need somebody to protect me."

"And if you did need protection, I'd be the worst one for the job. I'm just saying that Rick is a friend and I got hauled into this. I want to know he's okay. Besides, I'm half a journalist. There might be a story here for me, too."

Lisa chuckles, but not unkindly, at the notion of my being *half a journalist*. "All right, fine. I'll pick you up at eight in the morning."

That gives me pause. "There's an eight in the morning now?"

Then the laugh. I have no trouble picturing it. She throws her head back and her mouth is open, but the sound that comes out is lilting rather than harsh. It puts an ache in my chest.

"I'll see you then," Lisa says, before ringing off.

I stare at the phone. Then I slip it in my pocket and go back to pay the check.

***

True to her word (and I had no doubts on that score), Lisa's rented Mustang pulls up in front of my building at eight a.m. sharp. The temp is in the mid-forties, so I'm waiting in the foyer, wiping the sand from my eyes. I huddle into my peacoat, probably looking like an ad for surliness. When I slide into the passenger seat, two coffees are sitting in the drink-holder. Lisa picks one up and hands it to me.

"Thought you could use this," she says.

I take it in both hands. "You are an angel of mercy."

"Thank you. Probably the nicest thing I'll be called all day. Especially after we get through at Longson's campaign HQ."

"I will gird my loins."

The route takes us down Ramsey Hill, a steep stretch of road leading to both downtown St. Paul and Highway 35E. Lisa pulls the rental car onto the highway and heads south. I sip my coffee and try to pull out of my coma.

Lisa gives me a sidelong glance. "You never were a morning person."

"I was lucky to find a job that accommodates that."

"How late *do* you sleep?"

"I used to stay in bed until noon. Last couple years, I've tried getting up at ten. Makes me feel like I've slept in but haven't missed the whole day. You know what I mean?"

"In theory. I have to get up whenever the story tells me it's time to get up."

"Sounds rough."

"It's what I love to do." Although Lisa says it with less enthusiasm than she might.

Senator Bill Longson's campaign headquarters takes up two floors of an otherwise deserted office building in Edina; a snooty southern suburb whose high school hockey team is universally hated. I guess Longson feels more at home among his own entitled people. The building is on a forgettable stretch of road near Highways 100 and 494. The neighborhood is all office space and hotels and strip malls. I can't help thinking this is a little insight into the America a guy like Bill Longson would like to bring about. Greenpeace would throw up in their mouths just looking at it.

Lisa tosses her bag over her shoulder and leads the way inside. I get a rush of nerves, knowing we're entering enemy territory. For her part, Lisa looks as if she's reading a not particularly interesting novel. The front door is open. A glass divider separates the reception area from a sea of desks and cubicles. Campaign posters line the wall. Bill Longson smiles insincerely on one wall of the reception area. There is no receptionist at the desk, but a balding guy with a salt-and-pepper beard and bright blue eyes comes into the lobby as we arrive.

"Can I help you?" he says, his tone a little suspicious.

"I hope so," Lisa says. "I would like to talk to Madeline Hauser. My name is Lisa Cleary."

The guy turns the suspicion up to eleven. "May I ask what it's about?"

"It's something I need to discuss privately with Ms. Hauser. It should only take a few minutes of her time."

"My name is Roger Neill," he says, as if that's supposed to mean something. "I'm Madeline's assistant. I'm sure that anything you need to discuss with Madeline, you can discuss with me."

"Not in this case," Lisa says, an air of command moving into her voice. "It would be best to talk to Madeline. Trust me."

Roger doesn't say anything in response. He clearly knows who Lisa is. He's stuck between the consequences of throwing her out and the consequences of letting her talk to Madeline. He comes down on the side of letting Madeline make the decision.

"I'll see if she has a moment," he says, picking up the phone on the receptionist's desk.

Lisa and I step aside. "Five bucks says he starts wetting himself," I say.

"I told you: a visit from me usually isn't a welcomed thing."

Roger sets the phone down and fumbles with some paperwork. "I can take you back to Madeline."

"Thank you," Lisa says.

We take a couple steps toward the glass partition. Roger gestures toward me and addresses Lisa.

"I'm sorry, but this is…?"

Lisa answers for me. "Joe Davis. He's working with me on this."

Roger turns the fisheye my direction. "And what do you do for a living, Mr. Davis?"

"I fight crime with the help of my youthful ward and his faithful Native American sidekick."

Lisa covers her mouth with one hand. Roger's face crinkles, as if there's a bad smell in the room. He faces forward and heads for the office proper.

"Please follow me," Roger says.

I'm not sure what I expected in a campaign headquarters. The very term conjures up images of cigar smoke wafting through the air, spittoons lining the floor; men slipping off into corners to cut backroom deals. Then I realize it conjures those images for me because I watch too many old movies. Longson's offices could pass for the offices of a major corporation (which, viewed from a certain angle…). It's all desks and maps and tables and cubicles. Multiple images of Longson and his campaign slogan ("The Break of a New Day") line the walls. It's distressing to see the number of young people working here. Sure, they have the energy to do it, but what college-age kid is soulless enough to say *We need to get America back to what it was under Eisenhower?* Some things I'll never figure out.

Rather than leading us to Madeline Hauser's office, Roger takes us to a windowless meeting room near the back. A long table sporting an empty water pitcher and a white board serve as the only furniture. There's a TV on the wall, tuned to a local station. Bill Longson is giving a campaign speech. Madeline Hauser is standing near the table when we arrive.

Her voice has a smoky quality to it. "Please have a seat."

I feel dirty thinking this, but Madeline Hauser is a knockout. She's in her early forties, about Lisa's height, and has a mane of red hair cascading past her shoulders. Her brown eyes study us and her full lips provide no expression. The red suitcoat and the black skirt don't give me a complete view of her figure, but the outline is promising. If Rick *was* dating her,

I'll take my hat off to the man. Madeline takes a seat at the head of the table while Lisa and I situate ourselves in adjoining chairs. Lisa offers a hand.

"Thank you for meeting with us," she says.

Madeline briefly returns the handshake then turns to Roger. "Give us the room, please."

Roger's eyes flick from Madeline to us, as if questioning the wisdom of the request. One look from Madeline shocks him into compliance. He backs out of the room. I nod toward the TV.

"I'm surprised you're not with the Senator," I say.

"That was filmed yesterday," she says, "Senator Longson is currently meeting with his economic advisors."

I get a load of Longson's visage on the screen as he addresses his flock, um, *supporters*. He's got a round face, a thick nose and a prominent smirk. His brown hair is clipped short. The video doesn't convey it, but I know from his other TV appearances he's quite tall and bulky, falling in the six-five range and probably topping three-hundred pounds. Yet, he has a politician's good looks. If John F. Kennedy and Herman Munster had a baby, it would look a lot like Bill Longson. The closed captioning of his speech indicates he's railing against crime taking over the inner-cities (which is code for *those lousy African Americans don't know their place*). I look away from the TV, trying my damnedest not to imagine Longson's presidential portrait. Madeline picks up a pen and holds it between her fingers.

"So, Ms. Cleary," she says, "I enjoyed your work on Senator Kent."

If I recall, the work was a series of articles exposing abortions funded by a militantly pro-life senator from Idaho with a lust for campaign staffers and, apparently, a disdain for birth control. Given Madeline's likely position on the political spectrum—and former Senator Kent's friendship with Senator Longson—it's questionable as to how much she actually enjoyed the articles.

"Thank you," Lisa says. "I hope Senator Longson wasn't too upset."

"We haven't discussed it," Madeline says. "How can I help you?"

"I wanted to talk about Rick Michaels," Lisa says. "I understand he works for Senator Longson's campaign."

Madeline waves a hand toward the door. "As you probably noticed, we have quite a few people working on the campaign."

"I did notice that," Lisa says. "Rick contacted me three days ago, saying he wanted to talk about Senator Longson. We had a meeting set, but Rick didn't show. No one has seen him since."

If that concerns Madeline, she hides it magnificently. "I'm sorry to hear that. But it's a reality of this business, whether they're staffers or volunteers. People come and go all the time."

I prop an arm on the table. "Except we don't know where this one went. Or why."

Madeline turns toward me for the first time. "And, Mr. Davis, what is your interest in this? You write a…humor column, don't you?"

She says *humor column* in the same way one might say *German shit porn*. I wish there was water in that pitcher because my mouth has gone dry.

"Rick is a friend of mine," I say.

Madeline turns back to Lisa. "I'm sorry, I can't seem to place Rick Michaels. Perhaps Roger would be able to—".

"Really?" Lisa says, casually interrupting. "Because Rick's ex-wife is under the impression you and Rick were dating."

Madeline's eyes slide toward the floor. "That's absurd. Did Rick actually say that?"

"Not that I know of. It's an ex-wife's intuition."

"I believe *paranoia* would be a more appropriate word," Madeline says. "No, I was not dating…Rick was his name? I don't know who he is. In any event, it would be wildly inappropriate to date a staff member."

Lisa makes a mental note of this. "Would anyone here be able to talk to me about Rick?"

"I don't know off the top of my head," Madeline says. "Roger might. To be perfectly honest with you, we have our hands full right now. The election is less than a month away."

I lean forward, prepared to remind Madeline that Rick is a human being and not a missing stapler from the supply closet. Lisa, though, gives me a look, silently asking me to let her handle it. I sit back, my face feeling warm. Lisa returns her focus to Madeline.

"Do you have any idea why Rick would want to talk to me about the Senator?" Lisa asks. "Or what it might be about?"

"I have absolutely no idea," Madeline says. "Not to sound hard-hearted, but you would have to ask Mr. Michaels that."

Now why would *that* sound hard-hearted? The room is starting to feel cold (but maybe that's just me). Lisa seems unaffected.

"I don't suppose we could talk with the Senator?" she asks.

Not surprisingly, Madeline shakes her head. "I'm afraid that's impossible. The Senator's schedule is full. Besides, I can assure you that if *I'm* not that familiar with Rick Michaels, the Senator isn't." Madeline lays her hands firmly on the table. "Ms. Cleary, I understand your concern, but I would greatly appreciate it if you kept your distance from the campaign. As I've been trying to tell you, this is a critical time and I'd prefer the staff and volunteers—and certainly, the Senator—not be distracted by speculation."

This time, there's finality in Madeline's tone. I look toward Lisa, wondering what's going to come next. Lisa, though, gets up from the table.

"Thank you for your time," Lisa says. "Do you have a card? In case I have any follow up questions?"

Madeline frowns. Clearly, she wants less, not more, to do with Lisa in the future. "I don't have a card on me. I'll just give you my name and number."

She finds a nearby sticky note and pen and scribbles down the info. She has a little attitude as she rips the sticky note free and hands it over. Lisa doesn't take the bait. Frankly, I'm a little disappointed. I was hoping she would deal with Madeline's obstructionism by channeling *Scent of a Woman* Al Pacino. *If I was the woman I was five years ago, I'd take a flamethrower to this place!* Then again, I don't want Latter Day Al Pacino's voice coming out of Lisa's mouth.

Lisa leads the way to the door. There's a sudden movement when she flips it open. We look down the hallway. Roger is scurrying away, trying to appear casual. Lisa acts as if nothing happened. She assures Madeline we can find our own way out. Even there, I'm certain Madeline will be spying on us to make sure we leave without incident. Lisa and I say nothing until we get back to the car.

"I thought there might be more fireworks," I say.

"Seemed like time for a tactical retreat," Lisa says. "I just wanted to see how cooperative they were going to be. *Not very* is the answer to that."

"You get anything else out of it?" I ask.

Lisa buckles herself in. "Madeline knows who Rick is. She used his name casually, then doubled back and pretended like she didn't even know the name. I'm not sure if they were dating, but she's definitely covering something."

We sit back, getting ready to talk off. I look around the parking lot and spot something that interests me. I sit up.

"Looks like Ms. Madeline is chatting with someone," I say.

Lisa follows my gaze. Madeline stands by a side door, wearing a hastily-thrown-on gray overcoat. She's in conversation with a short, solidly built guy in a plain black suit. He's not wearing an overcoat, but the chill doesn't seem to bother him. His brown hair has been combed carefully into place. His head bows slightly, but his eyes bore into Madeline. Even from a distance, I can see there's something malevolent in his mastiff features. He's one of those guys who instantly give you the creeps.

"What do you suppose is going on there?" I ask.

"No idea," Lisa says. "You recognize that guy?"

"No. But to be fair, until I actually met Madeline, I couldn't have picked her out of a police lineup."

"The guy she's talking to might have stood in a few police lineups."

The conversation between Madeline and the new guy breaks up. He walks to a nearby black Dodge Avenger while she disappears back into the building. The Avenger exits the lot on the far side; too far for us to see where it's going or to have any chance of pursuing it. Lisa taps the steering wheel.

"Nothing we can do now," she says. "You know a decent place to get breakfast?"

"Madam, *I* can make you a decent breakfast."

"I have no doubt about that. But I'm perfectly willing to buy."

"Save your expense account. I'd be glad to whip up something. And it will be served to you by the finest tuxedo cat/butler in St. Paul."

"You have him trained that well?"

"No. But he'll be perfectly willing to hang around your feet and request food."

Lisa throws the car in gear. "To the Café Davis."

We pull out of the lot, the mood at least temporarily lightened. Back of this, though, is a sinking feeling I can't quite get a handle on. Maybe it's fear about what might have happened to Rick. Maybe it's that.

CHAPTER FOUR

SUMMER, BETWEEN JUNIOR AND SENIOR YEAR

The best summer of my life.

Maybe the notion is a cliché, but I think we all have a last carefree summer; one that's largely given over to enjoyment and fun before encroaching adulthood starts to hold sway. The summer between my junior and senior years in high school was exactly that.

Not that it was completely devoid of adult concerns. I worked at my father's hardware store every weekday afternoon and all day on Saturdays. Lisa took a job as a server at the Hub Diner after the Porter's Bay Times, *for reasons passing understanding, denied her application for a summer internship. Most every evening, I'd grab a thermos filled with my mom's lemonade and head over to the gazebo in Bennett Park. Lisa would meet me there, carrying whatever pie was left over from The Hub. I'd watch her walk across the lawn, silhouetted in the evening sun. Her mouth would twist into a little smile and the coy look in her eyes would tell me that smile was just for me. One night in particular, she slipped off her white sneakers and tossed them in the corner.*

"Sorry if my feet stink," Lisa said. "Long day at work."

"You realize you wouldn't be dealing with that if you took the job in your dad's office," I told her. Lisa had been offered a receptionist job in her dad's dental office but turned him down. "You'd just be sitting around all day."

"That's exactly why I didn't take it," Lisa said. "Smelly feet or a sore ass. I'll live with my decision."

I handed her a glass of lemonade, and we had a toast. Then she leaned toward me, and I kissed her. The best part of my day.

By this point, everyone knew Lisa and I were dating. We were barraged with observations about what a cute couple we were. The relationship made sense to everyone. Except me. I felt like I won the lottery, and someone was going to come along and take it all back. But that night, like all those nightly meetings in Bennett Park, I didn't think about that. I was just there with Lisa. We kissed and the kisses grew more passionate. Then she pulled back and stared into my eyes, a scared look on her face. Then she curled into me, and I was as reassured as I could be.

Shortly after that night, our attention turned to the Shore County Fair. My excitement about taking Lisa to it was interrupted by a visit from the Harvest Queen (a pageant winner crowned at the State Fair and consigned to touring Podunk county fairs such as ours) and the murder of her advisor. In the process of solving the murder (and I never doubted Lisa would), I managed to make an ass of myself by getting jealous of *her interactions with the Harvest Queen's brother, Eric. Lisa was mad at me for a few days, but she forgave me for it. I considered that a good sign.*

And I still got to take her to the fair, I'm not sure how impressed Lisa was. It probably struck her as a little shabby. But she certainly liked the enthusiasm people had for it. We went on the rides then bought ice cream cones and strolled along the midway, holding hands. We tried out a few midway games. I went to a throwing game and attempted to win a big teddy bear for Lisa. Since I threw sidearm and off my back foot (the exact way they teach you not to do it), I had to settle for a little Curious George doll. Lisa tried a basket shooting game and won a sizeable tiger for me. In order to assuage my male ego, she kept the tiger, and I kept the Curious George doll, and we pretended each had won them for the other.

We finally stopped at a bench and people-watched for a while. Lisa laid her head on my shoulder as we made up stories for the strangers who strolled past, each story getting more ridiculous until we were tied up in fits of laughter. Lisa wiped her eyes and put an arm on the back of the bench. She asked me about my jealousy toward the Harvest Queen's brother (a thing I had really hoped we were past). I was forced to confess to her.

"It's just…look…I really like you," I said. "And there are a lot of times when, no matter how happy I am, I say to myself, 'You've got this amazing, sweet, brilliant girlfriend. What have you done to deserve that?' So, it's…easy to believe it will all go away."

I looked down, too afraid to make eye contact. Lisa's hand gently lifted my face. She put her forehead against mine.

"I understand," Lisa said. "I can't believe I have someone so funny and warm and gentle. But it's more fun to go with it and not worry too much. Got it?"

"Yeah. Sorry I was an idiot."

Lisa took my face in her hands and gave my head a gentle shake. "Eric is a cute guy. And he can be really charming. But you know what he's not?"

"What?"

"He's not you." She kissed me and gave me another shake. "You idiot."

And that put that to rest. There was another issue to deal with, though. In the few weeks preceding this, there had been something Lisa had been meaning to ask me. She'd frequently bring the subject up after we'd been kissing, when she had that scared and uncertain look on her face. (Needless to say, this did nothing *to ease my insecurity.) This time, while Lisa still seemed a bit scared, her eyes looked directly into mine.*

"Here's the deal," she said, "My family's going out of town in a few weeks. They're visiting some friends in Madison. I can't go because I have to work at The Hub. I'll just have the house to myself."

The significance of what Lisa was saying went completely past me. "Sounds cool."

"I'll just be there. Alone. If you want to come over."

"That would great."

"Just the two of us."

I still wasn't getting it. "Sounds like fun. We could…" Then I got what she was saying. My stomach started fluttering. "Why, uh, why, that would be lovely."

Lisa laughed, the cat finally out of the bag, as it were. She hugged me, holding on for several long moments. I turned my head so that my mouth was close to her ear.

"Are you sure?" I asked.

Sometimes, I can still feel her hair brushing against my cheek as she nodded. "Yes," Lisa said. "Absolutely."

"You know I've never, uh…"

"Neither have I."

"And you're sure you want me to be…"

"Yes," Lisa said. "I wouldn't want it to be anyone else."

We sat in that embrace for the longest time. I honestly didn't know what to think or feel. I was scared and nervous and wondering if this was the right thing and if I was even ready for it. And I wasn't sure I could wait a few weeks.

Best summer of my life.

And I have a few things by which to commemorate it.

We're enjoying a leisurely morning at the Davis Estate. The cloud cover is gone. The cats lounge on the floor, enjoying the sunbeams coming through the window. I busy myself in the kitchen, making breakfast. Lisa sits on the arm of the futon, sipping a mug of pumpkin spice coffee. She spots something on the shelf over my desk and hops up to give it closer inspection.

"Is that the stuffed animal I won for you at the fair?" she says, taking George down from his perch.

I finish beating the eggs and glide over to the stove to get a look to the ham, onions, and peppers sautéing. "That is the one. You still have Tony the Tiger?"

"Maybe in storage somewhere."

Something about that makes my heart sink. Fortunately (and this might be the only time I say that), the buzzer sounds for the front door. I take off my apron and temporarily leave my cooking to answer it.

"As I recall, you gave me George to assuage my ego," I say. "I'm past that now. I am a fully formed adult male, not a child growing older." I hit the intercom and hear *It's Mike.* I jerk a thumb toward the intercom. "That job has been taken."

I make sure the door is unlocked and walk back to the kitchen. I pour the eggs on the ham mixture and begin scrambling them together. A moment later, the door flies open and Mike makes his way into the apartment. He whips off his leather jacket, revealing a dress shirt and slacks that befit his latest temp job.

"Joe, I got a problem," he says. Then he spots Lisa and stops. "Oh sorry. I didn't mean to interrupt anything."

"Of course you did," I say. "If I told you I had a guest, would that have stopped you?"

"We'll never know," Mike says. He turns to Lisa and offers a hand. "Mike Griffin. I'm a friend of Joe's."

"Lisa Cleary," she says, shaking Mike's hand.

"Nice to meet you. How do you know Joe?"

Lisa face tightens. "We…went to high school together."

"Cool. Joe and I went to college. Guess we just missed each other."

She holds up a finger and points at Mike. "You were accused of murdering someone. About two years ago."

"Yeah, that was a bullshit deal." He slips into the kitchen. "You got a second?"

"Probably not," I say, "but since you're here already anyway…"

He steps past me, going to the refrigerator for a grape soda. (Mike's taste for it is the only reason I keep that insipid beverage around.) He smells as if he was smoking right before he got to my building. "I've got a problem," he says.

"With Gillian?"

"Yep, with Gillian. Things are going south in the sack."

"And by *going south*, you mean…"

"Not in the fun way, no." He cracks open a grape soda and takes a sip. "Gillian is a hell of a lot less enthusiastic. It's like she's distracted. And that's when I can get her in the sack. Last couple nights, she's been wearing the No Sex ensemble to bed. Baggy sweatshirt. Sweatpants. Socks. Socks, for God's sake! She might as well be wearing a cast iron chastity belt."

I hold up a cautioning hand. "You might be reading too much into it. It *is* that time of the year. Weather getting cooler and all."

"No, it's something else," Mike says. "I think I know what."

"Your objectionable personality? Your excess body hair? Your lack of an actual career?"

"No. And fuck you. I think it's Moira. The twin sister. I think she's been badmouthing me to Gillian. Giving her the wrong impression of me."

"Are we sure it's the *wrong* impression?" Before Mike can take offense (which he absolutely should), I move to forestall it. "You sure you're not just being paranoid?"

"It's not paranoia if it's actually happening."

I go to the refrigerator for the cheddar cheese. "Have you thought about—oh, I don't know—actually *talking* to this Moira and seeing if everything is okay?"

Mike uses the soda can to bat the suggestion out of the air. "Are you out of your mind? Nobody gives you an honest answer when you ask them a question like that. They'll either dance around it or they'll lie to your face. Seriously, sometimes it's like you haven't met actual people."

"Forgive me. I'm a trainee."

Mike takes a large swig of soda and gives the matter some further thought. Something comes to him. (Oh, joy.)

"Got it," Mike says. "Jeez, it's really simple when you think about it."

"If you're thinking about it, it must be simple."

That one flies past him. "I have to win over the sister. If I do that, everything will be great. Moira will sign off on us. Gillian and I will be like peas and carrots. And fucking."

"It's all I've ever wanted for you," I say.

"Maybe this double date will help," Mike says. "You can convince her I'm a good guy."

"*I'm* not convinced yet."

He draws back a fist, knowing full well he'll never throw that punch (and that I know that as well). "Just think about it, okay?"

"I'll give it as much thought as it deserves."

Mike strolls away (leaving the half-filled soda can on my breakfast bar). "Gotta go. I'm having brunch with Gillian." He flips open the door. "It was nice to meet you, Lisa. Maybe I'll see you around again sometime."

Lisa slowly turns in the desk chair. She has George the monkey on her lap. "Maybe. We'll see."

Mike slips out the front door. I divide the Denver Scramble into two portions and slide them onto two plates. I set the plates on the breakfast bar.

"Breakfast is served," I say.

I fetch the forks and knives from the silverware drawer and grab the coffee pot. The cats come out of the bedroom and take their places under the breakfast bar. Lisa puts George the monkey back on his shelf and sits opposite me. A blush comes to her face.

"You just make stuff like this all the time?" she asks.

"Not all the time," I say. "It's fun to cook something special."

"You always knew how to cook."

I nod toward the desk. "Were you doing research over there?"

Lisa puts a napkin in her lap (I knew I liked her). "I wanted to get some more information on Roger Neill. The eavesdropper."

I treat her to my bad Orson Welles impression. "Who knows what evil lurks in the hearts of men?" Lisa joins me for the last part. "The Eavesdropper knows." I cut into my scramble. "What did you find out?" I ask.

"Not a lot," she says. "He has a poli-sci degree from North Dakota State. He's worked on several campaigns, has done some fundraising, a little lobbying. He worked on

Longson's campaign in the special election, and he's been on the Senator's staff ever since." Lisa takes a bite of the scramble. She holds a hand to her mouth. "Oh my God, this is delicious."

"Thank you," I say. "I imagine you don't get a lot of home cooked meals."

"Not if I'm doing the cooking. When we were in high school, the only thing I could do was heat up soup and maybe make a grilled cheese. I haven't gotten much better."

I use my fork to gesture toward the desk. "You find anything interesting? About Roger Neill?"

"Not really. I could only find one quote from him. It was just some innocuous stuff about Longson's vision for America, blah, blah, blah."

"Who quoted him? The Minnesota GOP newsletter?"

"No. It was the paper in Rochester. An article by someone named Zoe Court. Part of a bigger article that was basically fellating Longson and his desire to run for president."

"Please. I'm eating."

"Try to work on expressing your opinions about Longson. Don't keep things bottled up."

I concede the point. "I liked Mark Gardner. He was a good man. Good senator. To know he got killed by some survivalist whack-job like Jeremiah Kincade and replaced by this... *buffoon* has never sat well with me." I put a hand over my heart. "I will try not to let that influence my judgment."

"Very professional of you."

I take a bite of my breakfast. "Any idea why this Roger Neill guy was eavesdropping on the meeting?"

"Nope. Seems like something we should ask him, though."

I can't help noticing the *we* in that statement. I guess we're partners in this. And I'm just fine with it. "How we do that?" I ask.

"Let me do some more research." Lisa takes another bite. "I'd like to talk to him away from the campaign. If he knows anything about Rick, he's more likely to talk that way."

We go about finishing breakfast. Lisa sneaks Lenny a piece of ham, over my objections. I threaten to throw my napkin at her, and she threatens to pick up Lenny and put him on the counter (which is strictly verboten). George the monkey watches all this from his perch above the desk. Not sure, but I think he's smiling.

***

The idea of confronting Roger Neill away from campaign HQ conjured up images of any number of meeting places: back alleys, parking garages, hotel rooms, seedy bars. You can imagine my surprise when the site of our confrontation turns out to be The Stone Mill.

The Stone Mill is a restaurant/bar at the corner of Hennepin and Lake, right in the heart of Uptown, a hipster district near Minneapolis's chain of lakes (Harriet, Isles, Maka Ska, Zeppo, etc.). Its main feature is a huge stone fireplace, separating the bar area from the restaurant. Per Lisa's research, Roger Neill frequently stops here before going home. We grab a table near one of the picture windows and keep an eye out.

Roger strolls in just after eleven and parks himself at the bar. His tie is undone, and he looks haggard. We abandon the table and join him at the bar. Lisa plunks down on the stool to Roger's right. I take the one to his left. His head swivels between us.

"Wha…what's going on?" he asks.

Lisa props an elbow on the bar. "I was hoping we could talk."

"About what?" he asks.

"Rick Michaels. Among other things."

Roger's Dewar's and Soda arrives. He thanks the bartender and takes a greedy drink. Lisa and I assure the bartender we're okay with our drinks. Roger cups his hands around his glass.

"I don't know anything about Rick," he says.

"But you worked with him?" Lisa says.

"Sure. Doesn't mean I knew him all that well."

I fold my arms on the bar. "What did he do for the Senator?"

"A lot of things. He ran errands. Drove the Senator around. Provided protection."

Lisa poises her hand on her whisky glass. "That's interesting. Because Madeline claimed she didn't know Rick and that the Senator certainly wouldn't know who he was. But if he drove the Senator around and provided protection, it's pretty likely Senator Longson knows Rick."

Roger drains the glass, his hands shaking. "I don't know anything about that. You'd have to ask Madeline."

"But you're Madeline's assistant," Lisa says. "You'd know what she knows. Right?"

"You'd think that, wouldn't you?" Roger says, unable to keep the bitterness out of his voice. Then he sighs and says, "I'm sorry, I can't speak for Madeline. You'll have to ask her about that."

Lisa doesn't seem fazed. "Speaking of Madeline, I heard a rumor that she and Rick were seeing each other."

Roger shoots a look at Lisa. This isn't the cool denial we got from Madeline herself. Instead, he asks, "How did you hear that?"

"I have my sources," Lisa says. "Is it true?"

"I don't know," Roger says. "I'd see them together, occasionally. If they were seeing each other, they were mostly discreet."

"Mostly?" Lisa asks.

Roger winces, as if he'd love to backtrack from that statement. But he's gone this far. "I saw them having a conversation in the meeting room. The same one where you met Madeline. It...didn't look friendly."

I lean in. "An argument?"

"I don't know," Roger says. "Rick looked agitated. He was pacing and waving his hands. Madeline was her usual ice queen self. It didn't look settled when Rick walked out."

"Any idea what they were talking about?" I ask.

"No," he says. "I asked Madeline about it, but she said it was nothing. End of story."

Lisa and I exchange a look. We've caught Madeline in at least one lie. She wouldn't have a heated discussion with someone she barely knew. It gives us ammunition for the next time we speak to her. Lisa decides to open a new line of inquiry.

"What can you tell us about Zoe Court?" she asks.

Fortunately, Roger wasn't sipping his drink when she asked that or he probably would have done a spit take. As it is, he nearly drops the drink. He doesn't move for a few moments.

"How did you know Zoe?" he asks.

"I don't," Lisa says. "You were quoted in an article she wrote about Senator Longson. I thought there might be some kind of relationship there."

"Relationship? What do you mean by that?"

I'm starting to wonder who exactly is doing the questioning. Lisa takes it in her stride, calmly sipping her drink.

"There are all kinds of relationships," she says. "Professional, personal, what have you. I thought you must have some kind of relationship with Zoe for you to be included in the article."

Roger senses he's made a mountain out of this particular molehill (assuming it *is* a molehill). He retreats to the safety of his drink. "Zoe was a friend," he says, quietly. "She called me to do research and we met and hit it off. That's probably why she included me in the article."

Lisa tilts her head slightly. "Zoe certainly seems to have a high opinion of the Senator. Judging by the articles she wrote."

"I guess she admired him," Roger says. "He certainly makes for good copy."

"He does that," Lisa says. "Do you know how I can get in touch with Zoe?"

Roger's jaw hangs open slightly. "You don't know? Zoe is dead."

That's the first thing I've seen rattle Lisa. Her eyes get wide. She recovers herself and straightens her glasses. "What happened?" she asks.

Roger turns back to his drink. "Suicide. About three weeks ago. She threw herself off the top of a parking ramp in Rochester."

The question escapes me before I can stop it. "Why?"

"The police haven't really said. I don't think they found a suicide note or anything."

Lisa leans forward. "Did Zoe say anything to you? Did you see anything going on?"

Roger starts to answer, then closes his mouth and gives the matter some thought. He downs the rest of his drink and signals the bartender for another. "Something was bothering her," he says. "We spoke on the phone about a week before it happened. She said she needed to talk to the Senator, but he wasn't answering her calls. She thought she was being frozen out. She asked if I could help. Maybe put in a word to Madeline or Senator Longson. I mentioned it to Madeline. She didn't say much in response."

"What did Zoe want to talk to the Senator about?" Lisa asks.

"I don't know. But she told me I should think about leaving the campaign. She wouldn't tell me why." He clutches his drink glass. "Then she was gone."

Roger barely notices when the bartender sets another drink in front of him. After a moment, Roger releases the glass, allowing the bartender to take it away. He latches on to his new drink, guzzling it. I'd say the man enjoys his scotch, but you don't enjoy it when you're knocking it back like that. Lisa puts a hand near Roger's arm.

"You don't have any theory about why Zoe did it?" she asks.

"None," he says. "She had everything to live for. She was…she was beautiful." He wipes his nose. "Rick asked me about her."

I take the lead on this one. "What did Rick ask about?"

"How well I knew her. If I knew what she was working on. Stuff about her background. A lot of the same things you two are asking me. I told him what I'm telling you. Now Rick has disappeared."

"And you don't know where he's gone?" I ask.

"I don't," Roger says.

Lisa leans toward him. "When was the conversation with Rick?"

"Week, week-and-a-half ago." Roger pushes the glass aside and shakily slips off his stool. "I need to get going." He tosses some money on the bar. Lisa offers her card. Roger takes it and stuffs it in his pants pocket. "Ms. Cleary, I know you've made your reputation looking into…things. If I were you, I'd leave this alone."

"Really?" Lisa says. "Why is that?"

Roger looks around. "I just would. Have a nice night."

With that, Roger walks to the front door, weaving slightly, and exits. I slide over, taking the stool next to Lisa.

"What do you make of that?" I ask.

"I don't know. He was in love with Zoe Court. I can tell you that much."

"You know that for sure?"

"I know what it looks like," she says. Then she takes a breath and adds: "He's not telling us something. That's easy enough to figure out."

"Especially when everybody in Longson's camp seems to be doing it."

"Das ist richtig."

My eyebrows go up. "You know German?"

"I know *that* much German. And how to ask for directions to the hotel and the beer hall."

"I don't think anyone needs more than that."

We hold up our glasses in a toast. Lisa down the rest of her whiskey. "Would you mind chauffeuring me back to my hotel?"

"Just like old times," I say.

Something in that makes me sad. Don't ask me why. We both face forward and finish our drinks in silence.

***

Lisa is staying at the Ambassador Suites, a twelve-story hotel on the eastern edge of downtown St. Paul. It's familiar enough that my Saturn Ion can practically find the place on its own. I volunteer to walk Lisa to her room. The only parking spot is on the far end of the darkened lot.

"Where do we go from here?" I ask.

Lisa props her arm near the window. "We need to find Rick. His ex-wife doesn't know where he is. Everyone at the campaign acts like they were never properly introduced. And he didn't seem to have any other friends." She puts her hand in her hair. "You have any ideas?"

"Maybe something will come to me in the morning."

"Hope springs eternal," Lisa says, without a lot of enthusiasm. Then she squares me with a look. "You don't have to walk me to my room. I'll be fine."

"It won't take long. And it'll make *me* feel better. Okay?"

"Fine. Just don't tell Tucker Carlson."

We get out of the car and start across the lot. The night is crisp, trending toward cold. Lisa huddles into her suede coat. Once upon a time, I would have put my arm around her to keep her warm. But that time is *way* in the rearview mirror. I slip my hands into my coat pockets.

"Have you actually met Tucker Carlson?" I ask.

"I have."

"What's he like?"

"Exactly how you think he'd be," Lisa says, her tone flat, even frosty.

I laugh. Since Lisa is fairly (and understandably) guarded on her social media accounts, I'm tempted to ask what other celebrities she's met. That thought goes out the window when the first bullet flies.

The crack echoes in the darkness. A bullet crashes through the window of a nearby Camry. Another crack. This bullet pings off the rear quarter-panel of another vehicle. Lisa shoves me to the ground and follows me down. I switch positions, keeping myself between Lisa and our new friend, the gunman, wherever he may be. We're hidden between two cars. Lisa's face is calm, but her breathing has noticeably picked up.

"Good," she says. "I was afraid I was the only one hearing that."

I get into a low crouch, my heart pounding in my ears. "Where's it coming from?"

"The far side of the lot," Lisa says.

Everything is quiet. No sound from the street or the hotel. I duck-walk to the end of the vehicle we're using for cover. Lisa is right behind me.

"You see anything?" she asks.

"No. But this parking lot is really poorly lit. You should talk to management about this."

Lisa takes her cell phone out of her bag and starts dialing 9-1-1. I peek out, trying to track the gunman. A shot is fired. I duck back. The bullet flies into the night. Lisa grabs my arm.

"Are you all right?" she asks.

"Blood pressure skyrocketing. Bladder control maintained. No bullet holes. This is as good as I'm going to get."

"The police are on their way."

Two more shots are fired. We huddle between the cars. Nothing gets close to us. I don't think the guy is trying to hit us so much as drive us out into the open. Footsteps are heard, faintly. Getting closer.

Another shot. Footsteps getting even closer. No sign of a police cruiser. Lisa looks around. She scoops up a rock just a little smaller than a baseball. Before I can stop her, she stands and chucks it at the gunman. She drops down before any return fire can be offered.

Someone nearby shouts, "Ow! Fuck!" This is followed by the sound of a gun hitting the pavement.

Lisa looks that direction. "And my father said I couldn't throw to save my life."

I peek out again. A figure dressed largely in black is searching the ground, holding his shoulder as he does. Then we see flashing lights from an approaching police cruiser. The gunman takes off running, unarmed.

I step out from our hiding place and follow him, moving at full speed. Lisa tries to grab my arm but can't reach me.

"Joe, what the hell are you doing?" she says. "Leave this to the police!"

"They're not going to catch him," I say.

The gunman runs toward the far end of the lot, to a grassy field in front of a small building. Tenth Street and Wacouta Avenue lie beyond it. Highway 94 looms in the distance. It's hard to make out the gunman in the darkness (his wearing all black certainly doesn't help). I've always been a fast runner. The gunman might have a lead, but I'm gaining on him. The small building is round. The gunman circles it counterclockwise. I momentarily lose sight of him. When I next see him, he's hopping into a black Dodge Avenger.

A voice comes in from inside the car. "Stan, what the fuck happened?"

Stan, the gunman, shouts as he closes the door. "Just go, Mr. Reynard! Go!"

The Avenger accelerates away from the curb, disappearing down Wacouta. I stop and catch my breath. Then I slowly walk back across the parking lot. Lisa is now in conversation with the police. Both she and the attending cop, a jarhead-looking type who might be a new iteration of The Terminator, watch me approach.

"No luck," I say.

The cop scoffs. "You run after a guy who had been shooting at you and you live to tell us about it? I'd say lucky is *all* you are."

I'm willing to bet neither Lisa nor I feel lucky at the moment.

CHAPTER FIVE

SUMMER, BETWEEN JUNIOR AND SENIOR YEAR

It was two weeks after the Shore County Fair and Lisa's parents and sister had just left town on their trip. Lisa and I made plans to meet at her place and for me to probably spend the night. Assuming I didn't suffer heart failure in the process.

I put on a black collared shirt over the Soul Driver t-shirt Lisa had bought me with her Hub money. The night was warm, so a pair of khaki shorts and my sandals completed the outfit. I made sure my hair looked just right and I gargled more mouthwash than what might be healthy. I briefly considered wearing cologne but thought my parents might get suspicious.

My cover story was a sleepover at Sam's house. My dad was good friends with Andy's dad, but less so with Sam's. Ergo, the likelihood of getting caught in a lie was diminished with Sam's folks. The trouble was I had to let Sam in on this, thus subjecting me to all manner of Our little boy is growing up *jokes.*

I do remember feeling something strange as I was getting ready to leave that night. Dad was in his favorite chair, watching the news while

Mom was cleaning the kitchen. I was crossing a threshold in my life, but I couldn't tell my parents about it. On the other hand, I don't think they wanted to hear, "Mom, Dad, I leave you now to become a man." They probably would have grounded me.

I sufficed with, "I'm going over to Sam's now."

Dad didn't look up from the TV. "Have fun. Stay out of trouble."

Mom simply called from the kitchen. "Have a good time, dear."

Obviously, I was hoping to have fun and a good time. But as the experience would be totally new to me, I couldn't guarantee either. Staying out of trouble was probably all I had to offer. I headed out the door.

I parked my car (a beat up Ford Taurus my brother Kevin gave me when he left for college) just down the street from Sam's house (and not directly in front of anybody's house, lest it draw suspicion). As I walked past Sam's place, I saw him giving me a thumbs up from his bedroom window.

I tried not to rush to Lisa's house, lest I work up a sweat. I hustled up the front steps and extended my hand toward the doorbell. Lisa opened the front door before I reached the button.

"Hi," she said, slightly breathless.

My heart pounding, I said, "Hi."

She wore a gray dress that stopped about mid-thigh. She was fussing with one of the spaghetti straps, keeping it on her shoulder. Her hair had been miraculously tamed and flowed neatly past her shoulders. She wore her contacts, so her blue eyes shone. She bit her lower lip and laid a hand on doorframe. All the breath in my body seemed to be held tight in my chest.

"You look really pretty," I told her.

Lisa's eyes dipped. "It's just because I'm wearing my contacts."

"No," I said. "You're just…you're really pretty."

A corner of her mouth went up and Lisa took my hand. "Come on in."

She led me through the foyer and into the living room. The house, as always, was neat as a pin. (Lisa's mom was, like my mom, a stickler about cleanliness.) I had spent so much time with Lisa and yet this felt foreign. I took a seat on the sofa. Lisa gestured toward the kitchen.

"I, uh, I wanted to make dinner for us," she said. "I can make spaghetti noodles, but I haven't made sauce before. I can just heat up some marinara in a jar, if that's okay."

I sat up. "Do you have any ground beef in the fridge?"

"I don't know. Maybe?"

"Let me check. If you do, I can make the sauce. That is, if you don't mind me helping."

Lisa smiled, relieved. "I would like that. Yes."

I hopped up from the couch, feeling in my element again. Sure enough, there was a pound of ground beef in the fridge. Lisa filled a stockpot with water. I found a frying pan in a drawer on the bottom of the stove and inspected the spice rack.

"Italian seasoning, cayenne, red pepper flake," I said, "and I saw some black pepper on the dining room table. We're in business."

Lisa fetched the black pepper from the dining room table and handed it to me as I donned an apron I found next to the refrigerator. "Old family recipe?" she asked.

"Just something my mom taught me. And something I came up with myself." I started browning the ground beef and sprinkled in some Italian seasoning and black pepper. After working that into the meat, I added smaller sprinkles of cayenne pepper and red pepper flake. "My mom taught me to use the Italian seasoning and the black pepper. I started using the cayenne and red pepper flake myself. Just gives it a little kick."

Lisa folded her arms. "I'm impressed. A regular chef."

"Not exactly," I said, my face getting warm. "Just a guy who knows how to make spaghetti sauce."

We finished making dinner and decided to eat out on the deck. The sun was going down, bathing the yard in a golden glow. The night was warm and perfectly comfortable. Lisa's father had built the deck the previous summer, right after the family moved to town. There wasn't as much history here for Lisa's family as there was for me and my family in our house. Even still, there was a notable lack of enthusiasm in Lisa talking about any aspect of her family. I set my fork aside.

"Can I ask you something?" I said. "I get the feeling your dad doesn't like me."

"That's not technically a question. That's a statement."

"Fishing for something doesn't count as a question?"

Lisa reached to straighten her glasses before realizing she wasn't wearing them. "Sometimes, I wonder if he likes me. I know I'm his *daughter. I know he loves me. Great. But he never reads my stuff in the paper. He never says anything about my grades. He never asks about the stuff I'm involved in. But my sister Amy? He goes to all of her games. Volleyball, basketball, softball, he never misses one of them. He wants to spend time around Amy, and he never wants to spend time with me. He offered me a chance to work in his dental office. But that wouldn't be spending time. That would just be work." Lisa waved a hand, realizing she had gotten off track. "Long story short, I think he wanted me to date a jock. If I couldn't be a jock myself, I could at least be jock-adjacent."*

"I'm the only one in my family who doesn't fit that bill. Sorry."

"You don't have to apologize. It's my dad's thing, not mine."

I picked at my food. "Why do you think it's so important to him?"

Lisa took a bite of her spaghetti. "He was an athlete himself. In high school. Maybe he wants to re-live all that. Maybe he really wanted boys instead of girls."

"I'm glad he had girls," I said. "At least one, anyway."

Lisa reached for my hand. "I never feel like I have to prove myself with you."

"And you never will."

We finished dinner and put our plates in the sink. Lisa declined going back out to the deck, suddenly nervous the neighbors might see us and report it back to her parents. We lingered in the living room instead. Lisa offered to open a bottle of wine, but I wasn't sure. I was a little uneasy about anything that might make me lose control. (I can't believe I used to think that way.) Lisa then realized her parents might notice a bottle missing when they got home. After all, how the hell could she replace it? Instead, we grabbed some Cokes and sat on the couch.

Lisa played with the hem of her dress. I kept tugging at the neck of my collared shirt. Our nerves built as the sun went down and the night seemed to hold expectations. What was the protocol for deciding when to go to the bedroom? Was there a protocol? And did we even want to? After a sustained silence, I leaned toward Lisa.

"Are you sure you want me here?" I asked.

Lisa cupped her hands around my face. "I meant what I said. I wouldn't want it to be anybody but you. Nobody sees me the way you do. Why wouldn't I want to be with someone like that?"

I put my hands over hers, stroking them with my thumb. "I'm glad."

She gave me that smile that was just for me, then a shy, nervous look came over her face. She slid to the other side of the sofa. I picked up an unopened can of Coke from the coffee table. A thing I had neglected to remember was I had been rolling it between my hands during the silence stretch. So when I opened it, the damn thing exploded, catching me full in the face.

Lisa grabbed the can from me in order to bring it to the kitchen. She caught a look at me with Coca-Cola dripping off my chin and what I imagine was a befuddled expression on my face. She started laughing. Really hard.

"I'm sorry," Lisa said, gasping.

Within moments, the dripping can of Coke was forgotten about and Lisa collapsed back on the couch, holding her stomach. I found myself laughing as well, imagining what I must look like. Soon, I was doubled over as well. Finally, Lisa put her hand on my back.

"Everything okay?" she asked.

I tugged at my shirt. "It's fine. My parents wouldn't believe I spent the night at Sam's without getting a few stains on my clothes."

Lisa wiped away tears. Then she laid a hand against my cheek and said, "Kiss me."

I did. It wasn't, at first, unlike anything we had done already. The nightly visits to the gazebo in Bennett Park made us comfortable with this. Then it slowly built in intensity. Lisa let out a slow breath of air as I kissed her shoulder, carelessly knocking the spaghetti strap from her shoulder. Her lips brushed against my ear.

"Do you want to go upstairs?" she asked.

"Yes."

Lisa took my hand and led me up to her room. I found myself lingering in the doorway before I finally closed the door. Lisa crossed to the other side of the bed and turned on the lamp on her nightstand. We stood there, the bed between us. Lisa turned back the covers.

"I'll meet you in there," she said.

She grabbed the hem with both hands and pulled her dress over her head. I stood there, seeing her, a mix of fear and lust rushing through me. I took off my clothes and climbed into bed with her, the sheets cool against my skin. Lisa ran her hand down my arm.

"You're trembling," she said.

"I'm sorry."

Lisa's face was close to mine. She looked into my eyes. "It's okay. It's just me."

She brought my face to hers. Our hands glided over each other, exploring new territory. Lisa laid back, gently pulling me on top of her. I looked into her eyes. They were scared but inviting. I could see something deeper. I could see her. All of her. I brushed a strand of hair away from her face.

"I love you."

Lisa's eyes glistened. "I love you."

Then she reached over and turned out the light.

I flip on the hall light and lead the way into my apartment. As per usual, the cats come out from wherever they're hiding to greet me, ask about my day, demand that I feed them. Lisa closes the backdoor and leans against it.

"We didn't have to come here," she says. "I was freaked out for a minute, but I'm fine."

"Well, maybe I'm freaked out," I say, walking over to the liquor shelf.

The conversation with the police wasn't exactly fruitful, but I can't pin it on them. We couldn't describe the gunman. I gave them the make and model of the getaway car but couldn't tell them the license plate number. They bagged the weapon and found evidence of shots being fired, so they believed our story. But they couldn't promise much in the way of progress. Lisa didn't feel like going to her hotel room, so I brought her back here. She sits on the futon as I hand her a whiskey on the rocks and plunk down next to her, cradling a whiskey of my own. Lisa takes a gulp.

"Sorry," she says. "I don't know why I reacted that way. I've been in a warzone, for God's sake."

"When you were in a warzone, were any of those bullets directed at you personally?"

"Not that I know of."

"There you go, sport," I say. "This was personal."

Lisa tucks one leg under her. "You think Longson is trying to have us killed?"

"Us? You're the star reporter, madam. I just write glorified dick jokes."

She squares me with a look. "I wouldn't go that far. I read your column. I know about you saving your friend Mike. I know about the thing with the wrestlers. I know about you being accused of murdering…some woman's husband."

Lisa looks away when she says that last part. I'm not anxious to talk about the affair with Norah under the best of circumstances, and these hardly qualify. I knock back some whiskey.

"I don't know if it's Longson himself," I say. "But it's got to be someone with the campaign. It might explain why Roger Neill was so nervous when he was talking to us."

"And what might have happened to Rick."

That doesn't exactly lift the mood in the room, but Lisa might be right. We have to face the possibility something has happened to Rick. I cradle the whiskey in my lap.

"Where do we go from here?" I ask.

Lisa tilts her head. "I'd like to know more about Zoe Court. I can do a little research there. Probably won't get me anywhere."

"A dead end?"

"You know, I really avoided saying a thing like that."

"Too soon?"

"No," Lisa says, "I just hate puns." Lisa takes a smaller sip of her whiskey. "Maybe we need to check out Rick's place. See if we can find anything."

"You mean break in?"

Lisa has the old mischievous look in her eyes. "It's been a while. You still up for it?"

"It hasn't been as long as you think. Besides, I know an expert in the field."

"Who would that be? Don't tell me you and Sam still do this sort of thing."

"No, he's terrible at it. My friend Mike is the better choice."

"Understood. But let me call Rick's ex. He might have trusted Katie with his spare key."

Good idea. Funny how the simple solution often escapes me. It would save us the breaking, at least. The *entering* might be more problematic, particularly if Rick is hiding out there. I'll worry about that later, though. Speaking of hiding out…

"I'd rather you didn't go back to the hotel," I say. "I don't think it's safe there anymore."

"I'll be fine," Lisa says. "They're not going to come back tonight."

"What about the future?"

"I don't know. What do you think I should do?"

"You're welcomed to stay here," I say.

"You sure I'd be safer here?"

"I *do* have two vicious attack cats."

Lisa looks toward the comfy chair, where Lenny is currently licking himself and Squiggy is looking on with polite disapproval. "They don't seem particularly vicious."

"You haven't seen them at feeding time. Besides, I also have a crazy old guy who lives on the first floor who keeps an eye on everything. And he has a nice little gun collection."

"What about my stuff at the hotel?"

"We can go get it tomorrow, and you can check out. No sense running up expenses if you've got a friend you can stay with. I've got a spare toothbrush and you're welcome to take my bed. I can crash on the futon."

Lisa pats the sofa. "The futon will be plenty comfortable for me. Do you have spare bedding as well?"

"Of course."

"Why am I not surprised?" She then adds, quietly: "You don't have to do this."

"I want to. It would make me feel better. Besides, we're…we're in this together now."

"This is true. Okay, I'll stay."

The last of the adrenaline wears away from Lisa. She takes off her glasses and rubs her eyes. I fetch some spare bedding and an extra toothbrush from the hall closet. When I get back, Lenny has climbed up on Lisa's lap. She strokes his back and chats with him, mostly about his status as a good boy. (Squiggy sits nearby, keeping his dissenting opinion to himself.) I've probably lost their company for the night. It's okay. My loss, their gain.

***

My apartment isn't large, but sometimes that's a good thing. On a bright morning in the fall, for example, it doesn't take a lot of sunlight to make the place brilliant. The aroma from a simple pot of pumpkin spice coffee fills the entire apartment. The music (in this case, a Beatles playlist on Spotify) doesn't have to be blasting to fill the all corners. This is one of those occasions when my apartment is shown (literally) in its best light.

Lisa is at my desk, wearing yesterday's clothes and working on her laptop. (We'll have to get her stuff from the hotel soon.) She finishes up the article she was working on in Chicago before getting the call from Rick. The hash browns on the stove are coming along nicely. I finish beating the eggs in the mixing bowl and set them aside. I pick up the coffeepot and carry it into the living room to refill Lisa's cup. A corner of her mouth rises.

"You're spoiling me," she says.

"Just playing the role of a good host. Squiggy demands no less."

I return to the kitchen and put the coffeepot back. As I'm doing this, the front door opens, and Lars bursts into the apartment. Obviously, for all its comfort, my apartment *does* have its drawbacks...

"Hey brother," he says, gliding to the breakfast bar. "I was wondering when we're going to do another script session. I was hoping..." He spots Lisa. He spins on his heel and moves toward the desk. One hand smooths his floral print shirt while the other is extended toward Lisa. "My apologies, madam. I didn't realize Joe had a guest. My name is Lars."

Lisa spins the chair and shakes Lars's hand. "Lisa Cleary."

"Enchantée," he says, kissing her hand.

This is a rare occasion in which the use of French is just out-and-out gross. Lisa, though, tolerates it. Lars releases her hand and steps back.

"Sorry if I'm interrupting something," he says.

"Lisa's a guest," I say. "It's a long story."

Lars slips his hands into the pockets of his slacks. "How do you know Joe?"

Lisa's face falls. "We were…friends in high school."

He accepts this without asking follow-up questions (thank the gods). Lisa goes back to her article. I wipe my hands on my apron and return to breakfast.

"What brings you by, Lars?" I ask.

He plunks down on a stool at the breakfast bar. "Just hoping to talk about the movie."

"I don't know if I'm speaking to you on that front," I say. "Last meeting we had, you hung me out to dry. Ollie wants to do everything up to—and possibly including—crashing the Statue of Liberty into the Grand Canyon, and when I raise an objection, you sit there and make like Silent Bob."

"I know," he says.

"Ollie's got Michael Bay-sized ambition. And sadly, Michael Bay-sized talent. We'll go bankrupt before we have twenty minutes of footage."

"I am aware of this."

I turn away from the stove. "Then why aren't you saying anything?"

Lars rubs his hands together. "My friend, are you familiar with the idea of giving someone enough rope to hang themselves?"

"No, Lars. I only have a bachelor's degree and have been dragging a crank around this planet for thirty-five years. I have no idea what you're talking about."

"I see. It means that if you give someone enough space—"

"I know what it means, you fucking moron!" I say, trying (and failing) to keep my voice down. "How does it apply here?"

Lars holds up a hand, asking for my patience. "Ollie's potential destruction of this film is all part of my plan. You see, mon Ami, since we started this project, I've become more and more attached to the idea of directing the film. While working with you on the script, through many productive—"

"Not to say aggravating."

"—sessions, I began to get visions of how this film could come together. Sadly, Frankie and Fabio had already settled on Ollie as a director. After listening to him, I realized Ollie would be absolutely hopeless as a director. Frankie can't see it yet. I think she's enamored of Ollie. But I have faith that once Frankie emerges from her cloud of schoolgirl lust, she will see the truth. Ergo, my best approach is to do nothing and let Ollie talk his way out of the job." Lars takes a pair of shades from his coat pocket and slips them on. "Once our investors see the light, Ollie will be summarily dismissed, and I can swoop in and save the film."

I'll admit: I see the method in Lars's madness (when usually, it's the other way around). The front door buzzer sounds. (Jeez, Grand Central Station around here today.) I answer it and find it's Carol. I buzz her in and return to the kitchen. I grab a block of cheddar cheese, and begin shredding it on a plate.

"You sure this is going to work?" I ask. "Frankie and Fabio aren't generally the kind to say no. Frankie, particularly. And it's not like they're good with money. Their parents are really the ones bankrolling this thing."

"I'm counting on that last part. The parents are like a firewall in this thing. You've met Dr. Piper. If he gets a load of Ollie's ideas, he'll not only insist Ollie be fired, he might put a contract out on him."

I wish I had Lars's faith. My few meetings with Dr. Piper have given me the impression he's a no-nonsense guy.

But given that he has raised two idiot children and gone into business with Lars, his judgment is clearly not infallible. It's a mark of my own desperation that I'm willing to let Lars go through with this plan.

"Good luck to you, son," I say.

The front door opens and Carol steps in. As always, she's dressed professionally, wearing a white blouse and black slacks under her white coat. However, her hair is a little mussed and she looks tired. (Having a real job must take it out of you.) She notices the place is more crowded than usual. She spots the one new element in the room. Lisa turns to greet her. Carol's eyes widen.

"Your name is Lisa," Carol says. "You were Joe's girlfriend in high school."

Lisa's face lights up. "I was."

Carol extends a hand. "I'm Carol Ryan. I saw your picture in Joe's yearbook last summer. The bunch of us were up in Porter's Bay for his dad's retirement."

Lars whistles. "It was a crazy-go-nuts time."

Lisa sits back. "Joe showed you his yearbook?"

"Not exactly," Carol says. "I was visiting and found it on my own. Stumbled across the picture. I was really surprised." Again, Lisa's face falls. Carol senses she's stepped in something. She moves to remedy it. "You two really did make a cute couple."

Lisa smiles, wanly. "The cutest, according to our classmates."

"It's nice to meet you. What brings you by?"

I jump in. "Lisa and I are working on something."

Carol is curious but, with Lars in presence, she decides to let it go. She walks over to the breakfast bar while Lisa returns to her article. I fetch her a cup of coffee.

"I just finished a meeting," Carol says. "Thought I'd stop by." Carol turns to Lars and me. "What are we talking about?"

"The movie," I say. "It's our main topic of conversation these days."

"Mine, too," Carol says.

I cock my head to one side. "Oh? Why is that?"

"Because I've been seeing Fabio."

I nearly drop the cup of coffee. Lars tries to lean on the bar and misses. He narrowly avoids going ass over teakettle. I carefully set the coffee down.

"Please tell me *seeing Fabio* means you've been consulting him about the movie," I say.

"It does," Carol says. "When we're not having sex."

Lars flinches like he's on the receiving end of a wet willie. I hold up my hands and do a full circle in the kitchen. Carol looks singularly unrepentant. I put my hands on the breakfast bar.

"Please tell me you're joking," I say.

"I'm not," Carol says. "Fabio and I are having a good time. A surprisingly good time."

"I suppose this is the part where you tell me he's not the idiot I think he is," I say.

"No. He's absolutely the idiot you think he is," Carol says. "But he's very sweet. Like being with a dopey little puppy who's surprisingly good in the sack."

My hash browns could still use a few more minutes, so I'm stuck in this conversation. I hold my hands out, palms down. Mr. Reasonable.

"You know who this guy is, right?" I say. "He has no job, really. He lives with his parents. He builds his existence around getting high and hanging in da club. And I don't see that changing. In fact, if this movie is any kind of success, *all* of those things might get worse."

"I know that, Joe," Carol says, squaring me with a look. "I did *not* say I've found the great love of my life. This thing with Fabio is fun for now. There's nothing wrong with that, is there?"

There really isn't, but I retain the right to disapprove. While I appreciate Carol's friendship and recognize that I wouldn't have it if she hadn't taken up with Mike once upon a time, I could never figure out why she dated him. I thought it was an outlier. But now she's with Fabio, who makes Mike look like Neil deGrasse Tyson. Still, I hold up my hands in surrender.

"I wish you the best," I say.

"Thank you, Joe," Carol says, deadpan. "That means *so* much to me."

Lars hops off his stool. "I think it's great."

Carol snaps him a look. "You do?"

"Indeed," Lars says. "We need an ally in our fight against Ollie and you, Carol, can be that ally. I would imagine Fabio is but putty in your hands."

"Butt putty," I say. "I think I saw that on *Extreme Makeover.*"

Carol gives me an annoyed look and turns back to her other idiot friend. "Lars, I'm not going to manipulate Fabio just to help you guys with the movie."

Lars holds up one long finger. "Look at the big picture here. We all know how this thing with Fabio will play out. Sooner or later—probably sooner—you'll get tired of his personality. It will eventually override the great sex. When that happens, you will—I'm sure in the nicest way possible—kick Fabio's worthless ass to the curb. Am I right?"

Carol's mouth tightens. Then, slowly, the fight seeps out of her. "You're right."

Lars claps his hands together. "As I suspected. But while you and Fabio are, in the words of George Bernard Shaw, bumping uglies, maybe some good can come out of it."

My coffee stops short of my lips. "When did Shaw write *bumping uglies*?"

"*Caesar and Cleopatra*," Lars says. "It's in the subtext. Carol, help us out, huh? Remind Fabio what an idiot Ollie is. It won't be hard. Ollie will do most of the work for you."

Carol seems less than sold on this idea. "I don't know. It feels like I'm manipulating Fabio. That doesn't seem nice."

"You'd be doing him a favor," Lars says. "You'll save him unaccounted amounts of money and untold amounts of misery. If the relationship is doomed in the long run, can you think of a better way to let him down easy? *And* help out two good friends in the meantime?"

Carol lets out a long breath. "Fine. I'll help you out."

"I knew you wouldn't shrink at the last!" Lars says, slapping the breakfast bar.

"Sure, Lars, I really feel like I stepped up," Carol says.

I get up from the breakfast bar and check the hash browns. They're looking just about ready. I turn back to Lars and Carol.

"It's great to see a plan come together," I say. "Okay, breakfast is ready and I only made enough for two. Ergo, I would like to—in my most polite and winning manner—ask the two of you to fuck off out of here."

They move toward the front door. Lars assures Carol they will talk again. Carol looks like she's just made an appointment for a particularly uncomfortable mammogram. They say their goodbyes to Lisa before leaving. I pour the eggs into the frying pan and slowly combine them with the hash browns. A few minutes later, I add some cheese over the top. While it's melting, I get out plates and silverware and set the breakfast bar. A look back tells me we're ready to go.

"Soup's on," I say.

Lisa gets up from the desk, while I use the spatula to dish up breakfast. She looks over what I've made before sitting down.

"What is this?" Lisa asks.

"It's an Earth Breakfast. Your basic eggs, hash browns and cheese, scrambled together."

"Something your mom used to make?"

"Nope. Got the recipe from a local breakfast joint."

Lisa takes a tentative bite. She smiles widely, sets her fork down, and braces herself against the breakfast bar. She says, "Oh my God that is delicious."

That gives me a lift. I toss aside my apron and join Lisa at the breakfast bar. Lenny and Squiggy mill around our feet in case we decide to share anything. After a few minutes, Lisa tilts her head.

"You've known Mike since college," she says.

"Met him about five minutes after I got there."

"So, about seventeen years. How long have you known Lars?"

"Since I moved in here. About seven years."

"And Carol?"

"Roughly five."

"These are your closest friends?"

"Absolutely."

Lisa straightens her glasses. I fumble with my napkin, left to draw my own conclusions. My three closest friends, all of whom I've known for several years, either don't know Lisa or barely know her. It requires an explanation. But I don't have one. At least, not one I want to get into. It's clear we need another topic of conversation. I come up with one as I retrieve a jar of salsa from the fridge.

"You find out anything about Zoe Court?" I ask.

"A little," Lisa says, running back to the desk to get her notes. "She was a reporter for the *Rochester Herald*. Worked there for almost five years. She was one of the first to identify Bill Longson as a potential political contender. She wrote a series of articles that stopped just short of being campaign ads. Longson gave her several interviews, before and after he became a senator." She returns to her seat at the breakfast bar. "She was clearly a fan."

Lisa takes out a photo she's printed and slides it over to me. A picture of Zoe Court. She's thin and blonde, slight overbite, in her late twenties, maybe early thirties. Her eyes carry a certain confident that I've seen before. The woman on the other side of the breakfast bar possesses them as well.

I slide the photo back to Lisa. "You find out anything about her death?"

"Not a lot. She didn't leave a note. Co-workers said she'd been distracted lately, possibly depressed. Her editor said her work had dropped off. She didn't have a lot of friends. Family hadn't been in touch with her lately."

"Not anything that would contradict a suicide."

"Not that I can see."

I spoon some salsa onto my eggs. "Any idea why she wanted to talk to Longson? Or why she told Roger Neill to leave the campaign?"

"No. I don't mind floating a theory, but I need a hell of a lot more than this before I try."

"Nothing about a connection to Rick?"

'Nope. I looked pretty thoroughly. He's not quoted or mentioned in any of her articles."

Shazbot. I offer the jar of salsa to Lisa. She declines. I take a bite of my breakfast and think things over. There's no evidence that Zoe Court's death has anything to do with Rick's disappearance, although Rick *did* ask Roger Neill about Zoe. How could that be coincidence? And how does it relate to Rick's disappearance?

"Your research tell you anything else?" I ask.

"I called Rick's ex-wife," she says. "Katie has never heard of Zoe Court. As far as checking out Rick's place, she doesn't have his spare key. She's not sure who does."

"We're going with the break-in then?"

"Looks like it. Unless you're not up for that kind of kid stuff anymore."

I tuck my hand under my chin. "When have I ever let that stop me? As a wise man once said, 'You're only young once, but you can be immature forever.'"

Lisa laughs. "Did a wise man really say that?"

"Well, he was a pitcher for the Philadelphia Phillies, so I'm not sure how wise he was. But that is an actual quote."

She raises her coffee cup in a toast. "To the wisdom of the Philadelphia Phillies."

We clink coffee cups and finish our breakfast. After all these years, she and I are going to stage another break-in together. We really haven't outgrown this stuff.

Same old, same old.

***

"I wanted Moira's approval," Mike says. "It think it backfired on me."

No surprise there. Mike's plans generally backfire before they explode entirely. It's the way of things. *How* things backfired with his girlfriend's twin sister is the only X factor here.

"What happened?" I ask.

Mike makes sure Lisa is out of earshot. "Moira wants to sleep with me."

I nearly stumble, and there's only the tile floor to trip on. We're in the lobby of a high-rise apartment building in downtown St. Paul. Rick's place is several floors above us. We're walking toward the elevator, Lisa trailing us by several steps. Mike is updating me on his f'ed up love life while also acting as point man on the coming break-in. I try to keep things on the downlow.

"Sleep with you?" I ask. "Moira's the twin sister, right? I didn't mess that up?"

"Yes, she's the sister," Mike says, chewing his goatee. "And yes, things are messed up. Moira wants to sleep with me. Although, I don't think she's planning to do any sleeping."

"Okay, I need some context. How did we get from Moira doesn't like you to Moira wants to bop 'til you drop in the hot city?"

"That a reference to something?"

"Rick Springfield. I'm not proud of it. Move on.'

We're closing in on the elevator, so Mike has to rush. "I met Moira for coffee this morning. Thought it might break the ice. I'm trying everything I can. Then, out of the blue, she says she wants me. Said something about making sure I was the right guy for Gillian. She wants to…try me out."

"An audition. That *is* pressure."

"Joe…"

"Sorry."

"It's crazy, right? She's the sexual gatekeeper for her sister? You think it's always been like that?"

"Not enough to evidence to make a call," I say. "What did you tell her?"

"That I had to think about it. I'm worried if I don't sleep with Moira, she's going to tell Gillian to drop me." Mike runs a hand through his hair. "I don't know what to do."

"And I don't know what to tell you," I say. "I've never been in a situation like that."

"What about Renee and Tina?"

"They were roommates. And one of them had a boyfriend. Totally different story."

"Keep telling yourself that."

We finally reach the elevator. Lisa catches up, and Mike and I take on a furtive sort of demeanor. Lisa looks us over.

"Everything okay?" she asks.

"Peachy," Mike says.

"Jiffy swell," I say.

She's smart enough to know something is going on and not to ask about it. The elevator ride takes us to the fifteenth floor and is conducted largely in silence. Rick's apartment is near the end of the hall. There is no sign of a neighbor and minimal noise coming from the other apartments. We are, for the moment, free to do our fiendish work. Mike stops in front of Rick's door and calmly assesses the situation.

"Door shouldn't be a problem," he says. "I haven't seen a security camera, but that doesn't mean it isn't there. Stick close to me. Cover what I'm doing."

Lisa and I crowd around. My head is on a swivel, making sure the coast is clear. I hope someone doesn't come out of their apartment and wonder why there's a sudden huddle around Rick Michaels's door. Mike goes to work and, as per usual, it's but the work of a moment. The door flips open.

"Have fun," Mike says.

Lisa and I step into the apartment. It's a simple one-bedroom affair. A spacious living room, kitchen, bedroom, bathroom, hardwood floors. The walls are white, and the furniture is black. While this might be our show, we aren't the first to mount it. Someone has been here before us because the place is trashed.

Couch cushions are overturned. Paperwork is scattered around the floor. Desk drawers hang open. Cabinets have been gone through. Clothing is tossed over various pieces of furniture. The motivational posters on the wall are knocked askew. Even the refrigerator and the pantry have been ransacked. Foodstuffs cover the kitchen floor and counters. Lisa and I come to a halt.

"You think somebody grabbed Rick?" I say.

"I don't think so," she says. "This isn't a sign of a struggle. This is someone trying to find something. I'm guessing they didn't have any luck."

"You think we will?"

"Let's hope."

I'll give Lisa credit: she's not dainty in looking around (not that I thought she would be). She tosses things about and goes through the paperwork on the floor. I briefly consider checking out the kitchen, but the thought makes me nauseous. I peek in the bedroom, hoping I don't find Rick's body there. Thankfully, I don't, though the room is equally trashed. I return to the living room. Lisa is looking over a newspaper clipping.

"Find something?" I ask.

"It's an article from the *Rochester Herald*. By Zoe Court."

Lisa hands me the clipping. It's from about a month ago. Far from being the puff piece Zoe seemed to specialize in, this one talks about Longson's disdain for his predecessor.

He describes Mark Gardner as *a sawed-off little egghead professor*. According to Longson, Gardner was just another *bleeding heart giving away taxpayer money to minorities with their hands out*. When asked if Gardner's death was a break for him, Longson says *It was a break for everyone. We're better off.* No mention of Gardner's bereaved family.

I hand the article back to Lisa and say, "Quite the statesman."

"It's the kind of boorish shit Longson usually says. The difference is, it's in one of Zoe's articles. She usually wrote about him like he was a cross between Teddy Roosevelt and Abraham Lincoln. Like she was trying to balance out the way most of the media portrayed him."

"Fair and balanced?"

"Don't even." Lisa scans the article. "This is the first thing I've seen Zoe write that didn't make Longson look godlike. And Rick has a clipping of it."

"Maybe it's part of his opposition research."

"Maybe," Lisa says. "It just makes me wonder why Zoe turned on Longson like this."

"Maybe her depression was fueling it."

"You think she was depressed?"

"She committed suicide by throwing herself off a parking garage," I say. "It's not the sort of thing one does if they're walking on sunshine."

Lisa stuffs the article in her coat pocket. "I'll look into it a little more. Let's see if there's anything else to find."

We go through the trashed apartment as quickly and thoroughly as we can. Mike stands by the door, keeping an eye out. After a few minutes, I find something on the floor by the desk. It's an old handheld tape recorder. Lisa comes over for a look.

"My God, they still make those things?" she says.

"Apparently," I say. "Maybe Rick was the one keeping the industry afloat."

"If he has a tape recorder, he must have some tapes. Maybe that will tell us something."

We go through the place, but a funny thing happens on the way to discovering outdated technology: we don't find any tapes. It's not for a lack of looking. I finish digging through the bedroom closet and toss aside several items of clothing in disgust.

"Nothing," I say. "Do you think Rick took the tapes with him?"

"Would they be any good without the player?" Lisa asks, going through the bathroom.

"Probably not." I toss aside the last of Rick's abandoned clothing. "Maybe whoever ransacked this place found them."

"Maybe," Lisa says. "I'm still betting they didn't find anything. That's why they're looking for Rick. And why he's hiding." Lisa's voice sounds intrigued. "This is interesting."

I step into the bathroom. "What have you got?"

"A little love note to Rick." It's scribbled down on a sticky note. Lisa reads it aloud. "*Thank you for last night, stud. Just what I needed to relax me. M.*"

"Probably not M from the James Bond series?"

"I wouldn't bet on it," Lisa says, digging in her jacket pocket. "Let me check something."

Lisa holds up the sticky note on which Madeline Hauser wrote her phone number. She holds it next to the love note found in the bathroom. The handwriting is a match, particularly the distinctive *M*.

"I guess Katie's intuition was right," I say. "Rick was hooking up with Madeline Hauser."

"That's *two* lies we've caught her in," Lisa says. "First, there's the conversation Roger Neill saw, meaning she knew Rick better than she let on. And we have this." Lisa taps the note. "Telling me she knew him *a lot* better than she let on."

"You think this…" I say, indicating the general destruction, "is her handiwork?"

"If not hers directly, she might have contracted out." Lisa pockets the two notes. "I'm going to hold on to these."

Suddenly, we hear voices from the hallway. Lisa and I step into the main room and find Mike in conversation with someone standing just outside the apartment.

"Are you with the building?" an unfamiliar voice asks.

Lisa stiffens. I hold up a hand, cautioning her. If this new person is talking to Mike, it's best to let Mike go about his fiendish work. I step toward the front door, trying to get a look at the conversation. Mike is talking to a bald, heavyset man in his forties. The guy's floral print shirt and tan cargo shorts indicate he's either on vacation or working from home today. Mike has his arms folded, telling me he's in control of the situation.

"I'm afraid that's classified," Mike says.

The neighbor flinches like Mike just cut one (which is not out of the realm of possibility). "Classified? What are you doing that could be classified?"

Mike tosses up a hand. "If I told you, it wouldn't be classified, would it?"

The neighbor, though, is not easily dissuaded. He peeks past Mike and into the apartment. I try to stay out of the line of sight (though I'm sure the neighbor has seen me).

"Who the hell are you?" the neighbor asks.

Mike looks around, making sure nobody is in sight. The neighbor inadvertently looks as well. Mike seems to be debating an answer (which is exactly what he wants this guy to think).

"This stays strictly between you and me," Mike says. "Because if it doesn't, I know who to come looking for." He takes a breath. "I'm with the company."

"The company?" the neighbor asks. "What company?"

"*The* company."

The neighbor's eyes get wide. "You mean the CI—"

"Don't say it!" Mike holds up a finger, quieting the neighbor. "Just know that we've got business here. Don't ask me what business. I can't tell you. Well, I could tell you, but then I'd have to kill you. I don't have a problem with killing you. But I don't want the aggravation, and I sure as hell don't want the paperwork. You understand what I'm saying?"

"I...I think I do. Sure."

"That's good." Mike puffs himself up. "Now, here's what you're going to do. You're going to go back to your apartment and forget you saw anything. Don't tell anybody. Don't even think about it yourself. Do what you need to do to relax. Make yourself dinner, a drink, take a shower, jack off, I don't care what it is. But know that we have your best interests at heart. Unless we have to kill you."

"Uh, sure," the neighbor says. "Those two in there. Are they..."

"More willing to kill you than I am? Shit, yes. I'm the *good* cop. Remember that."

"I will, I will," the neighbor says, backpedaling, "I'll be remembering. And forgetting. Whatever you need me to do."

Mike waits to make sure the neighbor has vacated the area. A door is heard, faintly, opening and closing. Mike looks into the apartment and gives us the thumbs up. A look of admiration plays on Lisa's face.

"He's good," she says.

"No, he's awful," I say. "But he's good at *that.*"

We give the room another once-over, but it's clear we've found everything of interest. Besides, we don't want any more neighbors getting stories of CIA assassins. We head out.

Mike leads the way back to the car. I can't help wondering if our entire escapade has been caught on video. This seems like the kind of place to have surveillance. But no security guards accost us. Lisa glances at her phone. Something causes her to let out a little gasp. We stop.

"Roger Neill," she says, vacantly.

"What about him?" I ask.

"He's dead."

Wow. What are the odds the CIA is involved in *that?*

CHAPTER SIX

SEPTEMBER, SENIOR YEAR

Looking back, the beginning of our senior year was a little unusual. Yes, we were vaguely aware that much of what we were doing was being done for the last *time. Graduation and the huge void of adulthood lay on the not-too-distant horizon. But if childhood taught us anything, it's that the school year takes* forever. *Why worry about that stuff when it's so far away?*

As such, Lisa and I and our friends easily fell into our usual activities: working on the school newspaper, working on the yearbook, going to football games on Friday night, hanging out at Arthur's Diner after school, considering auditioning for the fall play and ultimately rejecting it because it was a musical and the thought of singing in front of others was simply too terrifying. Same old, same old.

Per Lisa's advice from the summer, I took things slow and enjoyed every day that came along. Of course, when sex is part of the equation for the first time in your life and *you're in love with your partner, living in the moment feels rather easy.*

The hard part for us was finding…quality time. Yes, there were nights when my parents and Owen would go to the movies, and I had the house to myself. Similarly, there were nights when Lisa's parents and sister were out (usually at one of her sister's volleyball games). But those evenings weren't nearly as frequent as one would hope. It was a good thing we started going up to Revelation Bluff.

As advertised, the place was a bluff with a spectacular view of Lake Superior. There were picnic areas and parking spaces and a few campsites. It was mostly wooded, and the campsites and picnic areas were in little coves. Mostly, it was a place teenagers could hide from the prying eyes of adults.

This particular night, we had Lisa's parents' station wagon, which was a gift from the gods. (Those who have attempted to make love in the backseat of a beaten up Ford Taurus will know what I'm talking about.) We found a relatively secluded space with a view of the lake. We climbed onto the hood of the car, just to spend some time before…spending some time. Lisa cuddled into me as we gazed at the vast darkness of Lake Superior. The leaves were beginning to turn color. The night was crisp but not cold. The warmth of our bodies would suffice.

I kissed the top of Lisa's head. "Going to the football game on Friday?"

"I have to," Lisa said. "I'm taking photos for the Bay Breeze. *"*

"You taking pictures of a football game," I said, unable to hide my amusement. "You hate *sports."*

"*I know how to use a camera. That was the only qualification Mr. Somrock needed.*" *She looked up at me.* "*You think we're going to win?*"

"*Against Denton? Probably not. In case you haven't noticed, our team isn't very good.*"

"*I don't know. Eric Carter and Jack Jordan are pretty good tight ends and Denton's linebackers have struggled in coverage this season. Jon Hooper is a pretty good quarterback in short distance. We can move the ball against Denton if we nickel-and-dime our way down the field.*" *Lisa must have noticed the shock on my face.* "*What? You think I'm just out there looking at the players' butts?*"

"*Actually, I wasn't thinking that at all. Are you?*"

"*Just through the camera.*" *Lisa rubbed my arm.* "*I prefer your butt, hon.*"

"*Both of us thank you.*" *I looked out over the lake again.* "*I don't think any of the boys' teams are going to be good this year. All the best athletes graduated. Not what I wanted for my senior year, but I don't have much say in it.*"

Lisa lay her head against my chest. "*It's strange. I say* we *and* us *when we're talking about Porter's Bay. But it still doesn't feel like* my *school. And this will be my alma mater.*"

"*You've been here a year and you've managed to become a star reporter for the newspaper, solve two murders, and get involved in more activities than eighty percent of the student body.*"

"*And found you.*"

"Well, that was my *favorite part."*

We kissed for a while, becoming steadily more intense. When we parted, Lisa kissed me on the tip of my nose: the international signal for Let's slow down a minute. *We resumed cuddling. The bluff was peaceful enough to hear something, faintly, not too far away. We turned and looked toward the end of Revelation Bluff.*

"Sounds like Rick is entertaining another visitor at The Fields of Gold."

The Fields of Gold *was what Rick Michaels named his little corner of Revelation Bluff. It was the farthest from the streetlights, ergo the darkest section. Perfect for whatever deeds might be dreamed up by consenting (near) adults. The sounds Lisa and I heard were rather distinct.*

"Here's to Rick," Lisa said. "And…who is he dating?"

I gave it some thought. "Not sure. I saw him with Sharon Polaski at Arthur's the other night. Maybe her?"

"Or a player to be named later."

"Listen to you with the sports lingo."

"My education continues."

We shifted our attention to the waves crashing against the rocks below, giving us at least the illusion of leaving Rick and his date in peace. Lisa again laid her head against my chest.

"Are you going to miss Porter's Bay," she asked, "when it's time to leave?"

"I don't know. It's weird. I grew up here and, at the same time, I've never felt like I belonged here. My brother Kevin likes to talk about

how you can love some place and outgrow it at the same time. I used to think that was just Kevin being Kevin. He's always wanted to be bigger than anyone else. Lately, I've started to think he's right. I've seen a lot of people around here graduate high school and go nowhere. They find a job and settle in and never leave."

"You don't want that to be you?"

"No, I don't. Sure, I could go work in my dad's hardware store and probably do that the rest of my life. It would be easy. But I wouldn't be happy."

"Does your dad know that?"

"Yep. He doesn't want me working there if it's not what I want to do with my life. He told me that."

Lisa's voice seemed distracted. "Must be nice."

"How about you? I can't imagine you want to be here the rest of your life."

She snorted. "I want to be a journalist. I don't think I'm going to be too excited to attend city council meetings and write feature articles about a new antique store."

"Wow. One year here and you've pretty much got Porter's Bay pegged."

"I'm nothing if not insightful, honey." Lisa cupped my face. "I'm sorry if it sounds like I don't like this town. I'll be honest: I wasn't happy when my parents told me we were moving here. I didn't know anybody. This seemed like the middle of nowhere. The only people I did know were my parents and my sister and…you know how we all get along.

Finding someone like you was the last thing I thought would happen. But it's been the best thing."

We kissed. Things gradually got more intense. I kissed her neck and Lisa let out a long slow breath. She slipped her glasses off.

"The sleeping bag is in back," she said.

"This isn't exactly The Fields of Gold."

"But it's good enough." Lisa's eyes were soft and wide. "I love you,"

"I love you."

We slid off the hood. We crawled into the back and into the sleeping bag. After that, it didn't matter where we were.

After the bombshell about Roger Neill, we run back to my place. I do the driving (which includes dropping off Mike) while Lisa makes a round of phone calls. These continue after we get back to my apartment. The cats are on high alert, sensing something urgent is going on. I busy myself by wiping down the counters and sweeping the kitchen. Finally, Lisa spins away from the desk and joins me at the breakfast bar. I set a cup of coffee in front of her, and she takes a sip while still focusing on her notes.

"It looks like a single car accident," Lisa says, her voice calm despite the pace of her movements. "Roger Neill veered off the road and wrapped his car around a light post. There were no traffic cameras in the area to capture the actual accident. Based on what they found at the scene, the police believe it was alcohol-related."

"Which is plausible if not for the fact Eden Prairie isn't exactly on Roger's route home."

"The police don't have an answer for that yet. And I don't get the impression they're trying too terribly hard."

"Open and shut case?"

"That's what it looks like." Lisa tosses her notes on the breakfast bar. "I tried calling the Longson campaign, but, shockingly, no one there will talk to me."

"Maybe they're all in mourning," I say, almost sounding sincere.

"Of course," Lisa says. "They're so grief-stricken, the Senator is going ahead with his campaign rally in downtown Minneapolis tonight."

I scoff. "Minneapolis is a Democratic city, but Longson thinks he's so charming he can win them over. He's walking into the belly of the beast."

Lisa taps her pen against her lips. "Maybe it's time we did the same thing."

"Appeal to a base we have no chance of winning over?"

"No," she says, bopping me with the pen. "Walk into the belly of the beast."

It takes a few seconds for me to put that together. "You want to talk to Longson? What makes you think he'll see you?"

"I don't *know* that he'll see me. But how many times can I come around before they realize they have to stop stonewalling me? They have one campaign staffer who's dead and one who's disappeared. If there's no story there, best to quash it before I turn it into one. That's the bargaining chip I can use to get a minute with Longson."

I'm torn. On one hand, I like the idea of going for an audience with Longson. On the other hand, it might make a dangerous situation even more dangerous. Longson's people may have gone after Lisa once. If she rattles their collective cage, they might go after her again.

"I don't know," I say.

Lisa reaches for my hand then stops. "You don't have to come along. Between Rick and Roger Neill, the pattern isn't very promising. I can't guarantee your safety."

A soft look comes into her eyes; one I'd almost forgotten about. Almost. I flick my hands, dismissive.

"Safety isn't worth having if it means not doing the right thing," I say. "Besides, I was with you when the guy took a shot at you. I was with you when we went to Longson's campaign HQ. I was with you when you talked to Roger Neill. If something *is* going on, they're not going to give me a pass."

A corner of Lisa's mouth rises. "We'll leave in a few hours."

She returns to my desk to continue working. I step into the kitchen to inventory the contents of the pantry and the fridge and come up with an idea for dinner. I should make it a good one. At the rate we're going, it might be our last.

***

The rally for Senator Bill Longson is held at the Minneapolis Convention Center, a pleasant but undistinguished circular building near the eastern edge of downtown Minneapolis. While Minneapolis is overwhelmingly blue, it has enough right-wingers to fill the hall. Lisa and I position ourselves near one of the backdoors, putting us in the midst of the acolytes awaiting Longson's arrival. A misty rain slickens the streets and reflects the glow of the streetlights. A large church hovers nearby and Highway 94 is visible beyond. I feel out of place amidst the throng carrying red *Longson* signs. (Shockingly, no rainbow flags or Black Lives Matter signs to be seen.)

The Senator's limo and a few adjoining vehicles pull up about a half hour before the rally is scheduled to begin. While there are a few other security personnel involved, it's not as if Longson has full Secret Service protection. And it's not as if they would have a lot of luck keeping him out of sight. When Longson emerges from the limo, he stretches to his full six and a half feet in height. His hair has been clipped into a spiky buzzcut and, I'm assuming, dyed brown in order to keep the gray roots from showing. Some flecks of gray have been left at the temples to give us a *wise old owl* effect. Longson greets everyone with his usual smirk (despite many press photos that reveal he has a perfectly good set of teeth). Everyone except his devoted followers can read contempt in it. Longson strides away from the limo, ignoring his security personnel. (Nobody "handles" him.) He steps in front of his aides, making sure no one else gets the spotlight. Despite the rain, he wears no overcoat. Only the dark suit stands between the precipitation and his wealth of belly. Lisa gets as close as security will allow.

"Senator Longson," she says, her voice clear and commanding. "Lisa Cleary, Metro Communications."

Longson glances Lisa's direction but doesn't stop. Madeline Hauser, wearing a blue raincoat, her hair slightly damp, is promptly at the Senator's elbow. She indicates the way inside. Lisa moves down the line of security, staying with Longson.

"Senator, do you have any comment on the death of Roger Neill?" Lisa asks.

Longson again looks Lisa's direction. So does Madeline. Her eyes are cold as she brushes some damp hair out of her eyes. They keep moving toward the entrance.

"It was a tragedy," Longson says, his tone making it clear this will be his only comment.

Lisa keeps going. "What about the disappearance of Rick Michaels?"

Longson stops and consults with Madeline. He points an emphatic finger toward Lisa then stalks into the Convention Center, leaving Madeline behind. Slowly, she approaches Lisa, looking as if someone in the vicinity has just cut one.

"What is it that you want?" Madeline asks.

"I'd like to talk with the Senator. One on one."

"That's impossible."

"Is it? I'm putting together a story. I'd think he'd want to comment on it."

Madeline's face tightens to the point of implosion. "There is no story."

"Then let the Senator tell us that," Lisa says. "I'd be glad to quote him."

The campaign manager looks toward the entrance. If I had to guess, she's received some instruction from the Senator that she doesn't agree with. Finally, she turns back to Lisa, her shoulder sagging.

"It won't be one on one," Madeline says. "I'll be there as well." She looks over at me, as if I just showed up. "Is *he* going to be there?"

"Yes," Lisa says, without hesitation, "I prefer to have the numbers even."

"Fine," Madeline says, her voice icy. "I'll make arrangements. After the Senator's appearance."

"Thank you," Lisa says.

Madeline marches into the Convention Center. Lisa turns away from security, and we walk down the sidewalk, ignoring the stares from staff and security. I lean toward Lisa.

"You think we're getting anywhere?" I ask.

"We'll have to take a shot."

"As long as nobody takes a shot at *us*."

***

The conference room assigned for the meeting is large, colorless, and impersonal. A long table dominates the room. Sitting at the head of it can make someone intimidating, but Lisa and I will do our best to maintain bladder control. It's the professional thing to do, you understand.

Madeline Hauser opens the door to the room and steps aside. She's dispensed with the blue raincoat, revealing a simple blue suit. Security hovers outside the door. Senator Longson makes his way into the room. His grim look is replaced by another smirk, this one designed to convey both amiability and superiority. Lisa and I rise as he steps to our side of the table.

"Nice to meet you both," he says, extending a hand toward Lisa. "Thank you for coming." As if this meeting was *his* idea. "Lisa Cleary. I've enjoyed your work."

Lisa gives Longson a pleasant face. "That's good to know."

The Senator engulfs my hand in a dry (and somewhat weak) shake. "And you are…?"

"Joe Davis. I write for *The Daily Bugle*."

"I've heard of it," Longson says. "Big commie rag, right?"

"We try."

Madeline leans toward the Senator. "Mr. Davis writes a humor column."

Longson's eyes get beady with suspicion, "Kind of funny you're along on this."

Not exactly the kind of funny I strive for. "I'm helping Lisa."

The Senator shows no more curiosity. Why tax your brain more than necessary? He drops his bulk into a chair at the head of the table. Madeline sits to his right, a placid porcelain doll. Longson turns to Madeline.

"Can we get some chicken nuggets in here?" he asks.

"They're on their way, Senator," Madeline says.

That doesn't entirely content Longson, but he accepts the answer. He turns to us and folds his hands on the table. "You get a chance to watch the speech?" he asks.

"We didn't," Lisa says, "Sorry."

"Too bad," Longson says. "You missed a good one. When I hugged the flag? Not a dry eye in the house. And when I talked about cleaning up the immigration problem, I had 'em in the palm of my hand."

I have, against my will, soaked up some of Longson's campaign rhetoric online. "Send 'em back where they came from."

Longson smiles. "You got it. Secure the borders. Do whatever it takes. Mexico's going to have to learn to play ball."

"Have you talked to the Mexicans about that?" I ask.

He flips a hand. "Why should I? It's Mexico, for crying out loud. I say jump. They say *How high, senor?*"

On the bright side, the Senator didn't do a Speedy Gonzales impression while quoting a "typical Mexican." The room is largely silent. Lisa pretends to look over her notes. Madeline gazes at the blank walls. I give Longson an indulgent nod.

"Interesting," I say. "Reminds me of the scene in *Henry IV, Part 1* where Glendower blusters about being able to call spirits from the vasty deep and Hotspur says, 'Why so can I. So can any man. But will they come when you do call for them?'"

Longson squints at me. "I don't know what in the blue hell you're talking about."

"No. I didn't think you would."

Lisa covers her mouth. Madeline squares me with a look. Longson stares like I just came down from the planet Vulcan and I'll melt his brain if he doesn't ask Elaine to the Enchantment Under the Sea Dance. Lisa recovers in time to get the interview back on track.

"I just wanted to ask you a few questions, Senator," she says.

"Of course. Like I said, I enjoy your work Ms. Cleary."

If Lisa is thinking what I'm thinking, there is a large doubt Longson has ever read Lisa's stuff. Most of what he knows about her likely comes through the occasional attempts by Fox News to discredit her work. He's flattering Lisa because he thinks he can charm her.

"I appreciate that," Lisa says.

Longson sits back, his bulk threatening the chair's structural integrity. "How can I help you?"

"I wanted to talk about Roger Neill," Lisa says.

The Senator shakes his head, gravely. "That's a tragedy. Drinking and driving."

"Then you *know* it was alcohol-related?" Lisa asks.

Longson turns to Madeline. She sits up, her mask of control still in place.

"That's the preliminary report," Madeline says. "The Eden Prairie police and the highway patrol will have more complete information."

Lisa makes a note. "Why was Roger in Eden Prairie? That isn't close to his home. And he was spotted at the Stone Mill in Uptown a few hours before the accident. Doesn't that seem strange?"

Madeline's voice is tight. "Again, I'll have to direct you to the authorities."

Longson's smirk has drooped, and he fidgets. I get the feeling he's like this if he has to sit for too long. Madeline keeps her concentration on the Senator. Lisa taps the pencil lightly against the notepad.

"What about Rick Michaels?" she asks.

Longson's face flushes. "What about him?"

"He's missing," Lisa says.

"I know that."

"He scheduled a meeting with me. He had something to share about the campaign."

"What was that?" Longson asks.

"He didn't say. And he didn't show up to the meeting."

Longson's smirk regains its mojo. "Sounds like you got stood up."

He waggles his eyebrows for added effect. I assume this is his idea of being charming. Madeline looks away. My hands, resting below the table, ball into fists. Lisa ignores the Senator.

"Did you know Rick?" Lisa asks.

"Heard the name," Longson says, drumming his fingers on the table. "I have a lot of people working for me. You should see my campaign HQ."

"I have. What did Rick do for the campaign?"

Longson spreads his hands wide. "I don't know right off the top of my head. Roger might've known, but…" He adds a melodramatic sigh. "What a shame."

"According to Roger, Rick drove you around sometimes," Lisa says.

"He might have," Longson says. "A lot of people drive me around."

"Is there anyone else with the campaign who might have known what Rick actually did?" Lisa turns to Madeline. "For example, Madeline, you were sleeping with Rick. You must have *some* idea what he did for the campaign."

Longson looks toward Madeline, who appears stricken. She immediately recovers.

"I have told you, Ms. Cleary, that—"

"We have reason to believe you weren't being…entirely truthful with us," Lisa says. "You and Rick *were* seeing each other, weren't you?"

Before Madeline can answer (assuming she's even going to), the Senator dismisses the whole thing with a contemptuous wave. "It doesn't matter what was going on with who. We all have our hands full right now. The election is less than a month away. We can't spend time yakking about something like this."

I now get a clear picture of the frustration of the average reporter. You have no authority, really. You have no subpoena power. No one takes an oath regarding the questions you ask. All you can do is dig around and hope to outmaneuver your target. Truthfully, it's a lot like the amateur investigator hack jobs I've been doing recently. Madeline and her boss aren't going to give us straight answers and there's nothing Lisa can do to compel them otherwise.

"What about Zoe Court?" Lisa asks.

Longson's face instantly turns red. Sweat jumps out on his brow and his hands grip the table. Any trace of a smirk is gone. Madeline half-reaches for him. He turns a murderous glare on Lisa.

"What about her?" he asks, his voice low and guttural.

Lisa keeps going. "She was a reporter—"

"I know what she was."

"She wrote very favorably about you."

"She did. So what?"

"She died as well," Lisa says. "Just a few weeks ago."

"I know that."

"How well did you know her?"

Longson stands. His height would be intimidating enough if he wasn't also leaning over the table, looking like

Mighty Joe Young flunking out of Anger Management class. I sit back in my chair. Lisa holds her ground. Madeline gets to her feet as well. Longson stabs a finger at Lisa.

"What the hell kind of story are you digging around for?" Longson asks.

Lisa sets the notepad on the table. "One of your campaign staff members is dead and one is missing. You aren't concerned about that?"

"I'm concerned. I just don't see where it's my problem."

"It is *your* campaign, right?"

Longson slams a clenched fist on the table. Madeline and I jump. Lisa remains unperturbed. Which is more than you can say for the Senator. The mask of civility is gone, revealing the barely concealed thug beneath.

"You listen to me, lady—"

Madeline puts a hand on his arm. "Senator…"

Longson pulls away. "You think you can come in here and ask me a bunch of insulting questions? You have any idea who I am?"

"I have a very good idea," Lisa says.

"I am a United States fucking Senator, and I am going to be the fucking President! And when I am, people like you— the whole fucking woke mob of you—are going to be held accountable for the shit you write. For everything you did to come after me and try to take me down. You understand?"

Lisa doesn't bat an eye. "And regarding the First Amendment?"

"Fuck the First Amendment and fuck you!"

Longson waits for a reaction from Lisa. His anger hasn't spent itself. Madeline stands by, helplessly. I look to Lisa, wondering if I need to step in and what the hell I could do even if I did. Lisa simply consults her notes.

"Regarding Zoe Court…" she says.

The Senator cuts her off. "You think there's a story there? There isn't." He slaps a hand on the table. "Who do you think you are, you little cunt. You got your fucking Ivy League education. You think that makes you somebody?"

"Actually, I went to NYU."

"Who gives a shit? You're still a dime-a-dozen cum rag who doesn't know her place!"

I pop to my feet and shout, "Hey!"

Longson straightens to his full height, a good head taller than me. "What do you think you're going to do, junior?"

Lisa holds up a cautioning hand. "Joe…"

Back in college, some friends and I played a game where we imagined things that would give someone mystique. Getting married for a week. Having a child out of wedlock. Spending a night in jail. They all look pretty tame now. But trading hands with a United States Senator? That would definitely give one whole heaps of mystique. I may be seconds away from clinching that one. (And I'm vaguely aware how out of my league I am.) However, Madeline Hauser moves to the door and flips it open.

"Security," she says. Two black-shirted, burly security guards appear at the door. "Please show these two out."

I stand there, dumbfounded. "I'm sorry, *we're* out of line?"

The security guys, though, don't seem remotely interested in assessing the true nature of the situation. They make their way over to us. Lisa calmly picks up her stuff and pushes up her glasses (heroically refraining from using her middle finger to do so). She steps past the Senator as if he isn't there (which has to further cheese him off). I try to give him one last tough guy look, but it's awfully hard when you have to look up to do it. I follow Lisa to the door.

"Thank you for your time," Lisa says to Madeline, before stepping out.

To their credit, security is professional about the whole thing. They walk us to the door without any pushing or shoving or other attempts at intimidation. One of them is even polite enough to open the door for us. Lisa calmly buttons her coat against the crisp night air. Personally, I'm fuming enough to ignore the chill.

"I don't know how you stay so calm when he talks to you like that," I say.

"He wants me to lose my cool," she says. "He expects it. I won't give him the satisfaction. He's not the first man to try that. And he won't be the last."

"Clearly, you have a trick for staying calm that I don't have."

"I let them rant. Pretend it's a child who has to get a tantrum out of their system." She takes a breath. "And I imagine nailing their hide to the wall the first chance I get."

"Maybe I need to develop that technique."

"Takes a lot of getting insulted first. I don't recommend it."

"Noted."

We walk in silence. The streets are relatively peaceful. The crowd from the rally has dissipated and there are no other big events in downtown Minneapolis tonight. A corner of Lisa's mouth rises.

"You can quote Shakespeare?" she says.

"*To be a well-favored man is the gift of fortune/But to write and read comes by nature.*"

"Okay, now you're just showing off."

"I am."

"Nice to know you didn't spend all your time in college drinking and whoring."

"Well, not *all* of it."

For a moment, Lisa seems distracted, as if she finds the response not entirely to her liking. I hate to think I've offended her, but I don't ask about it.

After all, I can't be the *most* offensive male she's run across tonight.

***

I'll be the first to admit I'm protective of my living space. I've already talked about how I keep it neat as a pin in order to write. I don't necessarily need things situated in a certain way (that might be what saves me from OCD), but it's understood among my friends that certain areas are off limits. No one goes into my bedroom without my permission. Certain activities in the bathroom are restricted. And no one sits at my desk but me.

Having Lisa here has thrown many of those rules out the window. And I'm surprised how little I mind.

Right now, she's sitting at my desk, wearing a pair of blue-striped pajamas, simultaneously doing research and negotiating with her editor. I'm in the kitchen, making breakfast. Having heard Lisa's gentle admonition about what my past few breakfasts must be doing to her cholesterol level, I've decided to go with English muffins and a small breakfast salad. There is bacon in the oven (sue me, there has to be *something* fun in this salad) and I'm dicing avocados when the morning, as frequently happens these days, is interrupted.

Lars bursts in the front door, his sudden appearance disturbing neither Lisa nor the cats. (Jeez, even she's getting used to Lars barging in.) He wears a suitcoat over a brown shirt and a bolo tie (one of his versions of formal attire). He carries a large stack of books, magazines, and DVDs. He drops the pile on the breakfast bar.

"I need you to hold on to my porn," he says.

I'm glad I halted dicing the avocados or I might have lost the tip of a finger. I gesture at the pile with my chef's knife.

"Let me try to put this politely," I say. "Why in the blue fuck do you need me to do that?"

"It's only temporary," Lars says. "Management is coming to talk to me and I have to purge my place of porn."

I go back to dicing the avocados. "This is about the complaint from Mrs. Hanratty?"

Lars hangs his head. "I thought it might go away on its own but no such luck. Management has expressed deep concerns that I might be making porn films in my apartment and they're coming to investigate the complaint."

"I would argue that *having* porn is not the equivalent of *making* porn."

"You and I are simpatico there, my friend. But I'm certain management feels differently. They wish to keep this building respectable, and they can't tolerate a tenant who's gone spront."

For the uninitiated (and I apologize for initiating you), *spront* is a code word my college friends came up with for porn. Lars was tickled enough to add it to his own vernacular. I motion toward the aforementioned spront.

"May I ask why you even have this stuff?" I say. "Everything is available on the internet. You just need to protect your search history."

"I know," Lars says, giving the porn stash an affectionate look. "But I've got a taste for the retro. Besides, I feel bad for the people who put this stuff out. A whole industry evolved away from them. All their hard work rendered meaningless. Who mourns for the poor smut peddler?"

I decide to *leap* away from this topic. "Are you going to tell management you're actually scoring porn films?"

"Oh God no," Lars says. "I'm going to deny everything. But my argument will be stronger if I don't have evidence—sexy, sexy evidence—hanging around my house."

"How long do you need me to hold on to this?"

"They'll be here any minute," Lars says, "By this afternoon, this stuff will be out of your life. I promise."

I know the relative worth of Lars's promises. But there is such a thing as helping out a friend in a crisis. It doesn't help that he's looking at me like a puppy in the rain. I use the chef's knife to gesture over my shoulder.

"Fine, stash it in the bedroom closet," I say. "Just put it as far back as possible. And I'm holding you to that *back by the afternoon* promise."

Lars slaps the top of the porn stack and offers me his hand (which I refuse to take). "Thank you, brother. I won't forget this." Although, he almost certainly will. He again looks lovingly at the porn. "Goodbye, my friends. We will meet again."

I roll my eyes while Lars stashes the spront in the bedroom. He's just come back when voices can be heard on the stairs. (It's easy enough, since Lars didn't close the f'n door when he came in.) Lars stiffens like a pointer sensing a bird.

"That's them," he says. He spins toward me. "Can I ask you a favor, brother?"

"You already have. That's why the Collected Works of Larry Flynt are in my closet."

Lars, as always, either ignores the snark or runs several seconds ahead of it. "Can you come down there with me? You've been a good tenant. You pay your rent on time. You keep the place clean. You—Larry Flynt, good one—you don't have any loud, wild parties." Would that our superintendent could say the same. "If management saw you there, they might be less skeptical of me."

"I don't know, Lars," I say, looking down at my sweatshirt and sweat pants. "I'm not really dressed for it. Besides, I've got a guest here. And I'm making breakfast…"

"They'll both keep," Lars says. "And you look very presentable. As always. This won't take more than a few minutes."

Lisa is still in the middle of her research, and I haven't tossed the English muffins in the toaster yet. Lenny and Squiggy can keep an eye on the place. For once, Lars is right. Everything can keep. I slip off the towel I keep over my shoulder when cooking and toss it on the counter.

"Lead the way," I tell him.

Lars throws an arm around my shoulders. "Thank you, my friend."

"Don't mention it. Seriously, don't tell anyone I did this."

I follow Lars out the front door. Our guests (or are we theirs?) wait on the landing outside Lars's apartment. It's an older couple and an even older woman. The man is an avuncular looking chap with a smooth bald head, a prominent nose, and bright eyes. He wears an old blue suit that has a slightly musty smell. The older woman is hawk-like, with a pinched face and stooped shoulders. She wears a tan coat over a matronly green dress. The even older woman wears a flowery dress and stands with her arms folded over her rather substantial bosom. She's heavy-set, with a 'do of wavy salt-and-pepper hair and a clamped jaw. Lars greets the older couple and ignores the even older woman.

"Greetings and salutations!" he says. "Please come inside my humble abode."

We step into Lars's apartment. It looks almost exactly like mine, save for a second bedroom and the décor. Lars's tastes run to various bric-a-brac, such as an African tribal mask propped on the floor and imitation broadswords on the wall. Surprisingly, it looks more picked up than usual. The older couple take up positions in the living room while I hang back near the door. The even older woman stands nearby, her brown eyes narrow with suspicion. Lars handles the introductions.

"Vic, Amanda, I'm sure you know Joe Davis."

Vic gives me a toothy greeting. "You live upstairs, right?"

"That's right," I say.

Amanda clutches her handbag. "Don't you write something on the internet? A blog or one of those things?"

"I do. Have you read it?"

"No," she says, sharply. "I don't like the internet. Never have."

Gee, I'm glad I came down for this. I turn to the even older woman, silently wondering if she's somehow chaperoning this event. "And you are…?" I ask, extending my hand.

The even older woman doesn't take it. "My name is Mrs. Hanratty."

Lars directs Vic and Amanda to places on the sofa, and he pulls up a nearby chair. Amanda's beady eyes sweep the room, obviously not liking what she's seeing. I grab a seat at the breakfast bar. Mrs. Hanratty remains at her post by the door. Vic undoes a button on his suitcoat and folds his hands on his knees.

"Now, as we mentioned on the phone," Vic says, "we're here because we've received some disturbing reports—" Here, he sneaks a look at Mrs. Hanratty, "—about the possibility that you're making…adult films…here in your apartment. Obviously, if this is true…"

Amanda jumps in. "Your ass will be on the street by the end of the day."

Lars seems perfectly relaxed. "I assure you, these reports are categorically false."

Mrs. Hanratty's eyes narrow. "Even though I heard things?"

"I'm not sure what people have been hearing," Lars says, trying to prop a foot on one leg and missing. "I can't be responsible for that. But I assure you everything here is on the up and up. And I mean that in its most wholesome sense."

Vic looks content with that answer. Mrs. Hanratty's face crinkles, as though there's a bad smell in the room. Amanda lifts her head slightly, taking on a judgmental sort of demeanor.

"We know you've been making a movie," she says. "Exactly what kind of movie is this?"

Lars changes his position in the chair and nearly falls out of it. "It's an independent horror-slash-heist film. Joe is the writer on the picture. He can tell you more about it."

Thanks, Lars. I give the visitors a brief rundown of the plot. Vic smiles, probably not taking in a word. Amanda loses interest halfway through. Mrs. Hanratty's appearance is similar to a dog being shown a card trick. When I've finished, Lars takes charge again.

"There you are," he says. "The only film we're working on is an edgy and thrilling masterpiece. We are certainly not purveyors of the perverted arts."

Vic pats his hands on his thighs, ready to end the questioning. Amanda makes no move to leave. I get the feeling she came here to try and convict (and possibly hang) Lars. She's not going to be easily dissuaded from that goal.

"Maybe you can tell me what Mrs. Hanratty has been hearing," she says.

Lars begins spinning a web of possible conspiracy theories regarding Mrs. Hanratty and her motivations for destroying him. These theories range from the plausible ("Mrs. Hanratty has simply never liked the look of me") to the less plausible ("I believe she is projecting her own repressed libido onto my activities") to the frankly absurd ("How do we know Ms. Hanratty has not been involved in the perverted arts herself?"). Mrs. Hanratty's face turns red. Lars, though, is moving too rapidly for her to refute his accusations. My eyes dart about the room, hoping Lars hasn't forgotten to remove anything.

And that's when I spot it, sitting on the floor below the front windows and just behind Mrs. Hanratty. A neck massager, which has probably been used on several portions of the anatomy, none of which are the neck. I'm not sure how Lars overlooked it (to say nothing of how it got in the living room), but it will likely mitigate any goodwill Lars is building with management. I clear my throat, trying to get his attention. It works. I nod toward the corner. And the stupid son of a bitch ignores me.

"So, you see, I am as innocent as a newborn babe," Lars says. "A fully clothed newborn babe. They must have those, right? Probably in England?"

Vic and Amanda weigh how much they should believe this nonsense. Meantime, I get off the stool and walk toward the window. Mrs. Hanratty takes a step away, as if I'm about to launch some sort of assault.

"I'm expecting a visitor," I say. "I just want to keep an eye out for them."

Vic and Amanda keep their attention on Lars. I stand at the window and see, as expected, that the front lawn is largely empty (and could really use a good raking). I try to come up with a plan for the neck massager. I can't just bend over and pick the thing up. A thought occurs to me. I do a double-take, looking out the window.

"Did the two of you drive here in a green Lexus?" I ask.

Vic turns toward me. "We did. Why?"

"There are some teenagers looking at. Surrounding it."

Vic rushes toward the window. Amanda follows, probably looking for opportunities to pursue legal action. Mrs. Hanratty throws up her hands, wondering what the hell this has to do with anything. I step back, nudging the neck massager along with my foot. While the others are looking out the window, I scoop it up and show it to Lars. His eyes bug out. He tries to straighten his bolo tie and rips it clean off. I hide the toy against my leg as Vic turns back from the window.

"I don't see any teenagers out there," he says.

"You sure?" I ask. "There were four or five of them. African American kids, if I recall."

Amanda clutches her handbag. "Oh my God. Maybe we need to call the police."

They spin toward the window. Mrs. Hanratty joins them, perhaps wondering if *her* car is in any danger. I hold up the sex toy again. Lars gestures toward himself, indicating he wants me to throw it to him. I lob it his direction.

And he drops the son of a bitch.

Lars falls on it like it's a fumbled football. He does this just as Vic, Amanda, and Mrs. Hanratty turn away from the window and see him on the floor.

"Are you okay?" Vic asks.

"Perfect," Lars says, squirming. "Just a little pain in my appendix. Happens from time to time. Ever since the war."

Amanda seems impressed. "You served in the military?"

"No," Lars says. "I was worried about getting drafted. Messed with my digestive tract."

Mrs. Hanratty issues a cluck of disgust. Amanda turns to Vic and says, "We probably need to get out of here. In case those teenagers are hanging around."

"Good idea," Lars says. "I trust we won't be having any more trouble."

He pops to his feet. And that's not the only thing popping. Apparently, Lars's master plan was to hide the sex toy in his trousers. There is now a bulge in his pants that would make Michael Fassbender weep with envy. Vic and Amanda recoil. Mrs. Hanratty is in shock. Lars approaches management, extending his hand (among other things).

"It was great seeing you both," Lars says. "Let's do this again soon."

Amanda whips open the front door and hauls ass down the stairs. Vic gives Lars a quick farewell and runs after his partner. Mrs. Hanratty glares at the bulge like she's getting her first peek at Rosemary's Baby. She turns around in time to realize management is gone.

"This isn't over," she says, shaking a finger at Lars.

"Au contraire, madam," Lars says, still proudly (and cluelessly) displaying the protuberance in his slacks. "I've proven once and for all that I am not the pervert you would have others believe me to be."

Mrs. Hanratty marches down the stairs, disappearing from view. I move to the door, grateful for an opportunity at escape.

"Well done, Lars," I say, trying to put at least half my heart into it.

"You think this will put me above suspicion once and for all?" he asks.

"No, I think it will put you right in the middle of suspicion on a five-year lease with an option to renew."

"You sure about that, brother? After the—" He jumps slightly. "Wow. This thing really presses against the balls if you turn just right."

I waste no time getting out the door. Lars closes it behind me. Just before he does, I hear him muttering, "Maybe we can work this into the movie." I run up the stairs.

Lisa turns away from the computer when I enter. She arches an eyebrow. "Do I want to know about any of that?"

"I can't begin to tell you how much you don't."

I toss the dish towel over my shoulder again and finish up breakfast. While the bacon crisps up, I chop some cucumbers, cherry tomatoes, and green onions. I drop the English muffins into the toaster, crumble the bacon into a bowl with the veggies, and toss it all with a light vinaigrette. I plate the operation onto the breakfast bar, along with some butter, jam, peanut butter, and two mugs of pumpkin spice coffee. Ina Garten, eat your heart out.

"Chow time," I say.

Lisa joins me at the breakfast bar, pausing only to pet Lenny. She gives me a look of approval when she sees what I've made. She sips her coffee and glances at the mug.

"*Writers Do It Between the Covers?*" she asks.

"I thought it was cute."

"It is."

We dig in. Lisa slathers some peanut butter and grape jam on her English muffin. She takes a bite and closes her eyes.

"I haven't had an English muffin in forever," she says. "Thank you."

"My mom made them from time to time when I was a kid. It was always a treat."

Lisa digs into the breakfast salad. "How is your mom?"

"She's doing great. Between you, me, and the wall, I think she's glad Dad became the interim mayor in Porter's Bay. It keeps him from getting underfoot around the house. She's run a tight ship all these years. She doesn't need him gumming up the works."

Lisa chuckles. "I loved your parents."

"They loved you, too." I pick at my salad. "How are *your* folks doing?"

"Fine, I guess. I don't talk to them too much. The advantage of being an investigative reporter: you're always busy with work. Sorry, Mom and Dad, no time to talk."

Lisa's face darkened when talking about her parents. Thankfully, a thought occurs to her, allowing us to avoid that subject. She sets her fork down and runs to the desk to get her notes. She riffles through them as she returns to the breakfast bar.

"I tried doing more research on Zoe Court," she says. "I didn't get too far. I'm going to call Rochester. Talk to people who knew her. Meantime, I did some looking into Madeline Hauser. And I *did* find something interesting."

Lisa gives me a mischievous grin. For all her *I'm just a working stiff* attitude, Lisa has a little flair for the dramatic. It reminds me she *did* do some theatre when we were in high school.

I set the English muffin down. "Okay, what did you find?"

"Madeline's address," Lisa says, sliding a page of her notes across the breakfast bar. "She lives in Eden Prairie. Just a few miles from where Roger Neill died."

Whoa. I prop an elbow on the breakfast bar. "No way that's a coincidence."

"Not bloody likely," Lisa says.

"That explains why Roger was all the way out in Eden Prairie. But what was going on with he and Madeline?"

Lisa takes the page back. "You think Madeline would answer if I asked her?"

"Not bloody likely."

"I know. And I obviously can't ask Roger. And the police think it's a traffic accident." She picks up her fork. "Even though Madeline's house is only a few miles from the accident, that doesn't necessarily mean anything sinister was going on. It could have just been a late-night campaign meeting."

I think about that as I take a bite of my English muffin. "Zoe Court is dead. Roger Neill is dead. Rick is missing. There's got to be a connection there."

"Probably. But Zoe is a suicide. Roger is a car accident. The only one that can't be explained away easily is Rick."

"And we don't know what happened there. What next?"

"That's an excellent question."

The silence returns while we work on breakfast. The situation with Rick will have to wait, at least for a minute. I pick at my salad.

"I still don't know how you avoided punching Longson," I say, "or even yelling at him."

"It's what I have to do," Lisa says. "One: if I fire back, anything I write about Longson after that is dead in the water. He and his people can—and will—claim bias. Two: you remember Beans Madden? The second he knew he got under your skin, he owned you. Longson is the same way. Three: it's the difference between men and women. If he loses his temper, he's powerful and commanding. If I lose my temper, I'm emotional and unstable. I can't be trusted to write the truth." She tosses her hands, lightly. "So, I pick my battles. Today, Longson and his people are probably talking about me—if they're talking about me at all—as some cold, frigid bitch. An ice queen. So be it."

We eat in silence. Lenny and Squiggy buzz about, looking for either affection or leftovers. I hum a little tune and start singing.

"I scween, you scween, we all scween for ice queen."

Lisa looks up at me. Then she throws her head back and gives me that lilting laugh. She throws her napkin at me. "You are such a geek," she says.

"Some things never change."

I take the empty plates off the counter and deposit them in the sink. Lisa's cell phone rings. She promptly answers. On her end of the conversation, she adds a few things, such as "I get it" and "Don't worry," and ending with, "I'll be there soon." I step back to the breakfast bar as Lisa rings off.

"What's going on?" I ask.

"That was Katie," Lisa says. "Someone broke into her place."

Ah. I guess *that* is what we do next.

CHAPTER SEVEN

NOVEMBER, SENIOR YEAR

As the fall went along, I noticed it was getting harder and harder to get a decent night's sleep. Talk of college increased. It was time to put in applications and take campus tours and all that. The reality that life was about to change, even if it was months away, was creeping in. Many nights, I laid awake in the dark, staring at my ceiling, listening to music, and wondering how I could slow time down.

The college fair at Porter's Bay High School was on a Tuesday night in the first week of November. It was held in the cafeteria of the high school (not the largest or most ornate room in the building). My parents had the novelty of accompanying me. My older brother Kevin had been recruited to play basketball at a Division II school. My younger brother Owen would be recruited to wrestle for a similar school. This turned out to be the only time they'd attend a college fair (for their least athletically gifted son).

It was a crisp and cold night, the kind that seems bitter in November but doesn't feel half-bad by March. It was threatening snow, which normally puts me in the mood for Christmas. Not this time. My parents led the way to the front door of the high school, a four-story brick structure that took up a whole city block. Its looming massiveness, even though I saw it every day, did nothing to calm my nerves. I lagged behind my parents, which was nothing new during my teen years. This time it wasn't out of embarrassment. It was out of hesitation. Fear.

The cafeteria was in the basement of the building. Like the rest of the school, it had marble floors and cement walls. The tables ringed the room in a U formation, allowing the various schools to set up shop. It was reasonably crowded. Parents and students milled about. The air, as always, smelled vaguely of pasta casserole (or as we call it in Minnesota, hot dish). My best friends, Sam and Andy, were not there. Andy had already decided on going to Tulsa University (an adventurous choice for a guy who would later wind up right back in Porter's Bay), and Sam had no interest in college at this point. (He would later choose dental school; something of a surprise to those of us who thought he would end up as either a standup comedian or a drug mule.) I briefly bumped into Rick Michaels, who said his grades indicated he was going to community college. Then I spotted Lisa.

She was with her parents as well. College was a thing we hadn't talked about yet. It was part of that deep dark future that lay at the end of the school year. I had no idea what that was going to look like. And I wasn't sure I wanted to know.

Lisa stood apart from her parents. I never felt comfortable around her folks. Her father's aggressive eyes looked on the proceedings with disdain. Her mother was sporting her usual inscrutable smile—one that left me wondering if she genuinely liked me or was simply tolerating me. (To this day, I can't tell you which it was.) I walked over to Lisa.

"Forget it," I said, sneaking up behind her. "Northwoods Community College maintains very high admission standards."

A corner of her mouth went up. "What? You have to find the address?"

"To say nothing of the front door."

Lisa spun toward me, and this produced an awkward moment. Normally, Lisa would greet me with a kiss. But her parents were there. And I was sure mine were behind me. We stood there and looked like we hadn't been properly introduced. The parents filled the introduction gap.

"Danny, good to see you again," my dad said, offering his hand. "How are you, Henry?"

The two of them shook hands, briefly. Dad's hands disappeared into Mr. Cleary's much larger hands. My mom looked at Mrs. Cleary, who remained on the other side of her husband.

"I love your coat, Iris."

"Thank you, Katherine. I picked it up in Duluth."

My mom turned to Lisa and put a hand on her back. "How are you, dear?"

Lisa broke into a wide smile. "I'm fine. Thank you."

My dad also took a moment to greet her. She stood apart from her parents, looking completely comfortable. Neither of Lisa's parents greeted me. Lisa grabbed my hand.

"Why don't you come with me?" she said. "I wanted to talk to you about something."

We slipped away, leaving the adults to figure out their own awkward situation. Lisa led me toward the tables on the opposite wall, her pace slowing, no real destination apparent. Her hand remained in mine. I leaned toward her.

"Everything all right?" I asked.

Lisa stroked my forearm. "It's fine. I just wanted to get away from my parents."

"What happened?"

"Nothing in particular," she said. "I just…I don't like the way they treat you."

"They've always been…" I was going to say nice to me, but I realized that wasn't really true. I finished with, "Polite to me."

"That's what I mean. When I talk about you, they're like, 'Oh, you're still dating him?'"

I'll be honest: that didn't surprise me. Dismayed me, yes, but didn't surprise me. When I was left alone with Lisa's dad, I generally withered under his glare. If he asked me questions, it was about how my brothers were doing, delighting in their various athletics. He only ever asked me one question about what I wanted to do, and I told him, "I'd love to have a column like the one I write for the school newspaper." He got a look on his face like a sewer pipe had broken. After that, he didn't ask me questions about my future plans. Or much of anything else.

"It's okay," I said.

"No, it's not," Lisa said. "You deserve better." Lisa leaned into me. "On top of that, there's my dad shooting down every school I want to go to."

This was a little bothersome. Lisa and I were both going to college, but we hadn't talked about where we were going. My parents made it clear they didn't have the money to send me any place fancy (not that my grades would get me into any place fancy). There were two or three local schools I was thinking about. Lisa had yet to express a preference.

I hesitated then asked, "What schools have you been talking about?"

"Northwestern. USC. NYU. Boston U. My dad says he can't afford any of those. I'm looking at scholarships and grants. With no help from him or Mom. I only came here tonight to humor them. Apparently, they think I'm going to see some local school and fall in love with it."

"No chance of that," I said. It almost sounded like a question, and a plaintive one.

"None," Lisa said. She looked over her shoulder. "My parents are coming over. I suppose you rode here with your mom and dad?"

"Not really. I drove my mom here. Dad came over from the store."

Lisa grabbed my arm like it was a lifeline. "Then she'll probably go home with your dad. You think you could give me a ride home?"

"Sure, that would be great."

She cocked her head. "Are you okay?"

"Yeah. I'm fine."

I said it too quickly. Lisa studied me, not buying what I told her. But for someone whose technique could be relentless, she never interrogated me. She rejoined her parents. Her father didn't even look her direction. After a few moments, I rejoined mine.

I wandered from booth to booth, collecting brochures and not paying much attention to anything I was told. I was on automatic pilot, fighting desolate emotions. Northwestern, USC, NYU, Boston U. None of those schools were close to Minnesota, which was where I was likely to find my school. What would become of Lisa and me? I had spent nine months seeing or at least talking to her every single day. The thought of spending one without her was depressing. The thought of spending a lifetime without her was more than I could bear.

"Adams College?" Dad said, tapping the brochure in my hand. "I've heard that's a good school. And it's only a couple of hours away."

It was among a pile of brochures in my hand. The guy at the Adams booth had talked about the school's English program and mentioned the possibility of my writing for the school newspaper. Then again, the people at every booth talked about their school's English program and mentioned the possibility of writing for the school newspaper. The Adams guy might have been talking about the school's commitment to alien mind probes. My head, needless to say, was not in the game.

"That sounds great," I said, studying the floor more than the brochure.

Dad took it from me, and he and Mom gave it a look. They liked what they saw.

"Seems like you can apply right online," Dad said, with a What'll they think of next *quality to his voice. His wonder at and distrust of technology were always at odds.*

"Maybe I'll do that," I said, watching Lisa wander from table to table.

We didn't stay much longer. I had collected all the brochures I was going to. Mom told me she would ride home with Dad. Lisa, also holding a large stack of brochures, let her parents know she was leaving with me. I was out of earshot, but their reaction didn't indicate they were pleased. Lisa hustled away from them and grabbed my hand before any real discussion could ensue. Just after we stepped out the front door of the school, she dumped her brochures in the nearest trashcan.

Snow had started falling. Lisa and I held hands as we walked to my car. I didn't say anything. We didn't always need to talk—we were perfectly comfortable with silence—but there was a strain in this. Lisa was too perceptive not to pick up on it. She stopped when we were halfway to my car.

"What's wrong?" she asked. "And please don't give me any of that Nothing *stuff. I know you better than that." The snow gathered on the sidewalk. Lisa slipped her hand under my chin and gently moved my head until I was looking her in the eye. "It's just me."*

I took a breath. "It sounds like you're going away to school. Far away."

"I want to get into a good journalism school."

"I get that." Though I probably sounded like I didn't.

Lisa ran a hand through her hair, brushing away some snow. "I want to be a journalist. And not just a journalist. I want to be the best. I need to do whatever I can to make that happen."

"I understand."

She laid her hands on my arms. "I don't want to hurt you. Ever. I hope you know that."

"I do," I said. "I just think…I would miss you." And that last part probably ranks as the greatest understatement of my life.

Lisa pulled me into an embrace. She whispered in my ear. "I'm here right now. I want your voice to be the last thing I hear before I go to sleep tonight. And I'll be here tomorrow. And the day after that. And the day after that." She looked up at me. "Let's just enjoy being here right now, okay? Just us."

It was hard to shake what I was feeling. But Lisa was in my arms. It made everything better. I kissed her on the forehead.

"I like that," I said.

We stood on the sidewalk, holding each other, ignoring the looks from passersby. We swayed lightly. Lisa snuggled into my chest.

"I love you," she whispered.

"I love you."

We stayed that way for a long time, swaying as if dancing, letting the snow accumulate around us.

Lisa and I are on the sidewalk outside of Katie's house. The place looks the same as it did before. Then again, I'm sure most of the damage is inside. That's been my experience, at least. We approach the front door, but before we can knock Katie is there to greet us.

"Thank you for coming," she says. "I wasn't sure who else to call."

"The police?" I say.

Katie winces. "It's not that simple."

We make our way into the living room. Katie locks the door behind us. She's wearing a gray hoodie, black leggings, and a pink headband. It looks as if she's just come from the health club. She leads us through the dining room and kitchen, and down the steep stairs to the basement. She points toward the corner, where Rick had left the two boxes. Both boxes have been opened and the contents scattered about.

"I met a friend this morning for coffee and a walk around the lake," Katie says, her face flushed. "This is what it looked like when I came back."

"Any sign of forced entry?" I ask.

"It looks like they popped open the backdoor," Katie says. "It wasn't quite closed when I got home. If someone comes through the gate and into the backyard, they're hard to spot."

"And you haven't called the police?" Lisa asks.

"They didn't take anything," Katie says. "Believe me, I looked. Before I called you and before you got here. All of the entertainment equipment. All of my jewelry. All the appliances.

Even the cookie jar where I keep extra cash. None of it was touched. Somebody just broke in here, rifled through Rick's stuff and left. Is that even worth calling the police about?"

"It might be worth filing a police report," Lisa says.

Katie doesn't seem convinced, but she says, "Maybe I should do that."

Lisa looks over the stuff. "Do you know if they took anything of Rick's?"

"No, I don't," Katie says. "I'm not completely sure what he kept in there. Did the two of you see anything when you were looking through them?"

I shake my head. "Just keepsakes, mostly."

Katie folds her arms, as if containing herself. No doubt, she's looking at her house with a sense of violation, the knowledge that someone else has been here. We go back upstairs and sit at the dining room. Katie's trembling slightly. It's possible the shock of the break-in is just hitting her now. Lisa sits next to Katie, takes her hand, and gives it a reassuring squeeze.

"It's going to be okay," Lisa tells her.

I nod toward the basement door. "At least they left the hockey stick. Gives you a weapon, just in case."

Katie chuckles, humorlessly. "That might be the most valuable thing in here. To some people, anyway."

"What do you mean?" I ask.

"That's *the* stick," Katie says. "The one he used to score the game-winning goal. To win the state championship."

Holy shit. It's like hearing someone say *Oh, that? Just a missing Shakespeare manuscript I keep next to the toilet.* (Okay, I'm exaggerating, but still…) I look toward the basement steps.

"The stick down there is broken," I say. "I don't remember the stick being broken when Rick scored the goal."

"It wasn't." Katie sighs. "We had a fight. We'd been drinking and one of us said something and things got stupid. Anyway, the next thing I know, we were both screaming at each other. I told him he was still trying to live down being a high school star, and he had to come to terms with it. He went downstairs and grabbed his hockey stick and brought it up here. And broke the damn thing in half."

My jaw drops. "He broke it?"

"Over his knee. Snapped it right in half."

"Over his knee? That must have hurt like a son of a bitch."

"It did," Katie says. "He had a limp for three weeks. Deep muscle bruise. He didn't want to talk about it. He had a friend fix the stick. It wasn't that hard. The friend hollowed out the spot where it broke and hinged it together. It didn't look great, but it was at least in one piece."

I whistle. "Bet you it's still worth something."

"To some people, yes," Katie says. "The high school, the Porter's Bay Historical Society, even the U.S. Hockey Hall of Fame. They all wanted it. Rick refused to give it to anyone."

"Why was that?" I ask.

"I don't know. The only thing he would ever say is, 'I'm not giving it up. It's mine.'"

Interesting. Seems like Rick valued the stick and didn't value it. Kind of emblematic of his whole relationship with that goal he scored. Katie goes into the kitchen and makes some tea to calm herself down. She offers some to Lisa and me, but we decline. Katie returns to the dining room and lets the tea steep. Lisa waits a respectful moment before broaching another question.

"Did Rick ever mention someone named Zoe Court?" Lisa asks. "Or Roger Neill?"

Katie takes a moment to think. "No, I don't think so. Are they with the campaign?"

"One of them was," Lisa says. "The other was a reporter. He didn't mention either of them?"

"I don't think so. Like I told you before, I wasn't all that interested in his job. The only person he ever mentioned was Madeline."

So be it. Lisa and I hang around and chitchat with Katie. She begins to visibly relax as she sips her tea. (I can't help wondering if she might have put something in the tea to speed that process along.) After a while, Lisa glances toward the door.

"Do you want us to hang around?" Lisa asks.

"It's okay," Katie says. "Nothing was taken. I'll get a new lock for the backdoor. That's all I can do for now."

Lisa and I don't feel great about it, but there's not a lot we can do. Lisa reminds her to call us if anything else happens or if she hears from Rick. Katie thanks us for our help. A minute later, we're out the front door and walking back to the car.

"This had to be Longson's people," Lisa says. "They tried Rick's place. Now they've hit Katie's house."

"In pursuit of what exactly?"

"Great question. Maybe Zoe had something. Evidence. Maybe Rick got ahold of it after Zoe died. Maybe that's what he wanted to talk to me about."

"And Longson's people are either looking for Rick or whatever Rick has."

"Maybe. There's just the small matter of having *zero* evidence."

We reach the rented Mustang and slip inside. Lisa tosses her bag into the backseat and positions herself behind the wheel. I stare at the house.

"You think Katie's going to be all right?" I ask.

"At this rate, are any of us?"

Good question. I wish she hadn't asked it, but it's still a good question.

***

Lisa and I return to my apartment. By the end of the afternoon, Lisa has done some further research into Zoe Court and decides she's done for the day. (Knowing Lisa's work ethic, she must be nearly exhausted.) She declines a drink, feeling her sleep would be improved with some chamomile tea. (*Now* she's in the mood for tea.) I brew some for her. (Yes, I keep chamomile tea around the house. I owe the public nothing.) Lisa settles on the futon and lets her mug of tea steep on the coffee table. I ease into the comfy chair.

"Research tell you anything?" I ask.

"Not a lot," Lisa says. "I talked to some of the people at the *Herald*. The longest conversation I had was with Jonathan, Zoe's editor. He said she did great work, but she was erratic near the end. Missing deadlines, showing up late for work. He wasn't sure what was causing it. He tried talking to her about it. She made some vague excuse about having a lot going on." Lisa picks up her tea. "He *did* say she wasn't suicidal. At least, he didn't think she was. I asked if he thought the police got it wrong. He hesitated and said he wasn't sure. That was pretty much the end of the conversation."

"So much for that."

I tuck my hands behind my head. Lisa looks toward the windows, tapping her notes against her chin.

"How far away is Rochester?" Lisa asks.

"Hour and a half."

"Think it's worth the trip? If we can find Jonathan and have a longer chat?"

"Assuming he'll chat with us."

"Only one way to find out," Lisa says.

She's got a point. It's not like we have many other leads we can follow. Or *any* other leads we can follow.

"Sounds like we have a road trip for tomorrow," I say.

The cats join us. Lenny stretches himself across my lap while Squiggy lays next to Lisa, his head perched on one of her legs. She pets his head.

"They're cute," she says. "How long have you had them?"

"A little over five years. Somebody who works at my health club had their parents and the parents had a litter. She found homes for all the kittens. She was originally going to keep Lenny and Squiggy because Lenny was the cutest and Squiggy was the runt of the litter. But she realized that wasn't going to work out, so she put up a notice at the club, looking for a new home. I saw the notice and…I don't know, I had an impulse. They've been here ever since."

"It was a good impulse," Lisa says, stroking Squiggy's back.

"I *did* wonder, though. First time I opened a can of wet cat food and almost threw up into it, I thought I might be in over my head. Squiggy just looked up at me, like, 'Sir, do you require my assistance?'"

"He really is your little butler, isn't he?"

"I like to imagine he is. I think he does, too. How about you? You have any pets back in New York?"

"God, no. It's not that I don't love animals. It just…doesn't seem like the kind of thing I'd be good at."

"You might surprise yourself."

"Probably not. I eat most of my meals from takeout. My apartment is cleanest when I haven't been in it for a while. I don't really have hobbies or anything. This…" She taps her notes. "This is my life. It's all I do."

"It's all you ever wanted to do."

"Maybe not all I *ever* wanted. But it's become that." Lisa leans back, settling into the futon. "You start to wonder, when you've done it long enough, is this it? Chase one story. Get it. Move on to the next one. Same thing, again and again and again." Lisa lets out a breath. "Sorry. It's being here. You're making me soft, Mr. Joe Davis. A good reporter needs an edge."

"Put it in your memoirs. *I was a nationally renowned journalist until I came to Minnesota and ran into a string of decent breakfasts.*"

Lisa looks for something to throw at me. She can't get anything without disturbing Squiggy, so she just shakes her fist. Lenny briefly opens his eyes, as if to say, *Do you mind? I'm napping here.*

"What about you?" Lisa asks. "Is this what you were hoping for?"

"Mostly. I love the column. I'll do that until five minutes after I'm dead if they let me. I love my friends, much as they can irritate the hell out of me. I love this apartment. I love the cats. Every now and again, though, I wonder, 'Is this what I'm going to do for the rest of my life? Do I want more? Should I want more?' I don't know. I suppose we all have moments like that."

"We do." Lisa's eyes drop. "I guess I want to know you're okay. We chat sometimes. But it's social media. You never know if someone is saying what they want you to hear."

"I get it. But I'm doing well."

"I'm glad. Because…"

A moment goes by. Lisa chooses not to finish that thought. I shift in the chair.

"Life goes on," I say.

"Then why don't your friends know who I am?"

I look down, trying to think of the best way to put it. "Because why bring up old hurts?"

Something flickers in Lisa's face. She looks away. We sit in silence for what feels like a long time.

"I hurt you," Lisa says.

"Yeah."

Lisa tries to give me a penetrating look, but she can't hold it. "This is the part where you tell me you got over it."

"It is."

But I can't. Lisa takes off her glasses and sets them aside.

"I'm sorry," she says, quietly.

"I don't want you to be."

Silence returns. After several long moments, Lisa gets up, dislodging Squiggy (which he deals with in his own stoical manner, stiff upper lip and all). She goes down the hall to the bathroom to brush her teeth. I grab the pillow and the comforter and make up her bed on the futon. Lisa returns. She stops when she sees what I've done.

"You're still spoiling me," Lisa says.

"Not a worry."

She steps past me, squeezing my arm as she does. I leave her to get changed for bed, turning off the lights as I walk toward the bedroom. The cats decide to bunk down with Lisa tonight. I close the bedroom door behind me. I try to clear my head, not think about anything.

If only it were that easy.

CHAPTER EIGHT

DECEMBER AND JANUARY- SENIOR YEAR

I love Christmas and always have. The only drawback is that it insists on being a winter holiday. I've never minded that so much, but during my senior year in high school, it became something of a bummer. Revelation Bluff no longer worked for quality time, as girls tend to want to keep their sweaters on under those circumstances. But Lisa and I had very much settled into our relationship. Sex was fun (and was becoming increasingly more so) when the opportunity presented itself, but it wasn't the be all and end all.

On a typical day, I'd pick Lisa up for school, and we'd meet with Sam and Andy before class. We'd eat lunch together in the theater. After school, we'd hang out in the Bay Breeze offices then join Sam and Andy for a burger at Arthur's Diner. Nights were filled various activities: the Winter Daze Dance, hockey games (though the team wasn't very good that year), going to the movies, what have you. On any occasion when our parents and siblings were out for the evening, we could get together for fervent and brief adult relations. There were mishaps, such as the time

Lisa's parents came home early, and I wound up putting her underwear on instead of mine, or when we lost track of time and barely got dressed before my parents found us. (To this day, I'm sure they knew something was up, what with our disheveled clothing and flushed faces. But it's not a topic of conversation my parents are willing to explore.)

Some nights, I'd park the car down the street from Lisa's house. Yes, it gave us an opportunity to make out. But it allowed us to just sit and talk; about what was going on in school, about what was going on in the news, about what was going on with our families. The future was about the only topic we studiously avoided.

One of those occasions was the day before Christmas break. Snow was falling fast, making me glad my drive home wasn't that far. Lisa was in my passenger seat, her feet propped up against the dash. (She was the only one I allowed to do that.) She was making another effort to go with her contacts, and I wasn't sure if it was them or the lateness of the hour that caused her to keep rubbing her eyes. She gazed down the street toward her house.

"I don't want to go inside," she said.

"I don't blame you. This car's heater is magnificent."

She swatted me on the arm. "My parents want to go to my grandma's house in Madison for the holidays. I don't want to go. But I really don't want another argument with them."

"They don't trust you to stay home by yourself?"

"It's not that. They let me stay by myself last summer. And Amy has to stay because she's got basketball. It's just more a control thing, I think."

This control thing of Lisa's parents wasn't new to me, but it was foreign. My parents had rules and discipline, but they never felt controlling or manipulative. While I would sometimes disagree with said rules, somewhere in my mind I knew my parents had my best interests at heart, even if I didn't agree at the time. Lisa, it seemed, never had that same assurance about her parents. I took her hand.

"Sorry about everything," I said. "I'll give you your Christmas present earlier."

Lisa rubbed my forearm. "You're my Christmas present. By the way, that was my present for you: corny greeting card lines."

"Cheaper than buying an actual greeting card."

"This is what I'm saying."

We sat as the falling snow cocooned us inside the car. Lisa laid her head on my shoulder and interlaced her fingers with mine.

"Sometimes I wish I could just stay with you," she said. "I like to hear your voice before I go to bed. I imagine you being there instead of on the phone. I think about what it would be like to wake up with you. To just...I don't know. Have coffee. Watch you eat breakfast." She wiped something on her cheek. "I would love that."

I kissed Lisa on top of her head. "I would love that, too."

For so much of my life, then and now, I'd think about the next thing I was supposed to do, the next idea I had, what have you. I was, and *am, typical of John Lennon's line about life being what happens when you're making other plans. I never felt that way with Lisa. When I was with her, just being there was enough.*

Finally, she slid over to her seat. "I should get going. I'll have enough of a fight as it is. No sense making it any worse."

"I suppose."

I flicked the wiper blades, clearing the window, and eased down the street, stopping in front of Lisa's house. The lights were on, and the silhouette of Lisa's dad was visible in the front window. Lisa turned in the seat, keeping her back to the house. She bit her lip.

"Are you tired of calling me every night before bed?" she asked.

"Not remotely."

"I'm glad."

Lisa kissed me, heedless of her father possibly watching us. After a minute, we parted, and she laid her hand on my cheek. We stayed that way for several moments. Finally, Lisa opened the car door.

"Talk to you soon?" she said.

"Absolutely."

I watched Lisa walk rather than run through the snow, going up her front steps. Her dad's shadow moved toward the front door. I wondered what Lisa was in for. I'd probably find out later. I threw the car into gear and drove home through the falling snow.

After a hastily eaten breakfast, Lisa and I get ready for our trip to Rochester. Since the morning is surprisingly temperate (if a little cloudy), I take my coffee out to the deck while Lisa showers and gets dressed. It's a little melancholy back here at this time of year. In the summer, I have lights crisscrossing the deck, the grill is out, and my deck table sits prominently in the center. All that stuff has been put away and won't be back until next May. Still, even without the usual accoutrement, the view is pretty damn nice. Downtown St. Paul is vaguely visible in the distance. The carriage house behind my building mercifully blocks the view of the alley. There is a glimpse of the trees lining Grand Avenue. My reverie, though, is interrupted by a phone call from Mike. I consider ignoring it, but it's probably best to get this over with.

"Pisces, Aquarius, Capricorn and Jones, LTD," I say. "This is Mr. Dolenz speaking. How may I help you?"

Normally, Mike would try to figure out what the hell I'm talking about. This time he blows right past it. His voice sounds tired. "I slept with Moira," he says.

I nearly drop my phone. "You what with who?"

"Slept with. As in sex. Y'know, coitus."

"With Moira?"

"The one and only. Except she's got a sister who looks just like her. But you get the general idea."

Whoa. I lean on the railing at the edge of the deck. "I may need some details."

"All right, I met Moira at the Blue Lounge last night. Figured I needed a place my friends never go. She made it clear what she wanted me or else she was going to tell Gillian to dump me. I didn't have a choice."

"Other than maybe trust that if Gillian really liked you, she wouldn't…y'know, now that I say it out loud, it *does* sound kind of silly."

"Exactly," Mike says. "It was either introduce Moira to the Great Shillelagh or I could forget about ever seeing Gillian again."

For those who don't know (and I envy each and every one of you), one of the few nods Mike gives to his Irish heritage, other than getting spectacularly drunk and vomiting every St. Patrick's Day, is the nickname for his wedding tackle. So much for the luck of the Irish.

"How was it?" I ask.

"It was amazing. Seriously. Wild, energetic, uninhibited. I don't know what I expected from her, but it wasn't *that*. I may have to see a doctor. I must have friction burns over most of the lower half of my body."

Speaking of things people don't need to know… "Is it over then? Moira's signed off on you and now you can date Gillian carefree?"

"I guess that's technically true," Mike says, not sounding enthusiastic. "But I'd hate to break things off with Moira. It was *really* good last night. It would be a shame to end things when we're just getting started."

Oh, for the love of pound cake. "If not for the fact you're dating her sister. Or are you planning on ending things with Gillian?"

"Are you crazy? Gillian's the sweetest, smartest, coolest girl I've dated since Car…well, in a long time. I don't want to break things off with her."

"And yet, you're sleeping with her sister."

"What does one have to do with the other?"

Dear Lord, please help me stay patient with…y'know what? I already promised I wouldn't bother You with stuff about Mike. Disregard. "You don't really think Gillian and Moira will be cool with this arrangement?"

"Moira might be. But not Gillian. Not at all. But if I break things off with Moira, she might tell Gillian."

"In which case, Moira would have as much to lose as you."

"This is true," Mike says, "You see? Everything will work out perfectly. I just have to keep dating Gillian and keep sleeping with her sister."

Pardon me, Mr. Abbott? It's Mr. Costello on line two. But there's nothing to be gained in arguing with Mike. You cannot explain morality to the penis-centered individual. It's like a tire fire. You just have to keep an eye on it and let it burn itself out.

"Good luck to you, sport," I say.

"Thanks, man. I'll keep you updated. Assuming I can get to the phone. I'm having a little trouble walking right now."

I ring off with Mike (who apparently needs to get some actual sleep) and return to the interior of the apartment. Lisa is at the desk, having just finished putting her still-wet hair in a ponytail. She closes the laptop and pops to her feet. "Ready to go?"

"I believe so."

She steps past me, toward the front door. "By the way, I heard you talking to someone out on the deck. Phone call?"

"My friend Mike. You really don't want to know what's going on with him."

Lisa opens the door. "Maybe I shouldn't be offended that he doesn't know who I am."

"Are you kidding me? You should give me a Nobel Prize." I follow her out to the landing. "By the way, I'll help you with the gas. No sense running up your expense account."

"Are you sure?"

"Yes. But any property damage, automotive damage or attempts on our life, we'll have to split fifty-fifty."

"Going Dutch on death," Lisa says, "Not a bad book title."

"I wouldn't use it."

***

Since I've lived in Minnesota my whole life and Rochester, home to the Mayo Clinic, is one of the state's most famous cities, you'd think I would be a lot more acquainted with it than I am. In point of fact, I've only been there once, and that was for a double date with my friend Stoner (who was ardently pursuing a girl from Rochester and needed a date for her best friend). I don't remember a lot about it, other than my date getting Richard Burton-level drunk and hurling in my lap. So, I'm not looking forward to a return trip.

Even now, I'm not certain what to make of it. I grew up in a small town and have lived in a city most of my adult life. Rochester doesn't quite feel like either. There are a few buildings over five stories and a small skyway system. It feels caught between its genteel past and its crass future. The downtown area is dominated by the monolith of the Mayo Clinic. The offices of the *Herald* are a few blocks away from the clinic, tucked into a four-story brown brick building. Lisa doesn't wish to draw any more attention than necessary to Jonathan, so walking into the offices of the *Herald* is out. Instead, I park down the street, and we stake out the place.

A minute later, a guy emerges from the *Herald* building. I'd put him in his early forties. His swept back hair has gone gray. His face is thin, like the rest of him. He's wearing a light coat over a sweater and slightly ratty jeans. His route takes him down an adjacent street, toward a couple sandwich places and a sculpture that looks like stacked volleyballs.

"That's Jonathan," Lisa says. "I got his picture off the paper's website."

A second later, we're out of the car and powerwalking toward Jonathan. We try to be unobtrusive, but it's a challenge when you're moving like characters from an old video game. We split so that each of us approaches him from a different side. He takes no notice of us until we're right up on him.

Lisa starts the conversation. "Jonathan Gilbert? Lisa Cleary, Metro Communications. We spoke on the phone."

Jonathan stops. He turns toward Lisa then notices me. His watery blue eyes dart about. His jaw works for a few seconds before any words come out.

"I…I didn't realize you were in Rochester," he says.

"Thought I'd stop in," Lisa says, "This is Joe Davis. He's with the *Daily Bugle*."

Jonathan looks confused. "Isn't that a website?"

"Aren't they pretty much all these days?" I ask.

His shoulders sag. "This is about Zoe?"

"Yes," Lisa says. "Do you have a moment?"

Jonathan probably wishes he had an excuse to put us off. All he's got is, "I was on my way to lunch."

"We can tag along," Lisa says.

Jonathan puts his head down and leads the way. The destination is a little coffee shop/restaurant at the end of the block. It's nothing fancy. Just a breakfast counter, a handful of tables and a picture window. The menu is soups, salads and sandwiches. The place filling up for lunch. Jonathan finds a table near the back. Our server, a thin redhead in her early twenties, greets Jonathan by name. He orders a turkey sandwich and fries while Lisa and I content ourselves with coffee. Once the server has left, Jonathan fidgets with a packet of sweetener.

"If you'll pardon my saying, Ms. Cleary," Jonathan says. "Zoe's death isn't the sort of thing you normally cover, is it?"

Lisa rests a hand next to her coffee cup. "It's part of an investigation into the disappearance of a staffer at Bill Longson's campaign."

Jonathan's face clouds. "I see."

"When we talked on the phone," Lisa says, "you said that Zoe's work was suffering. Before her death."

"I was hoping she'd get it back together. She told me she was working on something. But she only gave me a few details."

Lisa leans forward. "Such as?"

Jonathan looks toward the counter, probably wondering on the progress of his sandwich. "She was doing a story on Jeremiah Kincade."

My elbow nearly slides off the table. "The guy who killed Senator Gardner?"

"Yes," Jonathan says, "Don't ask me why. The national media beat that story to death when Gardner was killed and again when Kincade was executed. Nobody wants to know what his family life was like or anything like that. Zoe said she thought she had a new angle and she wanted to pursue it."

"Did she tell you anything else? I ask.

"No. She had been a good reporter. I wanted to give her some space. Maybe I gave her too much. But…she was special."

There's also a rueful quality to Jonathan's tone. If I had to guess, his interest in Zoe might have been more than just professional. But I keep that thought to myself. The turkey sandwich arrives, as do our coffees. Jonathan makes no move to start eating. I'm guessing we've put a dent into his appetite. Lisa lays her forearms on the table.

"Longson never commented on Zoe's death," she says.

Jonathan picks at the chips that came with the sandwich. "I seriously doubt Longson is concerned with anything other than his campaign and his image. Not necessarily in that order."

I swirl the coffee in my cup. "Do you believe Zoe's death was a suicide?"

"That's what the police say."

"But you don't agree?" Lisa asks.

"There were no witnesses," Jonathan says. "You never know. Maybe it was an accident."

"An accident?" I say. "She's doing some parkour on the top level of a parking ramp and *whoops*. That's what you're telling us?"

He looks down at the sandwich. "You don't have to be insulting."

Lisa rests a hand on my arm, backing me off. "If it wasn't suicide or an accident, that really only leaves one possibility."

To his credit, Jonathan doesn't make us spell it out. He takes a half-hearted bite of his sandwich and slips Lisa a look.

"I know what you're getting at," he says. "Maybe I spoke too soon when I said Zoe didn't commit suicide. It was a shock, yes. But…nobody really knows anybody, do they?"

Lisa and I exchange a look. It's clear we're thinking the same thing. Jonathan spoke up and now he regrets it. Maybe his emotions got the better of him. Maybe he believes Zoe was killed. Whatever the reason, Jonathan doesn't want what happened to Zoe to happen to him.

"Did Zoe ever mention Rick Michaels?" Lisa asks.

Jonathan cocks his head. "He's with the Longson campaign, right? I talked to him once. Right after Zoe died. He asked me about her tapes."

A jolt goes through me. Lisa's eyes widen, but she covers it with a quick sip of her coffee. She slips me a sidelong glance then returns her focus to Jonathan.

"A tape?" she says.

"Zoe had an old school handheld tape recorder," Jonathan says. "When she was in college, she used her phone to record an interview with some band. The whole file wound up getting lost. After that, she didn't trust a phone to record anything. She always used a handheld and kept the tapes in her apartment." Jonathan smiles, just for a moment, amused by the memory. "It was the same thing with her notes. She didn't like keeping anything on a computer. She kept everything in a file folder or a notebook. Anyway, Rick asked me if I knew anything about Zoe's tapes. I told him there were probably a few hundred in her old apartment."

Lisa tries to keep things casual. "What happened to the old apartment?"

"The family cleared it out," Jonathan says. "Hell, it might be rented by now. You know what landlords are like."

Shazbot. No sense in breaking into Zoe's apartment. Probably for the best, though. We don't have Mike along to help. Lisa rubs her chin.

"Any idea why Rick would be concerned about Zoe's tapes?" she asks.

Something in that question makes Jonathan more uncomfortable than he already is. "He didn't say, but..." He stares at his food. "It made me wonder if Zoe ever recorded Longson without him knowing."

"Why would you think that?" Lisa asks.

"Zoe had a tendency to use the recorder without people knowing. She'd hide it in her purse or in the pocket of her coat. Anyway, I told Rick I wasn't sure what happened to the tapes, and we left it at that. I haven't seen him since." Jonathan makes a show of looking at his phone. "I should get back to the office. I'll have this boxed up. I'm sorry I couldn't be more help."

He brings his plate to the counter and the server quickly boxes up the sandwich and chips. Lisa's face betrays nothing. Jonathan looks toward us, then bolts out of the coffee shop. Lisa turns to me.

"Zoe had tapes," she says. "Rick asked Jonathan about them. And we found a handheld tape player in Rick's apartment. Not going out on a limb to think it belonged to Zoe."

"How would Rick have gotten ahold of it?"

"Can't help you with that," Lisa says. "But if Rick as a tape—or tapes—that the campaign doesn't want him to have, that might be why they're after him."

"What could be on the tape?"

Lisa runs her hands over her face. "We'll have to find Rick and ask him."

"Back to square one."

"Right. Assuming we ever left it." Lisa gulps down more coffee. "I'll call Zoe's family. Just in case they know anything about the tables. If not, we can head home."

Lisa makes some calls while I look out the picture window. My eyes drift toward a parking ramp, probably not unlike the one from which Zoe Court fell to her death. I try not to picture it. And try to figure out what caused it.

***

Sadly, we strike out regarding any tapes or notes Zoe Court might have had. Her family disposed of any work-related items right after her passing. (Stupid Swedish Death Cleaning.) We're largely silent as we start the drive home. Lisa seems taken by the last gasp of fall colors visible on both sides of the road. We find ourselves on a deserted stretch of Highway 52.

"You get the feeling Jonathan knew something and wouldn't tell us?" I ask.

"He certainly suspects something," Lisa says, "but he's too afraid to mention it. He doesn't want what happened to Zoe to happen to him."

"Hell of a newspaperman, he is."

"That's what bothers me. That's why this whole Longson thing bothers me. As journalists, our jobs are supposed to be holding people in power to account. When we're too intimidated to do that, what do you have?"

"Sieg heil."

"Exactly."

Yeah, there's a pleasant thought. Meantime, I glance in the rearview mirror. A black Dodge Avenger is coming up behind us. Something about it looks familiar. I have a sinking feeling and I'm not sure why. (It's just a car closing in on a lonely stretch of country road. Nothing to see here, right?) Maybe I'm just being paranoid.

The car comes up alongside us. There are two guys in the front seat. I recognize them. The driver is the one I saw talking to Madeline Hauser in the Longson campaign HQ parking lot. The one in the passenger seat is the guy who tried to shoot Lisa. Passenger seat rolls down the window and aims a gun at us.

Okay, so I'm *not* just being paranoid.

I slam on the brakes just as the shot is fired. I don't know where the bullet winds up, but it misses us. I'll take that as a win. The Avenger goes up the road ahead of us. I swerve behind them. The shooter tries to position himself for another try. Lisa grips the dash.

"Who the hell is this?" she asks.

"Old friends coming back for a visit," I say, gripping the wheel.

The shooter tries a blind shot. It disappears into the ozone. I try to move around the Avenger. It blocks my path. I throw the wheel back and forth, moving the car in a serpentine pattern. The shooter can't get a clear shot. The Avenger slams on the brakes.

Two things happen in short order: 1, Lisa and I scream and at least one of us closes their eyes (I think it's me); and 2, I throw the wheel to the right, avoiding the Avenger. For a second, I'm waiting for the sound of crunching metal. Somehow, we get around it. (I assume we phased through the Avenger.) Another shot is fired, but it hits nothing.

Lisa looks over her shoulder. "Not exactly a marksman, is he?"

The countryside races past. "He only needs to get lucky once."

The Avenger is still coming. My eyes flick about, trying to figure out a move. The Avenger starts to go around my right, but I cut it off. The move proves to be a feint. The Avenger swings back to the left and comes up alongside. It swerves, trying to run us off the road. I slam on the brakes. The Avenger misses, and almost goes into the ditch. I punch the gas again and haul ass up the road. The Avenger is in pursuit.

Lisa's head is on a swivel. "Jesus, there isn't *anybody* on this road to see this?"

"I blame Rochester. It should be a better tourist destination."

Another shot pings off the rear of the Saturn. Lisa ducks down. I'm tempted to do the same. I continue the zigzag pattern. The gunman can't get a bead. An exit ramp is coming up. We have to get rid of these guys before they get rid of us.

I dive for the exit ramp. The Avenger follows my movement. Just before I get to the ramp, I throw the wheel to the left, missing the ramp and getting back on to the road. The Avenger tries to follow. But they turn too sharply. The car goes into a roll. It disappears down the exit ramp. I stomp the accelerator, going up the road as fast as I can. (What's the worst that can happen? I'll draw the attention of a cop?)

"That seems to have done the trick," I say.

Lisa looks out the rear window. "You think they survived that?"

"Finding it a little hard to care at the moment."

"Good point."

I bring the car down to a normal speed. Ten seconds after I do that, other cars appear on the horizon. (Assholes.) Lisa faces forward again. She pats my leg.

"Nice driving," Lisa says.

"Tell that to my friend Mike. He fancies himself the real driver in the group."

"He's got competition."

I'm gratified to hear that. Over the years, I've listened to quite a few smartass remarks about my driving. I'd be tempted to challenge Mike to some kind of competition. But the only way to really test us is to be chased by a gunman.

Frankly, I've enough of *that* for a lifetime.

CHAPTER NINE

FEBRUARY AND MARCH, SENIOR YEAR

While it was often a source of frustration, the most popular sport in Porter's Bay was hockey. Our players weren't necessarily the kind of rink rats you'd find in small towns on the Iron Range or in northwestern Minnesota. But Porter's Bay generally produced pretty good teams. However, after decades of high school hockey, all Porter's Bay had to show for it was a trip to the state tournament back in the Fifties and a lot of regional runners-up trophies. It was a dysfunctional relationship: fans gave abundant affection and got very little back in terms of success. (See also: Minnesota Vikings fans.)

There was nothing about the team Porter's Bay produced for our senior year that said this trend was going to change. In fact, this team was worse *than the three teams before it, all of whom could get no better than second place in the regional tournament. It had a few players worth talking about. Jon Hooper was a star center who was on his way to playing Division I hockey in college. Dave Anderson was a great playmaker who frequently set Hooper up for goals. Mark Brendon could be an excellent goaltender on certain nights. Andy Corelli was a big defenseman with a booming slap shot and mediocre ability at playing defense. Beyond that, the team was strictly pedestrian. And their barely .500 regular season record bore that out. They weren't expected to advance past the first game of the regional tournament. They confounded that expectation but were going to be destroyed in the semi-finals by Rust, an Iron Range team that was one of the best in the state.*

A funny thing happened on the way to sure destruction: Porter's Bay won. It was one of those strange games where Rust completely dominated the action, doing nearly everything except scoring goals. The one goal they did *get was a fluke deflection off Mark Brendon's back. Porter's Bay, on the other hand, collected three goals, the last one an open-netter that sealed up the win. The* Porter's Bay Times *called it one of the biggest upsets in the history of the program. For once, the paper could not be accused of hyperbole.*

Suddenly, the whole town was shaken out of its lethargy. A noticeably larger Porter's Bay contingent showed up for the regional championship game against Denton. They were rewarded with Jon Hooper scoring four goals and the Porter's Bay Cardinals getting their first trip to the state hockey tournament in decades. The whole town went, as my friend Sam aptly put it, batshit.

A certain delirium gripped Porter's Bay for the week before the tournament began. Businesses (including my father's hardware store) posted Let's Go Cardinals *posters. Adults and students made frantic preparations to get to St. Paul. Hotel rooms were arranged, tickets were purchased, and seats on shuttle buses arranged. When the team left for St. Paul on the Monday before the tournament, they were given a grand sendoff: a pep rally on the marble steps at the front of the school. The pep band played the school fight song (which sounded remarkably like the Notre Dame fight song), students lined both sides of the stairs, and the principal gave a short (and largely forgettable) speech wishing the team good luck.*

The prevailing attitude toward the team was: Hey, at least they got to state. *Certainly, such a Cinderella story made good copy (as the Twin Cities newspapers and TV stations reiterated), but, like the regional tournament, it was unlikely the Cardinals would get past their first game. Maybe they had half-a-shot at the consolation trophy, assuming whatever spell they had cast would not be destroyed by a quarterfinal loss.*

My friends and I couldn't afford hotel rooms and had no connections in the Cities. We were consigned to riding the shuttle bus down to St. Paul and coming back to Porter's Bay every day of the tournament. The shuttle bus in question was a school bus with only a fifty-fifty shot at making the eight-hour roundtrip. But what it lacked in reliability, it completely lacked in comfort.

The company, at least, was good: Lisa, Andy, Sam and Andy's sister Theresa (who was dating Sam at the time). We gathered in our little corner of the bus and kept each other entertained on the ride down. When we got to St. Paul, everyone jumped off the bus and ran in all directions. Small town high school kids set loose in the Emerald City. (Little did I realize I would one day live in a pedestrian neighborhood just up the hill.)

To the surprise of everyone (including, I think, the players) Porter's Bay was not eliminated in the quarterfinals. They knocked off a team from Bloomington, 5-2, and advanced to the semifinals. The following night, Jon Hooper broke a 1-1 tie with only thirty seconds remaining to lift Porter's Bay over a team from Rochester and into the championship game. Despite the shuttle bus not getting back to Porter's Bay until three in the morning, nobody slept on the ride home. Who could? We was in the state championship game!

The whole of our little town nearly shut down the next night. Every store except for the bars carrying the game on TV were closed. Even the State Theater, an old time movie palace on Howard Street, closed on a Saturday night for the first time in living memory. The caravan of cars and buses, all decorated in red and white, began pulling out early in the afternoon.

The ride down to the championship game was interesting. Everyone on our bus was chatty and exuberant. By the time we got close to St. Paul, the sun had gone down, and the mood on the bus had darkened as well. The tension was palpable. Had we really come this far—physically and emotionally—just to be let down?

The championship game pitted Porter's Bay against St. Patrick, a snooty private school known for recruiting its best players. They had been the favorites to win before the tournament even started. Certainly, facing an overachieving small town team wasn't going to change that. Public sentiment might have been with Porter's Bay, but that wasn't necessarily going to translate into a win.

Sure enough, St. Patrick got the first goal, less than two minutes into the game. Their top line swept in on a three-on-two and their slick passing shredded the Porter's Bay defense. The goal scorer completely faked out Mark Brendon and gently slipped the puck under him. St. Patrick's players didn't celebrate all that enthusiastically, as if this was how they expected the game to go. I sensed that some hack sportswriter was coming up with a line about midnight striking for Cinderella.

A couple minutes later, Jon Hooper intercepted a St. Patrick pass, raced right through two defensemen, and deposited a wrist shot in the upper corner of the net. The Porter's Bay section exploded. Midnight? Hardly. Andy, showing a side of his personality that only sports tended to bring out of him, stood up on his chair and shouted at the St. Patrick section.

"Game on, assholes! Game on!"

The first period ended in a tie. The second period, though, was a nightmare for the Cardinals. St. Patrick's dominated play and threw a huge number of pucks at Mark Brendon. Mark did what he could, but he let one get by him. Then another. Then another. It was 4-1 by the end of the second period. St. Patrick's fans taunted us with chants of "Why so qui-et?" We didn't have an organized response, though a goodly number of us offered the finger.

Lisa and I stared at the ice as the third period was getting ready to start. "Have we got any chance?" she asked.

"Plenty of time left," I said. "If we can get a goal in the first five minutes, then one in the next five, then one in the last five, we can tie it up."

It went without saying that Porter's Bay would have to play a hell of a lot better than they had in the second period for that hope to come true.

To their credit, Porter's Bay did play a whole lot better. St. Patrick's sat back a little, content to hold their large lead and play defense. Porter's Bay was sharper with their passes and more aggressive with their attack. But it didn't translate into goals. Five minutes went by without a score. Then five more minutes. There were only five minutes left and that 4-1 score looked more insurmountable with each passing second. Our section became more and more subdued as time dwindled away.

Porter's Bay was in the St. Patrick's end when the puck slid toward Andy Corelli, stationed near the blue line. Andy reared back and put everything he had into a slap shot. It was one of those blasts that somehow gets through traffic and finds the back of the net. The red light went on and the Porter's Bay section exploded, as much out of shock as joy.

4-2. Just under five minutes left. Maybe that would be enough to get the coach to pull the goalie in another few minutes. But was there enough time left to make a comeback?

A minute later, Dan Brendon, Mark's older brother and Corelli's linemate on defense, slipped a pass to Andy, who wound up and fired another puck at the net. It flew past two St. Patrick defenders and their screened goaltender. Again, the red goal light went on. Again, the Porter's Bay section exploded, this one putting the previous cheers to shame. Fans were hugging, standing on seats, pumping their fists.

4-3. Four minutes left. I was torn between belief and pessimism. Could they really pull this off?

The Cardinals put everything they had into their attack. St. Patrick's was in full backpedal, doing whatever they could to keep Porter's Bay from scoring (or Andy Corelli getting ahold of another puck). Time ticked down. Three minutes to go. Two minutes. Mark Brendon was pulled for an extra attacker. One minute to go.

With forty-five seconds left and the action in the St. Patrick's zone, Dave Anderson stole the puck from a St. Patrick's defender and threw it in front of the net. Jon Hooper grabbed it and faked a shot. The goalie dropped down, committing himself. Jon flipped the puck into the upper corner, tying the game. Porter's Bay had come all the way back.

Bedlam reigned in the Porter's Bay section. Andy hopped up on his seat and twirled his Porter's Bay scarf. Sam grabbed Theresa in a hug and hoisted her in the air. (A thing none of us had previously thought Sam capable of doing.) Lisa pounded on my arm. She hadn't shown much interest in hockey previously, but she was certainly a fan now. The St. Patrick's section, it must be said, was strangely quiet.

Regulation time ended with the game still tied. Our fans were buzzing. With the momentum on Porter's Bay's side, it seemed like only a matter of time before the Cardinals scored and the game ended.

We all should have known better. If this team had taught us one thing, it was that nothing was going to come easy.

The first overtime period was slow-paced. If the possibility of the game ending suddenly hadn't been in play, it would have been judged boring. St. Patrick's was still tentative, having been shell-shocked by the late Porter's Bay attack. For the Cardinals, they seemed to have expended their energy with that late rally. The listless period ended with the game still tied.

St. Patrick's found their footing again in the second overtime period and began to dominate play. For as much criticism as Mark Brendan took about his inability to play consistently, he was fabulous here. At one point, he slid across the goal mouth to make a pad save, then when someone tried to cash in the rebound, he jumped back across the net to make a stick save. The man was practically standing on his head to keep Porter's Bay in the game. It was still tied when the second overtime ended.

Everyone in the arena was tense. Lisa frequently found herself unable to look. I kept telling myself I would be okay if the Cardinals lost. The sun would come up tomorrow, I'd still have a great girlfriend, I'd still have my friends, I'd still have my column. If I could just avoid running off to the Canadian wilderness to get away from any trace of humanity, I'd be just fine.

The Cardinals started to show signs of life in the third overtime. Dave Anderson took a shot that rang off the pipe. Jim Kiel had a great opportunity that the St. Patrick's goalie barely managed to glove. All momentum came to a halt about halfway through the period when Rick Michaels was called for a tripping penalty.

Those two minutes felt like two hours. Mark Brendan was all over the place, stopping shot after shot. Andy Corelli threw himself on the ice to stop another. Jim Hooper got the puck and knocked it down the ice. When the penalty time ended, Rick scurried back to the Porter's Bay bench. We doubted he would be on the ice again.

The third overtime ended and the fourth began. The players were tiring. Passes were off target. Shots went well wide. It was looking as if a fluke goal would end the game.

Then it happened.

Jim Kiel bounced the puck along the boards to Pete Steele. Pete slipped a St. Patrick's defender and charged the net. He fired a low shot. The St. Patrick's goalie made a pad save, but the rebound flew away from him. Rick had been closing in on the net when he was tripped by a St. Patrick's player. He went flying through the air, his body perpendicular to the ice. Somehow, he got his stick down and reached the puck. It caromed off his stick and slipped past the goalie. The red light went on.

The Porter's Bay Cardinals were state champions.

I've never been in a riot, but this was the next best thing. Everyone was yelling, screaming, jumping around. The players were piled in a corner of the ice, Rick lying somewhere underneath all of them. This was the last I saw of my black stocking cap, as I threw it high in the air, and it disappeared into the crowd. Lisa hugged me and cried. Andy ran down the aisle, and we wondered if he was going to try to beat security and get on the ice. (No worries. He chickened out.) Sam sat on the back of his chair, his feet on the seat and his arms around Theresa, amazed at how this had become so important to him.

The players accepted their medals, the cheers for Rick noticeably louder than the others. The image of Rick's face on the big screen above the scoreboard is still imprinted in my mind. The kid with the sweaty brown hair and the disbelieving smile. The captains accepted the state championship trophy and paraded it around ice. They stopped in front of the Porter's Bay student section and exchanged handshakes and high fives with the students. Eventually, we made our way back to the buses and headed home. I doubt any of us slept that night. The trophy wound up in the center of the trophy case at Porter's Bay High. A picture of Rick's goal sits beside it, forever frozen in time. Porter's Bay would never forget that moment.

And no one would ever forget Rick Michaels.

Lisa and I sit on the futon and stare at the arch windows at the front of the apartment. We've come down from the adrenaline rush of the drive home. Personally, I can't lose the feeling someone will come through the door and start shooting up the place. Lisa calmly sips a mug of pumpkin spice coffee.

"Clearly, we're on to something," Lisa says. "I just wish I knew what it was."

"Don't we all?"

I take a sip of my own coffee. Lisa's eyes hold a certain amusement. "And to think, I had to teach you to like coffee," she says.

"My blood pressure and I thank you."

Lisa taps her notes against her chin. "Rick has a tape or tapes from Zoe. But they barely knew each other. How would one of her tapes get into Rick's hands? Zoe was also working on something about Jeremiah Kincade. She must have had notes or a file on the story. I wonder what happened to those?"

"You think her family threw them out? When they cleaned her apartment?"

"Maybe. I can contact them. See if they saw anything." Lisa lays her head against the back of the futon. "A new angle on Jeremiah Kincade. I wonder what that could be?"

"Maybe he was an avid cook in his off hours," I say. "*The Racist Redneck Asshole's Guide to Better Barbecue.*"

"*The Joy of KKK.*"

"*Mastering the Art of Cross-burning.*"

Lisa looks over at me. "Should we be making these jokes?"

"That or we break down crying. I choose this."

I realize those jokes aren't in great taste, but you have to give us a little room here. We're both freaked out from the shooting. It's not the first time either of us has been shot at, but that doesn't make it any easier. It makes you acutely aware there may be a *last* time you'll be shot at, and it may not end well for you. Lisa set her notes on the coffee table.

"Two attempts on us," she says. "Both involving someone loosely connected to the Longson campaign."

"Or at least Madeline."

"I seriously doubt there's much to Madeline outside the Longson campaign. Not only is she dedicated, but her boss requires a lot of looking after."

"No more than the average aircraft carrier."

Lisa gets up from the futon. "I'm going to call Zoe's family again."

"Speaking of dedicated…"

She gives me a little look back. "It's that or I sit around and think about how close I came to dying. What would you do?"

"Me?" I say, getting up. "I'd get dinner started." I give her my best (by which I mean, my worst) Jackie Gleason. "And a-way we go."

Lisa sits at the desk. I go into the kitchen, rummage through the cupboards, and contemplate dinner. Maybe some soup. I have everything I need for minestrone. (Might have to run to the store for some breadsticks to go with it, but otherwise…) Before I get to it, though, I stand at the breakfast bar and watch Lisa work.

We could have died. That was certainly the intention of the guys who came after us. And they may be back again. What if something happened to her? Or to me? Do I let her just think I hated her and that's why I kept my memories of her at arm's length? Or do I tell her that I pushed her away because I'd never get on with my life otherwise?

But I don't tell her anything. Nobody wants an old boyfriend pouring out their heart and forcing you to give them some kind of *Ah, it's so nice that you feel that way* in return. Nobody wins in that case. I slip away from the breakfast bar and get dinner started.

***

I do the vast majority of my work at home, but that doesn't necessarily make me a homebody. Sometimes, I take my show on the road. When I do, I usually hit Glacier's, my favorite local coffee shop. It's a converted café with checkerboard tile floors, brass rails and picture windows. It draws the young and artistic denizens from the upscale side of Cathedral Hill. I'm here now, pecking away at an article. Lisa left a couple messages for Zoe Court's family last night. As of this morning, she still hasn't heard back. I let her use my desk, but I'll never get any writing done if I'm sitting at the breakfast bar. Hence, my journey to Glacier's.

The table is on the other side of a wall, in a back hallway that leads to the restrooms. From where I'm seated, I get a view of the main room and the front door. Said view is mundane—it's late morning and the place is only half-full—until I see Mike coming through the door. Mike doesn't usually visit Glacier's. He spots me and makes a beeline my direction.

"Glad you're here," he says, sliding into a seat. "I might need help."

"I've been telling you that for years. You just coming around now?"

Mike gives me the stink eye, but he's too distracted to put his whole eye into it. He peers back around the wall, toward the front door. "I'm meeting Moira."

"Here? Isn't there some sleazy motel or gas station bathroom you'd normally use?"

He clenches a fist. "You want to cut the shit? This is serious."

"Fine. What's going on?"

"I thought about what you said, and I'm going to break things off with Moira. We slept together, and it was great. But I can't do this. I want things to work with Gillian. That can't happen if I'm doinking her sister."

"Y'know, I love that that's your version of integrity." I sip my coffee. "How do you think Moira is going to take it?"

"Not well," he says, his foot bouncing a thousand times a minute. "That's why I need you here. I can't face Moira by myself. I need some moral support."

I'd mention the difficulty of offering moral support to someone who has no morals, but I think I've teased this particular dog enough. "When does she get here?"

"Any minute now."

Mike hustles to the counter to order a coffee. While he waits, he waves to someone coming through the door. This must be Moira. I have to admit, when it comes to Mike and women: life is not fair. Yes, Mike is a good looking guy with a gift of gab (when he wants to have one). But there is no way he deserves some of the women he dates. Moira, for example, is a knockout. Flowing dark hair, thick eyebrows, pert nose, full lips, piercing blue eyes. She wears a black jacket over a black sweater that hugs her chest like an old friend. And, for crying out loud, she's got a twin sister. And Mike has slept with *both* of them. If I ever get to meet St. Peter, this is going to be on my list of grievances.

Mike grabs his coffee and greets Moira. She gives him a slight smirk, the closest approximation of human warmth she can muster. They make their way over to my table. Moira's smirk disappears.

"I didn't realize someone was joining us," Moira says.

I offer a hand. "I'm Mike's friend Joe."

Moira doesn't look at me. "I know who you are."

Great. Thanks to my weenie bit of celebrity, I'm used to being recognized. Thanks to my friendship with Mike, I'm used to not being welcomed. Rarely, though, have the two dovetailed so neatly. What a moment.

Mike slides into his chair. "Joe was hanging out when I got here. I thought he might want to join us."

"Yeah," Moira says. "*You* thought."

I'm tempted to pour my latte onto her lap, but what would that solve? (Beyond the sweet, sweet satisfaction it would provide.) We settle into an awkward silence, broken only by the incessant tapping of Mike's foot.

"I was doing something thinking," he says, "about…stuff."

Yep, off to his usual eloquent start. Moira props an elbow on the table, facing Mike and ignoring me. "What kind of stuff?" she asks, her voice slightly sardonic. "The weather?"

"I…I don't know about…"

Moira slides her hand along the table. "Because I heard the weather is going to get very…rough." The hand moves to Mike's forearm.

His voice comes out higher pitched than normal. "Getting rough, huh? That's too bad."

"Oh no. I like it when it gets rough. When the air is swirling, and the wind is…blowing."

Mike might start hyperventilating. "Blowing?"

"Blowing so hard."

We talk about the weather a lot in Minnesota, but rarely does it inspire the woody Mike is now likely sporting. For my part, I feel like I turned on the Ten o' Clock News and a porno film was being shown instead. Mike's resolve for breaking things off with Moira is clearly weakening, so there's no point in my being here. I need to make a clean getaway. (Although, I could probably get up from the table and walk away and neither of them would notice nor care.) Before I can do that, Mike's phone rings. When he sees the name on the caller ID, his eyes bug out. He answers, delicately.

"Hi there," he says. "What's going on?"

Gillian's voice, bubbly as you like it, can be heard at our little table. "Nothing much. Just wanted to see what you're up to."

"I'm, I'm just hanging out," Mike says. "I'm at Glacier's. It's a coffee shop on—"

"I love that place!" Gillian says. "I'm just a couple blocks away. I'll join you!"

Mike looks as if he wants to protest, but his words (and possibly his lunch) are caught in his throat. Gillian rings off before he can respond.

Moira doesn't look any more pleased than Mike. "What are we going to do?" she asks.

Mike snaps his fingers and gestures toward the empty chair next to me. "You join Joe. Pretend the two of you are together."

If Mike had suggested she run naked through a high school football team's locker room, Moira could not show less enthusiasm. Not that I'm thrilled, either. (*I would rather run naked through a high school football team's locker room*). But we agree to the deception. Moira drops into the chair next to me and gives me a look that says *If you try to hold my hand, I'll slug you.*

Gillian walks in a few moments later. She's not hard to spot since her mirror image is next to me. Gillian wears a tan coat over a white sweater and tight tan pants. Her hair is pulled back and kept in place by a white clip. Mike peeks around the corner. Gillian gives him a little finger wave as she approaches the table. She greets Mike with a peck while Moira looks away.

"What a cool coincidence!" Gillian says. She sees Moira. "Hey sis. What are you doing here?"

Moira speaks through gritted teeth. "I'm here with Joe."

Mike jumps in. "I was just in the neighborhood and wanted to get a coffee. Ran into the lovebirds here. It's a whole day of coincidences."

Gillian seems delighted. "Wow. That's so cool."

"I know," I say. "It's all very…convenient."

Gillian shucks off her coat and slides in next to Mike. She takes his hand and snuggles close. Moira's fingernails claw the table. Gillian's eyes shift between me and her sister.

"I had no idea you two were dating," Gillian says. "How long has this been going on?"

Moira jumps in first. "It's pretty new."

"Very, very recent," I say.

"That is so awesome!" Gillian says. "We can double date now."

I try to join in the mirth. "We sure as hell can."

Gillian hops up. "I just need to run to the restroom. Sis, do you want to go, too?"

"No, I'm fine," Moira says.

Gillian seems thrown by her sister's refusal. (Women stalk restrooms in packs. For guys, the bodily function is a lonely hunter.) She recovers quickly and bounces down the hall. As soon as Gillian is out of sight, Moira glares at Mike.

"I need to talk to you," she says, practically snarling.

Mike agrees, perhaps sensing that if he doesn't, this will end with his penis being thrown clear of his balls. They get up from the table and walk to the front door. The conversation takes place outside, in front of the picture window. After a few minutes, Gillian comes down the hall from the restroom. I look toward the picture window. Mike and Moira are furiously making out on the sidewalk.

Wait, what?

I manage to contain my reaction so Gillian won't think something is wrong. She will likely come around on my right to retake her seat at the table. This will give her a clear view of the picture window and the sight of her sister and her boyfriend turning fifty shades of gray. I spring up as Gillian approaches and pull out her chair, as if rising to greet a lady. It allows me to strategically block the view of the picture window. Gillian beams at me.

"What a gentleman," she says.

"Ah, y'know…" I peek over my shoulder. "Somebody has to be."

Gillian slides into her chair. I sit across from her, keeping an eye on the front window. Mike has Moira pressed against the glass as they relentlessly snog. Give them another minute and we may have a misdemeanor on our hands. Gillian looks at the empty seats.

"Where are Moira and Mike?" she asks.

"Uh, Moira had to make a phone call."

"What about Mike?"

"He…left something in his car."

"Oh? What?"

Any sense of restraint, if the view in the picture window means anything. "I'm not sure."

If Gillian were the suspicious type, she'd have plenty to work with here. But she's willing to take me at my word (for what it's worth).

"You and Moira," she says. "That's awesome. How did it start?"

Okay, Joe, keep it casual. Don't commit to a big love story. "I saw her a couple of times and thought she was really cool. I asked her out and here we are."

Gillian sets her chin in one hand. "I love that. What first attracted you to her?"

Easy, Joe. Deep breaths. "That's a really good question. The thought that keeps coming back to me is, 'This woman could really be a...'" Outside, a cop approaches Mike and Moira to throw a bucket of metaphorical (and perhaps soon to be literal) cold water on them. "Cop," I say.

Gillian's head retracts. "You thought Moira could be a cop?"

"No, no. Sorry. Just got distracted by a...thing."

"Oh?" Gillian says, starts to turn. "Is there something going—"

I smack the table. Gillian spins toward me, startled. I rub my chin and try to answer Gillian's question as if nothing happened.

"What did I see in Moira?" I say. "I'm not quite sure."

My eyes cut toward the door, just in time to see the happy couple reentering. Mike looks toward me, and I tap the air with my index finger, my hand still on the table. It's an old signal between us. It tells Mike to slow down and create some separation with Moira. He goes with it, letting Moira get well in front of him. She slides into the chair, looking, if nothing else, more radiant than when she left. Mike returns to his seat, carefully straightening his hair and tucking his shirt back into his jeans. Gillian pats Mike on his leg and turns to her sister.

"Who did you have to call?" Gillian asks.

A flicker of annoyance plays on Moira's face. I put my life on the line by taking her hand.

"I was just telling your sister you had to step away for a phone call," I say. Then I muster up the courage to add: "Honey."

Moira avoids looking at me. "I just needed to give my boss a call."

"I get it," Gillian says. She scrutinizes her sister. "Are you okay? You're very flushed."

Moira's hand tightens on mine. I avoid wincing, not wanting to give anything away. "I'm fine," Moira says. "It's just a little warm in here."

Gillian turns to Mike. "How about you, hon? Did you get what you needed?"

Mike's eyes bug out. I tap the table, getting his attention. "I told Gillian you had to run out to your car," I say. "What was it that you needed again?"

"Needed," he says. "Outside. I needed…my…smokes. I apparently needed my smokes."

Gillian's face wrinkles. "It's a filthy habit, hon. I wish you'd give it up."

"I will give that some serious consideration," Mike says.

Moira's grip on my hand is reaching tear-inducing levels. If I don't get out of here soon, Luke Skywalker and I will have the same number of operational hands. I turn to her.

"Sweetie, this has been fun," I say, "but I think we should get going, don't you?"

Moira, thank the gods, releases my hand and stands up. "That sounds nice. Let's go somewhere and…leave."

Gillian bounces up and grabs her coat. "We should get going, too." Mike helps Gillian into her coat. "This was fun," she says. "We should do it again real soon."

"Sure," I say. Sometime next millennium maybe.

Mike guides Gillian ahead of him. Moira grabs his ass. Mike lets out a high-pitched yodel. Gillian, and the rest of the place, stares at him. Mike keeps the yodel going, trying to approximate singing (if singing was a sort of torture device). Gillian puts a hand on his arm.

"Honey, what are you doing?" she asks.

"I'm just singing," Mike says. "*The Lion Sleeps Tonight.* Isn't that the song on the PA?"

"No," Gillian says. "It's *Seven Nation Army.*"

"Ah," he says, snapping his fingers. "I always get those two confused."

Gillian lets it go. She and Mike head toward the front entrance. Moira speaks to me out of the side of her mouth.

"Don't get the wrong idea about this," she says. "There is *no* chance anything will happen between us."

"Can I get that in writing?"

***

I let myself in through the front door and climb the stairs to the apartment. Lisa is on her laptop, exactly where I left her just a little while ago. She spins the chair around to greet me. Squiggy appears at my feet, as if to say *Sir, may I take your coat?* I know his real mission.

"You hungry, Squiggs?" I ask.

"I just fed him and Lenny a little while ago," Lisa says.

"You didn't have to do that."

She waves a hand toward Squiggy. "Look at that face. Could you deny that face?"

The blue eyes with the dash of white between them gaze up at me. "No, I never have been able to do that."

"We are powerless in the face of such cuteness."

I hang my peacoat on the coat tree by the door and step into the kitchen, Squiggy close on my heels. As soon as the sound of my opening the plastic bin containing the kibble can be heard, Lenny appears, as if out of thin air, and shoulders Squiggy out of the way. (What an adorable little complete asshole.) While the cats eat, I take a seat at the breakfast bar.

"How goes the research?" I ask.

"Didn't get anything new out of Zoe's family," Lisa says. "They disposed of all her files. I get the impression they didn't approve of her being a reporter. For obvious reasons, we didn't get too deep into that." She tilts her head. "I think it's time we talked to Madeline Hauser."

My eyebrows go up. "Just because she tried to have us killed?"

"And with everything going on, maybe it's time Madeline answered a few questions."

"There *is* the small matter of Madeline not wanting anything to do with us. And her being surrounded by legitimate security."

Lisa kicks her feet up on the arm of the futon. "Did you know Madeline Hauser's parents are major contributors to the state Republican Party?"

"I did not. But there is nothing in that statement that surprises me."

"Tonight, they're having a fundraiser for Senator Longson at their house."

Not sure I like where this is going. "What would you like to do with this information?"

"Seems like an opportunity to talk to Madeline. Make her a captive audience, so to speak."

"Interesting idea. Assuming, of course, we aren't shot on sight."

"They won't do that," Lisa says. "We're ticketholders, after all."

This is like high school again, when I was always felt like I was running ten minutes behind whatever Lisa was plotting. "How did you get tickets?"

"I have my connections." The buzzer for the front door goes off. Lisa peeks out one of the arch windows. "Those would be our clothes for the evening. I looked at your suit in the closet and figured out the size for your tux. I hope that was okay."

"No problem. As long as it contributes to our likely incarceration and possible deaths, *mi casa es su casa*."

"It'll be fine. Trust me."

She disappears out the front door. *Trust me* she says. In the old days, trusting her usually got me into a shitload of trouble, saved only by a narrow escape. The funny part is: even with that knowledge, I *do* trust Lisa. Implicitly.

✳✳✳

The home of Dr. and Mrs. Stephen Hauser is a brown brick house on a hill in the northern section of Edina. The driveway winds up from the road, stopping before a front door framed with white columns. Expensive cars line the driveway and the winding street below, all parked by valets in black windbreakers and dress pants, stuffing miniscule cash tips into their pockets. Looking at the countryside, the house was likely the only one in sight when it was first built. Various McMansions have sprung up around it over time. I'm not certain why the Hausers have not abandoned Edina for the more remote climes of Lake Minnetonka or Eden Prairie. Perhaps it's the old money prestige of Edina, in all its snooty suburban glory. Perhaps it's proximity to the country club. I doubt I'll get a chance to ask them. Lisa and I park within view of the house. Even from a distance, the place is lit up like a distant ocean liner cresting a wave. I rest my hand on the steering wheel of the rented Mustang.

"I suppose it's best if we walk up?" I ask.

"They might look at us funny," Lisa says. "But not as funny if we pulled up in an obvious rental car."

"Too bad your expense account doesn't afford you a better car."

"It does. I blew it all at the track."

We start toward the house. The black tux and trench coat fit surprisingly well. Lisa has a gold coat over a slinky black dress with spaghetti straps. It's not entirely appropriate to the weather, but it's stunning. Her hair is up, and she's left the glasses at home. She slips her arm into mine as we make the long climb toward the house. I reach into my inner coat pocket and pull out the tickets.

"How did you manage to score tickets to this thing?"

"I have a few connections in the GOP. People kind enough to supply tips when needed."

"I thought most of the GOP equates you with the devil."

"Funny how that changes when someone wants to leak something to their advantage."

"Politics and bedfellows."

"Indeed."

We make it up the steep driveway with a minimum of fuss. If this were December or January, all bets would be off. The person working the door, a blonde woman with a severe ponytail, doesn't bat an eye as she scans the tickets.

"Thank you," she says, her voice clipped and professional. "Have a wonderful evening."

Not bloody likely. We step into a small foyer, where an attendant takes our coats and provides us with tabs we can use to reclaim them later. We're directed down a long hallway to the dining room on the south side of the house, where the fundraiser proper is being held.

For me, the term *dining room* brings to mind the modest-sized room where my family routinely ate dinner. The dining room at the Hausers' is larger than the gymnasium in our old high school. The ceiling is impossibly high and features a skylight with a view of the darkness. Pictures of Senator Longson line the walls. (I had no interest in the rubber chicken dinner, but my appetite is definitely gone now.) Round tables are spread across the floor. Guests are mingling, the conversation likely greased by the open bar. Lisa and I stand in the doorway, realizing how far out of our element we are, both in terms of political views and portfolios. Lisa steels herself with a breath.

"You see Madeline anywhere?" she asks.

"No. I see the man of the hour, though."

Senator Bill Longson is in a far corner; head, shoulders, and gut above the rest. There's nothing particularly avuncular about the man. He stands as regally as he can while potential donors crowd in around him. He's a monarch among supplicants. Lisa grips my arm.

"We should probably mingle," she says. "We're going to look conspicuous."

"More conspicuous than if we mingle?"

Lisa drags me into the crowd. I keep my head on a swivel, wondering if anyone will recognize us. We exchange nods with a few couples. They don't seem to know instinctively that we're out of our element. Other than being potential targets for murder by the guest of honor, we fit right in. I look longingly toward the bar, but some instinct tells me I need to stay sharp. Lisa comes to a sudden halt.

"I found Madeline," she says.

I follow Lisa's eyes to where Madeline is standing, on the far side of the room. She's glad-handing a group of party guests, probably coolly describing the methods by which the Longson campaign will not only return to the Senate in triumph but capture the presidency in the near future. She wears a low-cut green gown that exposes lots of creamy skin, so I doubt she's getting a lot of eye contact for her efforts. I turn to Lisa.

"Any ideas how we're going to get her alone in this mess?" I ask.

"Not yet. But I'm sure the opportunity will present itself."

I wish I had her faith. But I've trusted Lisa this far. We just have to wait for Opportunity to stop by, say hi, and maybe offer us a drink.

"Hi there," a voice behind me says. "How you doing tonight?"

I stiffen up. That's not Opportunity. That's Senator Bill Longson. He's right behind me, in conversation with a middle-aged couple who have likely given up on sex (at least with each other). His broad back is turned to us.

"Have you tried the vodka?" the Senator asks. "It's a special Longson brand. You can buy it on my website, exclusively. It's gonna be huge."

Uh-huh. Probably made in a barn with a fading American flag and some scripture painted on the side. Filtered through a pair of Longson's skivvies. His worshipers would love that. Meantime, Lisa and I slip into the crowd. A (for now) clean getaway.

The move puts us in front of an older couple. The man has a full head of gray hair, neatly swept back, and an equally gray mustache. His face is slightly red and boozy. The woman has straight brown hair that flows to her shoulders. Her eyes are cold, her eyebrows have been plucked, and her face has been spending time with her friend, Mr. Botox. She wears a matronly, yet fashionable black and gold gown. Lisa attempts to get around them. The woman stops us.

"Welcome to our home," she says, in a voice that may have once belonged to Joan Crawford.

Holy crap. These are the Hausers, Madeline's parents. What are the odds there's a hole in the floor we could drop into? Lisa politely shakes hands with Mrs. Hauser.

"You have a lovely home," Lisa says. "Thank you so much for having us."

"The doctor and I are big supporters of the Senator," Mrs. Hauser says. "We were thrilled when Madeline went to work for him."

"I'm sure," Lisa says.

"The doctor and I believe very strongly in Senator Longson. He has the stuff to lead this country back to greatness. Close the borders. Cut taxes. Get rid of these entitlements. Keep out the terrorists and make people work for a living. It's not complicated. It just took someone with the guts to actually say it."

I look toward the bar. "Boy, he sure did."

"He's already made his mark," Mrs. Hauser says, "He's one of the most accomplished members of the Senate."

Lisa feigns confusion. "What was that big piece of legislation he passed?"

That stops Mrs. Hauser short. Her visage is hard to read, since the Botox limits her range of expression. "I'm not entirely sure," Mrs. Hauser turns to her husband, "Do you remember what it was?"

Dr. Hauser sips his whiskey and gives us a learned, "Nope."

"I'm sure it was important," Mrs. Hauser says, flipping a hand, "Everyone on Fox News has been singing his praises. He's going to be an excellent president."

Just the thought makes me shiver. Lisa grips my arm tight. I follow her look. Madeline has spotted us. She makes her excuses to the people in her conversation and moves our direction.

Mrs. Hauser chooses this moment to talk *to* us rather than *at* us. "I'm sorry. I didn't catch your names."

Probably because we made a point of not throwing them. Since I'm relatively certain no one in this room would recognize my name, I do the honors. "I'm Joe Davis."

Dr. and Mrs. Hauser briefly shake my hand, still concentrating on Lisa. She clears her throat, hoping her celebrity status only travels so far.

"Lisa Cleary." She half mumbles it while shaking their hands.

Dr. Hauser gestures with his drink. "Lisa Cleary. That name is familiar. Where would I know it from?"

For possibly the first time in recorded history, Lisa falters in giving a response. It's up to me to leap into the breech.

"Lisa Cleary," I say, as if it should be obvious, "Of the bauxite and bathroom fixtures Clearys."

The Hausers brighten in recognition. Lisa turns up her forced smile. Madeline reaches the conversation. Mrs. Hauser beams through her medically induced facial paralysis and lightly places a hand on Madeline's shoulder.

"Thank you for coming over, dear," she says. "I don't know if you've had a chance to meet these people. This is Lisa Cleary, of the bauxite and bathroom fixtures Clearys. And this is Joe Davis. I'm sorry, Mr. Davis, I don't know what you're in."

"I'm into all sorts of things," I say. "Some of them even legal."

All of the Hausers freeze, like prairie dogs with the scent of an enemy. Madeline puts a hand on my back and guides Lisa and me out of the conversation.

"He's hilarious, isn't he?" Madeline says, not sounding remotely amused. "If you'll excuse us for a minute, I'd like to talk to Ms. Cleary and Mr. Davis."

The Hausers seem confused as Madeline drags us toward a corner of the room. She leads us through a small door, into what must be Dr. Hauser's study. The walls are painted a deep green that matches Madeline's dress. There's an arch window behind the oak desk. The bookcase is lined with medical volumes. It feels slightly musty, but then, I don't think Madeline hauled us in here to show off the décor. She closes the door behind her.

"What the hell are you two doing here?" is how she opens the conversation.

"We have tickets," I say.

"You don't expect me to believe you're here to support Senator Longson."

"It was a long shot," I say.

Lisa steps forward. "We thought it was time to talk about a few things. This seemed the only way to do it."

Madeline opens her mouth but doesn't say anything. She knows as well as we do that we couldn't have gone through official channels to set up a meeting. The campaign is actively avoiding us. Madeline deflates slightly.

"What do you want to talk about?" she says.

"Roger Neill came to see you the night he died," Lisa says. "That's right, isn't it?"

Madeline takes a moment to decide how cooperative she will be. "Yes, he did. He called and said he needed to talk. He didn't want to get into it over the phone. It was the end of a long day. I told Roger he could come over if he wanted to. And he did."

"What did you talk about?" Lisa asks.

"He wanted to talk about Zoe Court. And Rick Michaels."

It sends a little jolt through me. Roger *did* suspect something about Zoe and Rick. And now he's dead. Is Madeline really going to tell us that's a coincidence? If Lisa gets the same jolt, she hides it magnificently.

"What did he want to know about them?" she asks.

Madeline lets out a breath through her nose. "First, you need to realize Roger had been drinking. That was a factor in his accident. But he was raving about Zoe working on something the campaign didn't want known and that Rick must have known. It was an amazingly paranoid performance. I finally had to ask him to leave. The next morning, I heard what had happened. It was a shame. Roger was an excellent assistant."

I'm not getting an overflow of grief from Madeline, but we all experience these things differently. Lisa considers the information.

"You didn't think there was anything to what Roger was saying?" Lisa asks.

"Of course not. It was ridiculous on the face of it. Zoe was struggling at work. She was clearly unstable."

"What makes you say that?"

"Does a well-adjusted person throw themselves off the top of a parking garage?"

Lisa takes that in stride. "Did Roger say what story Zoe was working on?"

"No, he didn't. My belief is that there was no story. Zoe was making it up in order to save her job. When it became apparent it wouldn't do that, she decided to end it all."

"Did you share that theory with Roger?"

"Not directly," Madeline says. "I asked him if he really believed there was a story. He seemed convinced there was. He was intoxicated, so I didn't feel like arguing with him. I left him to his delusion."

"According to Roger, Zoe was working on a story about Jeremiah Kincade," Lisa says.

That doesn't seem to faze Madeline. "Oh?"

"Is there any reason the campaign wouldn't want to see a story about Jeremiah Kincade?"

"None that I can think of," Madeline says. "The Senator has always expressed regrets that Mr. Kincade's actions created the special election."

"Uh-huh," I say. "Except on those occasions when he trashes Senator Gardner's memory."

Madeline looks nonplussed. "The Senator is entitled to his opinions."

Which he never hesitates to share. Lisa takes over, sensing I'm about to lose my temper.

"Did Roger say anything about Rick?" she asks.

"Just that it was odd he had disappeared," Madeline says. "Roger was trying to make some kind of connection between Zoe's death and Rick's running off."

"Do you think there *is* a connection?" Lisa asks.

"No," Madeline says. "As far as I know, Rick and Zoe weren't acquainted. What happened with one doesn't have anything to do with what happened with the other."

I slip my hands in my pockets. "Then why do you think Rick disappeared?"

"I don't know," Madeline says. "If you inspect his work history, you'll realize that dependability was not his strong suit. I'm sorry. I know you're friends of his, but that's a fact."

"It's also a fact you were seeing Rick," I say.

Madeline looks aghast. "That is—"

Lisa cuts her off. "The truth. We have proof."

That brings Madeline up short. She's probably wondering if we're bluffing and if she should call it. Finally, she decides to come clean. "Fine. Yes. We were." She squares us with a look. "Happy now?"

"Not particularly," I tell her. "You have any idea where Rick is?"

"No. It was just a fling. He never came over to my place, and I never went over to his. It was hotel rooms and the occasional weekend in Stockholm."

"You went all the way to Stockholm?" I ask.

"Stockholm, *Wisconsin*," Madeline says. "It's a little town on Lake Pepin, just across the border. My parents have a summer house there. When they weren't using it, Rick and I would meet there. Sometimes." She shakes her head. "I don't know where Rick disappeared to."

Strangely, I believe her. I get the feeling she's looking for Rick just as much as we are, though for wildly different reasons. Lisa studies Madeline.

"Roger Neill saw you having a conversation with Rick," she says. "It didn't look friendly. It was right before Rick disappeared. Do you remember that conversation?"

"I do. And it *was* unpleasant. I was breaking things off with Rick. Seeing him was a mistake. It was best to end things and move on."

"And Rick didn't take it well?" Lisa asks.

"He was upset, certainly. I doubt this was the first time a woman had broken things off with him, but that didn't seem to matter. Maybe he and I simply saw things differently. Rick…he must have been under the impression it was something more. It upset him, as I said."

"That was the last you saw of him?" I ask.

"That was it," Madeline says. "I assume he got upset and left the campaign without a word. That's how we're treating it, anyway."

Of course they are. "Why didn't you tell us this the first time we talked to you?"

"Because it was embarrassing," Madeline says. "A couple reporters come in and start asking questions about me seeing one of the employees. Do you think I want that dragged into the light?"

Lisa surrenders the point. "Rick said he had something about the campaign. What would that have been?"

"I'll tell you what I told you before: I have no idea. Maybe it was something about the affair. Maybe he thought that would make a difference. I'm sorry, Ms. Cleary, if he wasted your time by bringing you up here, but it's possible that's all it was."

A perfectly plausible theory, viewed from a certain angle. It doesn't explain the break-in at Katie's, the ransacking of Rick's apartment, or the multiple attempts to kill Lisa. That's a little heavy for a simple lovers' snit. Lisa seems to follow my line of thinking.

"We saw you talking to someone in the parking lot of your campaign headquarters," Lisa says. "We have reason to believe this man has twice been involved in an attempt to kill us. Can you tell us anything about him?"

Madeline scoffs. "I'm sure I don't know what you're talking about. I'm approached by people all the time. Some I know, some I don't. Can you be more specific about who this man is?" Lisa gives her a physical description, but as could be expected, it doesn't ring a bell with Madeline. "I'm sorry. I can't help you. That man doesn't sound familiar to me."

Why am I not surprised? When it comes to any potential criminal activity, Madeline Hauser and the rest of the Longson campaign remain deaf, dumb, and blind. Lisa tries to mask her frustration, but the flush in her face gives her away.

"So, you're saying—"

Madeline, though, steps toward the door, guiding us gently, but firmly, by the elbows. "I'm saying you've taken up enough of my time and I would like you both to leave before I have to have you escorted out. It would make such an ugly scene."

"Unlike your boy's campaign rallies," I say.

She ignores the gibe. "Please leave quietly."

Lisa acquiesces more gracefully than I do. It will take a Herculean effort to avoid knocking over vases or stealing knick-knacks on my way out. Madeline walks us to the front door, smiling at the guests, and hands us over to a security person. She walks away without another word. Lisa and I are silent as we walk down the driveway. The night has turned chilly (not that it had far to go). The security guard departs only when we've left the grounds.

I run a hand through my hair. "That was…everything we should have expected."

Lisa pulls her coat tight against the cold. "At least we *know* Roger Neill was at Madeline's the night he died. And Madeline confessed to dating Rick."

"You think their little argument was about them breaking it off?"

"My gut says no. The evidence says I have nothing to contradict that."

I stop at the car. "This would be so much easier if people just confessed and threw themselves on the mercy of the court."

"Where's the accomplishment in that?"

For Lisa, it's the accomplishment. For me, I just want to get out of this with my skin intact. And hope that Rick gets out of it the same way.

***

"I think we've definitely got Fabio in our corner," Lars says, leaning on the bar. "Our friend Carol here has been pillow-talking him."

"Do you have to put it that way?" Carol says, frowning into her Cosmo.

"What would you prefer?" Lars asks.

Carol shrugs. "I guess pillow-talking works. I want him to see Ollie is a moron."

I spin on my barstool. "That wasn't apparent to Fabio before?"

"I get the feeling a lot of things aren't apparent to Fabio," Carol says.

Lars sips his beer. "Sometimes, you need a guiding hand."

Carol levels a look at him. "Is that a sexual metaphor?"

"It didn't start that way," Lars says, stroking his beard, "but we can't control everything."

Nick, the bartender, brings a couple of pints for Lars and me. (Thank you, kindly inn-keep.) Our colleagues are gathering in the restaurant end of The Tav. The place is about half-full. We should have privacy for our production meeting. Fabio and Frankie are in conversation. Fabio gives Carol a little wave, which prompts Frankie to give him a dirty look. Ollie sits near Frankie, his head bowed slightly, and his hands clasped on the table. I take a bracing sip of my Grand Oktoberfest.

"You still have faith in this clambake?" I ask.

"Absolutely," Lars says, sipping his IPA. "By the way, *clambake*. Good word. We need to use it more often."

"Glad you like."

Carol slips off her barstool. "I'm going to say hi to Fabio before the meeting."

She ignores the bow Lars gives her and strides to the table. Honestly, I wish I wasn't here. Half (or perhaps more than half) of my mind is on the case and where we can find Rick. Once Carol is out of earshot, Lars turns toward me.

"I appreciate her help," he says, "but I've also taken steps to ensure our success."

There's nothing in that phrase that comforts me. "Do I dare ask?"

"Nothing too bad. I decided to make peace with Ollie. I took him out for dinner earlier."

"All right…" I say, waiting for the other shoe to descend.

"We had drinks," Lars says. "Ollie had quite a few. As long as I was buying."

"You're trying to get him sloppy before the meeting?"

"I was hoping to intensify Ollie's personality by removing some of the barriers to his behavior. Getting him loaded seemed the easiest way to do that. Also, I helped this along by slipping him a Mickey Finn."

Ah, there is the Size 15 boot coming in for its scheduled landing. "You slipped him a Mickey?" I ask.

Lars uses his hands to tamp down the air. "Easy, my brother. Bar patrons don't like hearing about Mickey Finns. Kills the mood, you understand."

I do him the favor of lowering my voice. "What did you give him?"

"Just a little hallucinogenic. He'll be fine."

"As long as he doesn't go up to the roof and try to fly home."

"Trust me."

And why wouldn't I trust a guy who just admitted to drugging his dinner companion? "Fine," I say. "But you're in charge of getting Ollie home safely."

Lars accepts that with an air of resignation. "I hope Ollie remembers where he lives. Or that he has a permanent address."

We join the production team at the table. Carol gives Fabio a pat on the shoulder and returns to the bar. Fabio slips some paperwork out of his folder.

"Why don't we get started?" he says.

Everyone except Ollie consents. He doesn't raise his head. Frankie, sitting next to Ollie, lays a hand on his shoulder.

"Ollie, are you okay?" she asks.

The director finally looks up. His eyes are rimmed with red, and his pupils are dilated. He looks from one of us to the other, as if surprised we're here. It takes a second to find his voice.

"Hi," Ollie says. And he certainly is.

Fabio hesitantly gets us back on track. We go over some dry budget numbers, which make even Fabio look bored as he presents them. Ollie gazes into the distance. What he's seeing is anyone's guess. I'm starting to feel sorry for him.

"The car drop sounds cool," Frankie says. "We should get the money to make it happen. Do you think we can get the permits?"

Fabio exchanges a look with Carol. "Those might be a little hard to come by. I checked with the city, and they thought the idea was…"

"Innovative?" Frankie asks.

"Horrendous," Fabio says. "That was the exact word. I even had Dad call the mayor. They're golfing buddies, so I thought maybe Dad could put in a good word. No fucking way. That's exactly what the mayor said, word for word."

If there is such a thing as a mixed pall, that's what descends on the table. Frankie seems genuinely disappointed. Lars and I appear to be in sympathy, but we're secretly relieved this completely ridiculous stunt appears dead in the water (which may very well have been the result if the stunt had been allowed to go forward). Ollie's hands slowly extend across the table.

"Permission is an anchor on creativity," Ollie says, his words coming slow but not slurred. "They're limitations *we* set up. Nothing more."

I look toward him. "Unless, say, a municipality gets involved."

Ollie ignores me (whether by choice or impairment, I can't be sure). "Creativity is a free and floating spirit. You can't own it. You can't corral it. You can't *limit* it. The muse simply will not allow that."

Nobody at the table says anything, unsure how Ollie's ramblings relate to the film. I decide to venture in.

"What are you saying?" I ask, since a direct question is always best.

Ollie's eyes are saucers. "I'm saying no one can stand in the way of the creative spirit. If the city doesn't like our ideas, that's their problem. Why are we letting the city stop us?"

"There *is* the little matter of them putting us in jail…" I say.

"Jail?" Ollie says. "The only jail that can hold us is the jail we make for ourselves."

"I'll keep that in mind when I'm making meth in the toilet of my cell."

"The only cell you need to worry about—"

"I get the metaphor," I say. "We all do."

Frankie and Fabio exchange a look. "We do?" Frankie asks.

Ollie, though, is in the grip of the creative spirit and whatever primo shit Lars slipped him. "If we push past our barriers, we can do amazing work. Artists are the mirror held up to society. We are all that stands between truth and corruption."

I look up from my notes. "And dropping a car from great heights in service of a vampire heist movie accomplishes this…how?"

"It's artistic expression. Our own helplessness in the face of a world spinning out of control. Our greedy little possessions paling in comparison to the forces they're designed to distract us from. The inequity of wealth and privilege. International forces contending for superiority as they drag us closer to our doom. This is why we need the arts. And we have to ratchet up the spectacle to get our point across. We need explosions. Something to rip down the illusions we've created. We have to destroy in order to build!"

No one knows what to say. How do we decline Ollie's idiotic idea without triggering a tantrum that might result in him removing his clothes and destroying property? Frankie slowly bobs her head as she considers the matter.

"Far out," she says. "I love it."

I throw her a look. "And when the city comes after us?"

Frankie doesn't seem fazed by this. "Let 'em try. We don't need their permission."

"That's how it's done!" Ollie says, spilling some of his wine. "You get these barriers out of the way, and you grab this world by the balls. You know what I'm saying?"

I'm not sure if *Frankie* knows what Ollie is saying—big picture—but she likes the idea of blowing stuff up. She slips her arm into his, a gesture to which he is mostly oblivious. Fabio glances at Carol, who wags a finger at him. He puts his hands on the table, trying to be firm.

"I don't think that's a good idea," Fabio says. "We have to talk about ideas that are legal and within our budget." He holds up the paper containing the budget for emphasis.

Frankie slaps the table, startling all of us (particularly Ollie). She points Carol's direction. "It's her, isn't it? Ever since you started boning that bitch, you've been talking like some corporate suit. She's taking all the soul out of you!"

Frankie grabs the budget paperwork in her brother's hand. Fabio refuses to let it go. They play tug of war until it rips in half. Fabio stands up from the table.

"I can do my own thinking!" he says. "I'm my own man!" He turns to Carol, who has materialized behind Fabio. "Isn't that right?"

"Exactly, honey," Carol says.

I half-expect Carol to pat Fabio on the head. Frankie grabs Ollie's hand.

"Fine, brother of mine," Frankie says. "You let your corporate suit girlfriend tell you what to do. But Ollie is a true artist and I'm backing him a hundred percent. We'll see which one Daddy likes best!"

Frankie storms out, dragging Ollie with her. His legs won't quite lock, making him appear almost simian. Carol slips her arm into Fabio's and accompanies him back to the bar area. Lars and I are left to pick up the pieces (and apparently, the check).

"Was this part of your plan?" I say.

"Well, we're divided," Lars says. "I'm not certain we're going to conquer."

"Then we really haven't gotten anywhere."

Lars serenely sips his IPA and mutters, "Bugger."

***

When I get home, Lisa is at the desk but not working. Squiggy acknowledges my arrival, then goes over to Lisa. He does his usual trick of putting his front paws on her chair then reaching up to tap her on the arm, as if to say, "Madame, may I be of assistance?" Lisa's face lights up.

"That is so adorable," she says, picking Squiggy up and putting him in her lap. "That thing he does with his little paws."

"It is," I say, tossing my keys on the breakfast bar. "Although, it's a little less adorable when you realize those are the same paws he uses to tread in the litterbox."

Lisa sticks her tongue out at me. Squiggy remains curled up in her lap, supremely unconcerned with my jibes. I drop onto a stool at the breakfast bar and rub my face. Lisa looks up from stroking Squiggy's back.

"How did the meeting go?" she asks.

"Apparently, we're in a societal downward spiral from which only a vampire heist movie can save us." Not surprisingly, Lisa starts to ask a follow-up question, but I stop her. "I'm sorry, lady of the press, but I'm not taking any further questions at this time. What were you up to while I was gone?"

"Thinking about the story. As always." She sits back in the chair. "If Zoe was killed, maybe the Longson campaign had something to do with it. Maybe Rick got a hold of the information Zoe had. He confronted Madeline about it. Then he called me and set up a meeting. Maybe something happened and he had to run."

"How does Roger Neill figure into it?"

"He was close with Zoe. Maybe he knew what she had. Or at least suspected it. Maybe he confronted Madeline about it, and she called her friend with the gun to take care of it."

"Very plausible," I say, "Just one little problem."

"A complete lack of proof?"

"That's what I'm thinking."

"I know," Lisa says, blowing out a sigh. "It feels like it's right there under our noses. If we find Rick, it will all fall into place. We don't know where to look."

I wave a hand toward the kitchen. "I didn't get anything to eat at The Tav. I'm going to make a grilled cheese. You want one?"

"I could eat."

I could eat. The time-honored Minnesota response when you're hungry but don't want to put somebody out. You can take the girl out of the Gopher State, but you can't take the Gopher State out of the girl.

I get a couple frying pans out of the cupboard and warm them on the stove. That done, I grab a block of cheddar cheese and a block of gruyere out of the fridge and start shredding them. I think about the situation with Rick while I work. Lisa's right. We need to find him if we're going to get at the truth. But we only know bits and pieces. His asking about Zoe Court. His affair with Madeline. The two of them sneaking around and…

I have no idea why the thought pops into my head. It's something that happened a long time ago and involves three idiots who have nothing to do with this case. And yet it starts me down the road to figuring something out. I walk to the end of the breakfast bar, dinner all but forgotten. Lisa notices my reverie.

"What's up?" she asks.

"Did I ever tell you about…no, I'm sorry. I couldn't have. I haven't seen you in sixteen years." I sit on a stool at the breakfast bar. "I had these three friends in college: Robbie, Stoner, and T.J. After we graduated, they got a house together in Minneapolis. Whole arrangement lasted about a year. They spent most of the time at each other's throats. One of the problems was with T.J. He was one of those guys who'd get pissy about his privacy in the bathroom. If he was taking a shower, he'd freak out if someone stepped into the bathroom, even if it was just to take a whiz or brush their teeth. On the other hand, Robbie was one of those guys who'd be comfortable living in a house without walls. He'd be sitting on the toilet with the door wide open, having a conversation with you."

"Lovely," Lisa says. But she gives me the room to continue my story.

"Stoner was somewhere in the middle. But he was the most devious one of the three. And he finally got tired of all the arguing about the bathroom, particularly T.J.'s complaints. One day, when he was home by himself, he took a screw gun and removed the bathroom door. Then he hid it in the one place he knew T.J. would never think to look: under T.J.'s bed." I glance at Lisa, breaking my reverie. "You're wondering where I'm going with this."

"The thought had occurred."

"What is the best place to hide something? Right under someone's nose. Wouldn't the same rule apply to people?"

Lisa opens her mouth to ask a question, then stops. She sees where I'm going with this. She sits up in the chair.

"Where do you think Rick is hiding?" Lisa asks.

"You remember Madeline mentioning the summer house in Stockholm? The one nobody would visit until next spring?"

"The one she brought Rick to a few times. Might make a pretty good hiding place. At least temporarily."

"And Madeline might not think to look there." I get off the stool, unable to sit still. "You think you can find the address?"

Lisa arches an eyebrow. "It's not a matter of me finding it. It's how *soon* I can find it."

She goes to work on her laptop. A few snowflakes drift pass the arch windows. A mid-October snow. That's not going to make for a fun drive to Stockholm.

It might be even less fun when we get there.

CHAPTER TEN

SPRING, SENIOR YEAR

A triple date for prom seemed like the best plan. Lisa and I, Sam and Theresa, and Andy and his date, Elyse Erickson. We decided to meet at Arthur's Diner for an ironic burger-and-fries dinner and then carpool from there. I washed and even polished my crappy Ford Taurus before leaving to pick Lisa up. I took one last look at myself in the mirror. I tugged at the cuffs and tried to look like James Bond. Instead, I looked like a nervous kid wearing his first (rented) tux.

The day was sunny and warm. Perfect weather for prom (or most anything). The AC in the Taurus had regressed to substandard levels, so I had to keep telling myself, "Don't sweat, don't sweat, don't sweat." Somehow, I had command over that when I was a kid.

Lisa was still upstairs when I got to her house, so I was forced to stand in the living room and make small talk with her dad. He was polite but seemed to think this whole prom thing was ridiculous. Yes, he and Lisa's mother went to prom when they were in high school. But it was her mother's idea, not his.

Lisa came down the stairs a minute later, ending my chat with her father. She wore a black gown with gold trimming. Her hair was done up just so, and she wore just a bit of makeup. She was giving the contact lenses another try. She gave me a shy smile as she stepped carefully down the stairs.

She was stunning.

Lisa came off the stairs, followed closely by her mother. She tried to ignore her father's look of mild disapproval. She stood in front of me, biting a corner of her lip. Some of the breath came back into my body.

"Wow," I said.

Her face lit up as she looked down. I carefully (and slowly) pinned a corsage to her bodice. Lisa slipped unpleasant looks toward her parents, who seemed to want to get this prom thing over and get back to watching TV. She was much more adept in pinning the boutonniere to my lapel. As she did, she leaned close to me.

"You look very handsome," she said.

Okay, now I felt like James Bond.

We got out of Lisa's house quickly. (But not before Mr. Cleary shook my hand and told me to have a good time with a tone that suggested, "Touch my daughter, and I'll kill you." Safety and common sense dictated I not tell him that ship had already sailed.) We hopped in the car and Lisa tapped the roof like it was the roof of an old hansom cab.

"To the prom, Jeeves."

"As you wish, madam."

We had to stop by my place so my parents could take pictures and repeatedly mention what a handsome couple we made. I didn't care much for being the center of attention. (Boy, would that change over time.) It was nice to see how much more relaxed Lisa was around my parents than her own. My dad slipped me some money as he and Mom wished us off. I probably wouldn't spend it, but I appreciated the gesture. His slap on my back and wish for me to have a good time carried no subtle warning. It was genuine.

We met the rest of our party at Arthur's Diner. Somehow, we managed to cram all six of us into a booth. Guys on one side, girls on the other. We ate and jabbered, each of us nervous and excited. We kept the meal strictly to burgers and fries (Arthur's specialty) and were careful not to get anything on our formalwear. Just before we left, Sam, with great formality, loosened the caps on all the saltshakers.

We piled into a huge Cadillac on loan from Andy's grandparents. Andy did the driving while Elyse sat up front and the rest of us somehow crammed into the back. We got to the school in time to take our places in the grand march (and witness Beans Madden's attempts to bring a mule to the prom).

The gym had been decorated with streamers and ornaments. The lighting was low. Everyone walked under a red-and-white balloon arch when entering. Lisa and I took every slow dance together. She had less success getting me on the dance floor for anything up-tempo (since my dancing skills best resembled a bag of disconnected body parts being handled by a drunken marionette). Finally, I joined in for the last several dances. What the hell? I figured I might as well complete high school with no regrets.

After leaving prom, we headed to an after party at the beach. We first stopped by Andy's house to change into our swimsuits and t-shirts. Everyone seemed more relaxed when rid of the formalwear. Late May on the North Shore can range from freezing to balmy. Fortunately, we were getting the balmy end of things that night. The playground was on the southern part of the beach, near the entrance to town. It wasn't a huge gathering. Just our party and three other couples. Anything larger might have drawn the interest of the local constabulary.

The after party was reasonably tame. There was a lot of running around and loud conversation and a few people venturing into the water. (Not a good idea in Lake Superior unless it's July.) Someone did think to bring whiskey, but a pint was only going to go so far among twelve people. Lisa and I declined, sensing we might have to face her dad when I brought her home. (Both of us legal adults, both of us months away from leaving home. And yet, we were worried about getting grounded.)

Rick Michaels was among the people at the gathering. He was there with his date, Paula Povich, a rather pulchritudinous junior who had latched onto Rick after he achieved celebrity status. She cavorted about in a bikini top and jean shorts while Rick leaned against the monkey bars, standing apart from the others, a faraway look in his eyes. Lisa and I walked over to him.

"Happy prom," I said.

Rick forced a smile. "You guys having a good time?"

"Most definitely," I said.

"That's good," he said.

"How about you?" Lisa asked.

"Having a blast." His tone didn't sound as if that were remotely the case.

I looked around at the gathering. "I don't see anybody from the team."

Technically, Rick was part of Porter's Bay's baseball team at this point (they were about forty-eight hours from being eliminated from the regional playoffs), but the team, even at this early stage, would forever refer to the state championship hockey team. Rick shrugged at my observation.

"I don't much like to hang around them," he said. "And they sure as hell don't like to hang around me."

Lisa tilted her head. "Why is that?"

"I got the goal. I got the goal." He spread his hands out. "Third string left winger, nearly cost us the game with that stupid tripping penalty in overtime. They feel like they did all the work, and I was just in the right place at the right time." He shook his head. "It's no big deal. I was never tight with those guys in the first place." He pushed off from the monkey bars. "Hey, this is supposed to be a good time. Let's not talk about any of that stuff."

Paula came bouncing up to us. She ignored Lisa and me and grabbed Rick's arm. "Some of us are talking about going skinny dipping," she said. "Sound like fun?"

Rick slowly turned toward the looming blackness. "You want to go skinny dipping in that *lake? You need hypothermia that badly?"*

Paula tugged at Rick's arm. "C'mon. It'll be fun." She finally noticed Lisa and me. "You guys can come, too."

Over the years, I've learned that if you get a bunch of horny young people around a body of water, skinny dipping is likely to be a side effect. This was my first exposure, so to speak, to this phenomenon. But I was not prepared to get naked around anyone but Lisa, and I'm pretty sure she felt the same way. Besides, Rick was right. Sliding bare-ass on an ice rink would be warmer than jumping in Lake Superior around this time of year. Rick suddenly turned to me and put his hand on my shoulder, as if he was going to say something. Instead, his eyes slid away, and he walked off with Paula. (To this day, I have no idea what he wanted to say.) He gave us an apologetic look, as if to say, I've got to handle this. *Lisa and I gave him a wave as he left.*

"Have fun," I said.

Rick gave us a rueful glance and disappeared into the darkness.

Nobody from our group participated in the skinny dipping. Even Sam, and we thought for sure we'd have to drag him out of there. It was well after midnight before our little group left. Andy took us back to our cars, still safe and sound in the Arthur's Diner parking lot. I drove Lisa home. The adrenaline of the evening was wearing away, and we were both starting to yawn. Lisa held my hand as I walked to her to her front door. Her beautiful gown was folded in her arms. She turned her back to the door and gave me a sleepy smile.

"Thank you for a wonderful night," she said.

"It certainly was."

We kissed. Lisa kept her face close to mine. "I wish I could invite you in, but…"

"But you'd like me to remain alive and well and your boyfriend?"

"That's pretty much it."

We kissed again. Lisa leaned against the door. "Good night," she said. "I love you."

"I love you."

A flicker of something crossed Lisa's face. She quickly recovered her smile. She slipped inside. I walked back to my car, amazed by how quiet everything was, even by Porter's Bay standards. I watched the house. The light came on in Lisa's room. I imagined, briefly, lying down with her. Not sex. Just lying in bed. It was a nice thought. I started the car and drove home.

Lisa settles herself into the passenger seat. With the dark, not much can be seen, though we sense the bluffs looming on the left and the expanse of Lake Pepin (really, just a boa constrictor bulge in the Mississippi River) on the right. After our last car trip, no one can blame us for being uneasy.

"How much farther to Stockholm?" she asks.

"Last sign said five miles," I tell her, feeling a little uneasy myself. "You know where we're going when we get there?"

"As much as Google Maps will tell me, since I've never been there."

The tension in the car is palpable. I get the sense Lisa and I are trying our best not to take it out on each other. Personally, I'm not sure what the best-case scenario is here: we find Rick safe and sound and break the story, or we find nothing and drive home, safe and sound ourselves. Snowflakes glide past the window. The snow is light if unseasonal. Normally, I find snowfall relaxing, but not tonight.

"Even if we find Rick," I say, "do we have any way of protecting him?"

"If there's a story there," Lisa says, "I'm sure Metro can arrange some protection. If it's big enough, maybe the Feds can, too."

"Then we better hope it's big."

"That would be nice, wouldn't it?"

While Stockholm, Wisconsin seems to be a perfectly charming town, it's not the kind of place in which one arrives and says, "My God! We're here!" It caters to quaint in the same manner as Porter's Bay. The downtown has a few shops (antiques, what a surprise) and eateries. Just past downtown, we turn left to get to the Hausers' summer home. The road winds upward into the bluffs before we take another left onto a dirt road. It takes us past fields and into a small, wooded area.

The general upward trajectory gives the impression we're far above Stockholm.

The headlights of the Saturn fall on a small opening between two clusters of trees. A small A-frame garage is embedded in one of the clusters. Beyond the trees, a two-story house stands at the apex of a circular driveway. It's a tasteful colonial-type home. An enclosed porch wraps around the house and likely affords a spectacular view of Stockholm and Lake Pepin. A stone chimney rises from the roof. The circular driveway wraps around a patch of grass with an empty flagpole in the center. Barren trees and brush stretch out on all sides. The whole thing feels like a rich person's idea of rustic. I park next to the front door.

"Any ideas?" I ask.

"We look for Rick," Lisa says. "Hopefully, he didn't take off when he saw us coming."

"Unless he jumped off the bluff, I don't think he has many options."

We get out of the car and walk to the front door. I press the doorbell. Shockingly, there is no response. I try knocking. Same result.

"Should we call him?" I ask.

Lisa holds up her phone. "No cell service."

I cup my hands around my mouth. "Rick? Rick, it's Joe Davis! Lisa's with me. We're here to help."

Lisa follows my lead. We stroll around the grounds shouting out variations of that message. After a few minutes of getting no response, we meet back at the front door.

"I don't think he's here," Lisa says.

"Son of a bitch. We're right back at square one."

We stand there, trying to think of another plan. But there isn't one. Slowly, we walk back to the car. Just before we get in, a voice calls to us, faintly.

"Joe? Lisa? That really you?"

Since my directional hearing is for shit, it takes a moment to locate where the voice is coming from. Lisa points to the opening in the trees, at the entrance to the driveway. We jog that direction. Someone stands close to the tree line, trying to obscure themselves in the shadows. They don't make a move to run. We're about ten feet away when the figure holds up a hand.

"That's close enough," he says.

Even from here, we can see who it is. Rick Michaels, as we live and breathe. His voice is raspy. He looks around, paranoid.

"Did anyone follow you here?" he asks.

"We didn't see anyone," Lisa says. "We can make sure you're safe."

"I don't care about me," he says. "Make sure they don't get to Katie."

"Don't worry," I say. "She'll be okay."

Rick lets us come forward. His hair is a little shaggy, his eyes are glassy, and there's the shadow of a beard on his face. He wears a brown bomber jacket over a black sweater and blue jeans. He's clearly been wearing them for several days. But he's still in one piece.

"You've been hiding out here?" I ask.

"There's a room above the garage," he says. "Ditched my car in the woods, just in case someone came to check on the house. There's a bunch of canned goods in the pantry. It's a little primitive, but I'm doing okay."

Lisa moves closer to him. "Our meeting. It was about Longson. And Zoe Court. That's right, isn't it?"

Rick seems relieved. "I knew I called the right person. Sorry I had to stand you up."

"It's okay," Lisa says. "We can talk now."

He looks down, gathering strength. When Rick looks up again, his eyes are rimmed with red, and his voice is tight. "I was in Rochester when Zoe died. I drove Bill Longson down there. He said he had a meeting. I parked on the street, next to the ramp. He got in another car. Turned out it was Zoe driving. About ten minutes later, I saw her fall. She landed two cars away."

"How did you get ahold of the tape?" Lisa asks.

"The tape player flew out when she landed. I picked it up and put it in my pocket. I wasn't even thinking. I didn't tell Longson anything about it."

"What's on the tape?" Lisa asks.

Rick takes a breath. "Zoe had a file. On Jeremiah Kincade. She had been doing a story on his family. How they dealt with what he did. Turns out they had been getting money. Living expenses. It came from a charity. Zoe did some digging into it. The charity was a shell company. Longson's funneling money into it. And that's just the start. Turns out Kincade wasn't the monster. It's Longson."

Lisa lays a hand on Rick's arm. "You know what's in the file?"

"I saw it," Rick says. "Longson sent me to Zoe's apartment. He wanted me to clear the place out before anyone got there. I found the file. But I didn't give it to Longson. I tried talking to Madeline. She was…my boss. She told me to forget everything and get rid of the file. I couldn't do that. Not after…not after seeing Zoe fall. That's why I called you." He looks down. "I was going to give you everything. I hid the tape and the file. But then two guys came after me. Nearly ran me off the road. I had to get away. Didn't even have time to go back to my apartment and get the tape player. I'm sorry. Guess I was just thinking of myself. Like Katie always said."

"It doesn't matter," Lisa says, "You can still do the right thing."

A trace of a smile crosses Rick's face. He seems relieved. Maybe it's because there's someone to share the burden of the truth. Maybe it's just because there's someone to talk to. Before we can talk, though, we hear a car coming up the road.

It's moving slowly, and the headlights aren't on. Whoever is behind the wheel was likely intending to sneak up on the house. They couldn't have known we would be standing in the driveway. The three of us look toward it.

"You expecting anybody?" Lisa asks.

"Nobody I want to see," Rick says. "Hate to tell you this, but I think you *were* followed."

The car stops. We're bathed in the light. I raise a hand to my eyes, trying to block the glare. Then come the firecracker pops of gunfire.

I grab Lisa's hand and run for the trees surrounding the house. I look back but don't see Rick. More gunshots. We crash into the brush. My jacket and face are wet from the snow on the branches. My heart pounds in my ears. The edge of the bluff is visible, no more than ten feet away. There's nowhere to go. Lisa and I crouch down. I try to control my breathing. Two voices are heard coming up the driveway.

One is low, with a bit of authority to it. "Stan, you go up to the house and look around."

A younger voice, higher-pitched, answers. "What are you gonna do, Mr. Reynard?"

"Let me worry about that."

Reynard looks our direction. I try to hold still. If he spots us, we have no place to go. He walks toward the tree line. He's no more than a handful of feet away. Neither Lisa nor I move.

Then he spots us.

Reynard takes one step our direction, and I know we've been had. I hop out of the brush, my hands up. Reynard sticks the gun in my face.

"Where's your girlfriend?" he asks.

"She's…" I'm about to correct him on Lisa's status as my girlfriend, but that doesn't seem prudent. "She's not here. I don't where she went. Everybody scattered."

"Fuck you. I saw the two of you take off together. Last chance. Where is she?"

I'm trying to think something up when Lisa comes out of the brush and says, "I'm here."

Reynard flicks a look her direction. "Good thinking."

He grabs the collar of my peacoat and shoves me, none too politely, toward the driveway. He gestures with the gun and

Lisa follows. Stan is near the flagpole. His movements are twitchy and nervous.

"You get 'em?" Stan asks.

"Got two of them," Reynard says. He raises his voice. "We found your friends, Rick. You give a shit about them, I suggest you come out. I'll kill them both right here. Doesn't make a bit of difference to me."

For several long moments, there is nothing but silence. A void, dark and still. Finally, Reynard turns toward Stan.

"Hold on to the reporter," Reynard says. "This other motherfucker doesn't mean anything."

Stan pulls Lisa away from me. Reynard levels the gun at my chest.

"No!"

The scream comes from Lisa. She kicks at Stan, trying to get away. He struggles to contain her and keep a hand on the gun. She claws at his hands, trying to get out of his grip. Reynard looks their direction, annoyed. Stan tries to keep ahold of Lisa.

"Stop it, you fucking bitch!" Stan says, gritting his teeth.

Lisa does *not* stop it. She brings her heel down on Stan's foot. He lets out a grunt of pain. Lisa grabs his free hand and sinks her teeth into it. Stan bellows in pain. He uses his gun hand to throw her to the ground.

"You fucking *bitch*!"

Stan aims at Lisa. Reynard shouts for him to stop. I run toward Lisa, knowing I'm not going to get there in time.

Rick comes out of nowhere. He knocks Lisa out of the way just as Stan pulls the trigger. Rick catches it full in the chest. For a moment, Rick stands there, stunned. Then he drops to his knees and falls to one side, into the grass.

I stop running, stunned. Lisa is on the ground, looking at Rick. Even Stan seems surprised. He lowers his gun. I don't hear anything from Reynard. For a moment, it's as if someone put life on freeze-frame.

I'm the first to recover. I grab Lisa's arm and yank her to her feet. We run for the trees surrounding the driveway. Neither Reynard nor Stan take notice of us. We go several feet into the brush before we stop. Further movement might give us away.

Reynard stalks over to Stan, grabs his arm and spins him around. "You stupid motherfucker," Reynard says. "We weren't supposed to kill the son of a bitch!"

Stan's voice gets a little whiny. "I wasn't trying to do that. The bitch bit my fucking hand. What was I supposed to do?"

Reynard runs a hand through his now disheveled hair. He looks down at Rick. "How are we going to cover this? You got any ideas?"

"No, I don't."

"Really? 'Cause I do."

Reynard lifts his gun and shoots Stan. The gunshot sounds like a bomb going off. Stan falls face first to the ground. Reynard takes a handkerchief from his coat and wipes down the gun. He sets it next to Rick.

That done, he looks around, trying to find Lisa or me. We sit in the brush, trying not to breathe. Reynard mutters a curse and walks back up the driveway. A few moments later, his car disappears into the darkness.

Lisa and I charge out of the brush and run to Rick. He's on his back, lying on the snowy ground. His eyes are open but unfocused. The wound is right in the center of his chest. Blood spreads across his shirt. Lisa and I kneel on either side of him. He sees Lisa then me. His face lights up.

"Hey," he says, the breath barely escaping.

Lisa takes off her coat and lays it over Rick's chest. "It's going to be okay. We're going to get help."

Rick tries to raise his hand. "Stick…" he says.

"Absolutely," Lisa says. "We're sticking right here."

He tries to reach for her but doesn't have the strength. "Katie…"

"Katie's going to be fine," Lisa says, her eyes wet. "You, too. You're going to be okay."

Something in Rick's face tells me he knows better. I take his hand and squeeze it. He turns his face toward me.

"Get 'em…"

Then Rick's eyes go vacant. His hand goes slack in mine.

Lisa senses it happen. She calls Rick's name. He doesn't move. She looks around, as if help is nearby, as if something can still be done. Finally, the helplessness hits her. Lisa hangs her head and screams.

"Fuck!"

I slip my arm around her and guide her toward me. She cries into my shoulder. I keep hold of Rick's hand. Snow falls all around, dissolving as it hits the ground.

CHAPTER ELEVEN

GRADUATION DAY, SENIOR YEAR

Everyone should graduate on a day as nice as ours was. It was a sunny evening, warm but not hot or humid. There was a slight breeze off the lake but not overpowering (as it sometimes could be). The ceremony was held in Cheever Field, an ancient cement football and track field built on to the east side of the high school. All three hundred graduates were situated, in alphabetical order, on rows of chairs leading from a stage placed near the fifty-yard line. Normally, the last names Cleary *and* Davis *would have meant Lisa and I were seated near each other. But she got a spot on the stage. That's what you get when you're valedictorian. Guess I should have studied a little more. But I didn't mind. I was proud of her.*

It was your standard operational ceremony. The principal made some welcoming remarks. Brief speeches were made by a few members of the school board, none of whom we could pick out of a police lineup. Andy and I were only a few seats away and had trouble keeping our composure every time we made eye contact. The only time we behaved was when Lisa gave her speech.

The speech was not new to me. Lisa had practiced it in front of me for about three weeks. She hated giving it. Even then, she preferred to let her writing do the talking and to not have attention drawn to her. I monitored Lisa's delivery like a nervous stage director. I needn't have worried. She was poised throughout. It was everything Lisa wanted it to be: bland, non-confrontational, and short. There were statements of gratitude toward teachers, a thank you to all parents (which she noticeably rushed past), and an eloquent statement about following your dreams and making a difference. She sat down to a large round of applause.

The longest part of the ceremony was the awarding of diplomas (or the folders that would eventually contain our diplomas). I was in line behind Andy when we got to the stage. He turned and looked at me. I thought it was going to be another clowning around moment, but it wasn't. It was a strangely subdued look, as if he recognized that two guys who met in kindergarten had arrived at this moment. I wondered if our parents, sitting together in the stands, were thinking the same thing. Andy turned to receive his diploma.

When it was done, the school administrators made a production out of declaring us the graduating class. Then everyone's caps went in the air. Sam and Lisa found Andy and me, and we exchanged hugs. Our parents found us amidst the chaos, and we all posed for pictures. Lisa's dad solemnly shook my hand while her mom kept her distance. My mom wiped her eyes. Dad gave me a warm handshake and, for one of these rare occasions, a hug.

"I'm proud of you," he whispered.

After this, we headed over to the high school for the senior all-night party. Everyone got there by ten, and we were locked in for the night. At least we had the run of the school (under the watch of chaperones). It felt strange, as if this was the last time everyone would see each other. In some cases, it was true. We all had friends we'd see in school but not in our everyday lives. Even with the friends I would see over the summer, it felt like something was coming to an end.

Given the size of the school, it didn't take everyone long to spread out. Most of our same group from prom (absent Andy's sister Theresa, who would be graduating in a year) gathered together in the Bay Breeze offices. Lisa and I looked around, probably feeling the same thing but neither of us saying it. My last column had been printed during the final week of school. Lisa's final story (on the lack of funding for girls' sports) was in the same edition. Mr. Somrock saw us briefly on the field after the graduation ceremony. He told my parents, "If he doesn't become a writer, I'm going to track him down and kick his butt." I'm sure he said something similar to Lisa's parents. And here we were, hanging out for the last time in a place that had been the center of our world for the last few years.

Sam, who put himself in charge of keeping the party alive, hopped off the table he was sitting on. "You know what we need to do? We need to get on the roof."

Andy cocked his head. "The roof? How are we going to get up there?"

"Beans Madden told me how," Sam said. "It's easy. We just need to make sure nobody sees us. If word gets around, half the school will be up there, and we'll get busted. Come on."

Andy hung back, as did Elyse. (She and Andy really did make a nice couple. It was a shame they didn't work out.) I hesitated. Lisa joined in with Sam.

"Sounds like fun," she said, taking my hand. "What are they going to do? Expel us two hours after they gave us our diplomas?"

I couldn't argue with her there. Now that we had a majority, Andy and Elyse agreed to join us. (I always appreciated Andy's ability to knuckle under in the face of overwhelming odds.) We slipped out of the Bay Breeze offices, trying (and I'm sure failing) not to look as if we were up to something.

The fourth floor of the school consisted only of the choir room. We got up there without being detected. Sam led us to an adjoining room that consisted of little more than a fuse box and a ladder leading to the roof. Sam led the way up. A few moments later, we were on the roof, one of the highest points in Porter's Bay.

The view was great on all sides. Streetlights twinkled below us. Howard Street was visible in one direction, and the lake on two others. It was a view we had never seen before and would never see again. We tried to keep the conversation to a dull roar. You never knew when someone would be sharp-eared enough to hear us. Mostly, we reveled in the feeling of freedom.

Lisa and I slipped away and found a corner to ourselves. We held hands, our fingers loosely joined. We looked toward the lake, both of us quiet.

Lisa was the first to break the silence. "Graduation."

"Now summer."

"Then what?"

Ah, we were going to do this now. Then again, graduation night seemed like the perfect time to have the discussion we'd been avoiding. It was a testimony to our ability to compartmentalize that we had not had this discussion before now. Lisa had been accepted to NYU. She had enrolled and found student housing. I had been accepted at Adams College (which pretty much required writing to them and saying, "Hi, I'd like to go here"). Student housing and enrollment would be arranged over the summer. Lisa and I were going separate directions in the fall. It was only a matter of what would happen to us as a couple.

I wasn't sure how to address it. "You're going to New York."

Lisa nodded, sadly. "It's going to be great."

"I'd love to go with you."

"But you can't."

She was right. In a perfect world, I'd move to New York with Lisa. But I couldn't exactly live in the dorms with her. And I couldn't afford to move there on my own. Even if I found a job, there was no way I could work and go to school. Lisa would have to go to New York without me. I knew all this. I just didn't want to face it.

"I know," I said.

There was something big we had to address. But I couldn't make the words come. But I didn't have to. Lisa could read my silence.

"You're wondering what happens to us," she said.

"Yeah, I am."

She looked out over the darkness. "We're going to be in different worlds. Not just half a country apart, but college is going to be a completely different thing. I just don't think…" Lisa paused, as if she had more to say. As if she had a lot to say. Instead, she said, "I don't think it would work."

And there it was. The relationship was now finite. I stood there, my hand still loosely holding Lisa's, trying not to feel like the bottom had dropped out from under me. Somehow, I knew this was coming. Maybe some silly part of me hoped to avoid it.

"I get it," I said, my voice hollow.

"I'm sorry."

"Don't be." I turned to Lisa and put my other hand over hers. "Can we do this? Can we just…be how we are now until you leave for New York? Then we can go our separate ways."

A corner of Lisa's mouth rose. "I wasn't planning on hanging out with anyone else this summer."

I kissed her, partially out of relief, partially out of some primal need to hold on to her, even for just a moment. She stroked my cheek. All this prompted Sam to shout, "Get a room, you two," which prompted me to give him the finger. Everyone laughed. Lisa and I parted. Her hand was still on my cheek.

"Let's go join the party," she said. "Have some fun."

"Sounds good."

So we did. Eventually, everyone decided to climb down from the roof, since our absences might be noted, and someone might come looking for us. I was able to mostly shake off the conversation with Lisa and get back into the spirit of things. Video games had been set up in Miss Gilles's room. Thanks to a racing game, I proved to be a much better driver in virtual reality than in actual reality. The sun began to peek through the windows of the classroom. Everyone's enthusiasm was waning, maybe from tiredness, maybe from the fear of saying goodbye. We were to gather in the gym for the final ceremonies, with awards and drawings and such. Just as we were about to leave Miss Gilles's room, Lisa grabbed my arm.

"We haven't signed each other's yearbooks," she said.

Frankly, our sloth in that area was a little embarrassing. Not only had we been dating for over a year, we had both worked on the yearbook. Our books were filled with signatures and messages from various friends and teachers, but not from each other. We had brought our yearbooks to the party and left them in our now-empty lockers. We fetched them and stopped in the cafeteria to sign them. Lisa took mine and sat on one side of a cafeteria table. She gave me a sly look.

"No peeking at it until you get home," she said.

"Same here."

I took her yearbook and found a spot near the back, on an otherwise empty page. My pen hovered over it for a second, then I just wrote what was on my mind.

Lisa,

You will do great things. The world will hear from you, and it will know your name. It will know your brilliance, your huge heart, your bravery, your decency, your drive, your integrity. It will know all the things I know about you and love about you. I look forward to the world seeing that. Thank you for sharing it with me. I love you,

Joe.

I closed the book and slid it toward Lisa. A moment later, Lisa finished her writing and slid my book to me. True to our word, neither of us snuck a peek at what the other wrote. Lisa got up from the table and moved in the general direction of the gym.

"Let's go finish this up," she said. "Then we can get some sleep."

The final ceremony wasn't much, but it was still fun. Just some random drawings that allowed kids to cheer each other one last time. The biggest cheer was for Jerome Raymond, our unofficial Class Nerd, who accepted it with a nonchalance that gave us the impression he was a lot cooler than he ever let on. When the ceremony was done, they unlocked the doors, and we were allowed to go our own way. I said goodbye to Sam and Andy (although we already had plans to get together that night), then drove Lisa home. When we got there, I stopped out front. Lisa gave me a sleepy grin.

"We're going to have fun this summer," she said.

"Absolutely," I said.

"And that's all we're going to think about."

"Agreed."

Lisa leaned over, and we kissed. When we parted, she rested her hand on my neck and looked at me over her wire rim frames.

"I love you," she said.

"I love you."

We had one more kiss, then Lisa slid out the passenger door, promising to call me when she woke up. I watched her dash up the steps to her front door. A heaviness settled on my heart. I couldn't help wondering how many more times I would get to do this. What would life be like without her? I tried to ignore it, telling myself, "You just need some sleep. You'll feel better when you wake up." If only it had been that easy.

I pulled away from the curb and found myself saying out loud, "Time to start the rest of my life."

I would love to tell you Lisa and I immediately call the authorities and tell them everything we know. But we realize involving ourselves with the police will create more problems than it will solve. Why were we at the Hauser's summer residence? What was Rick doing there? What was Stan doing there? Who killed who? The police will just as likely take us into custody. After all, I seriously doubt the sheriff of a rural county in Wisconsin wants much to do with investigating a U.S.

Senator from Minnesota. And if we're in jail, who's going to figure out the rest of this?

Lisa is the first to take action. She searches Stan's body and finds a cell phone. She's able to unlock it as we run back to the car. (No real trick, since the damn thing is likely a burner.) She calls the police when we're clear of Stockholm and chucks the phone out the window before we cross the border. We make it back to St. Paul without further incident.

Our drive is quiet. When we get back to my apartment. Lisa sits on the futon, absently petting Squiggy, who has taken up position on her lap. I plunk down in the comfy chair and watch the snow falling outside the arch windows. I'm numb, like my mind and heart are saying *We've got an overload situation. We're going to shut things down for a little while*. Lisa finally breaks the silence.

"You want to get drunk?" she says.

"I thought you'd never ask."

I grab two lowball glasses from the kitchen, toss in some ice and pour in whiskey from the liquor shelf. I hand one to Lisa and sit next to her on the futon. She studies the glass.

"Drinking," she says. "That was something you and I never did together."

"Nope."

"Too bad. I'm really good at it."

"Me, too."

We clink glasses in a toast. Lenny barrel-rolls onto my lap, allowing me the privilege of rubbing his belly. Lisa strokes Lenny's tail. I get the sense she's as numb as I am.

I hold up my glass in another toast. "To Rick," I say.

Lisa clinks glasses with me. "To Rick." We drink. Lisa's head sinks onto her chest. "It feels over. All this and we still didn't get the tape or the file. And I don't know if Longson's people have it."

Before we left, Lisa checked out the apartment over the garage. She was quick and thorough. She didn't find anything other than the spare key to the Hauser's house. We checked the house and didn't find anything there, either. I turn toward Lisa.

"It's not over," I say. "Those two guys. They're connected to Longson's campaign."

"You have any proof of that?"

I open my mouth, then close it. She's right. We saw Reynard talking to Madeline, something she denies. We have no picture of them together. No evidence at all.

Lisa's voice gets quiet. "Rick sacrificed himself for me. I didn't ask him to, but…"

"That was who he was."

"I wonder if *he* knew that." She takes a sip of her whisky. "When he came to see you, to get my number, he must have had Zoe's evidence by then. Did he say anything?"

"About Zoe's stuff? No."

"Anything personal? Sounds like it wasn't just business."

I hesitate. "He asked if you and I had stayed in touch over the years. I told him we just chatted on social media every now and again. He said that was a shame."

"It is." A beat. "But I guess that's how you wanted it."

I'm tempted to fire back. But she's right. We've barely communicated in sixteen years because that's how I wanted it. I run my finger around the rim of my glass.

"I guess I did," I say.

Lisa turns toward me. "Do you hate me?"

I prop an arm on the back of the futon. "No. All these years, and I'm still holding a grudge? What kind of life would that be? And I don't want to hate you. I just…don't."

A moment passes. Lisa doesn't seem entirely satisfied with that answer. "I thought after what happened that summer—"

"It was just a thing," I say. "Besides, you got what you wanted."

"Excuse me?"

"Sorry. I meant New York. NYU. Metro Communications. Being a star journalist. That's what you wanted."

I stop, having walked right to the edge of what I wanted to say. Lisa, though, knows where it's going from there. She sits back on the futon and sips her whiskey.

"It wasn't anything you would have wanted to be a part of," she says. "Sharing me with the job. Not seeing me for days or weeks at a time. Wondering where I'm at. What I'm doing. If I'm okay." She looks toward the ceiling. "Who I'm with. Then, when I *am* there, realizing I'm not really there. I'm thinking about the next story. Or the last one."

"Sounds like you learned from experience."

"The hard way. Yes."

I have no idea what to say to that. I'm not sure why Lisa is bringing this up now. Maybe it's a way out of her own numbness. I don't know. We sit in silence, sipping our whisky. Lenny and Squiggy abandon us and cuddle up together in their kitty bed in the corner. Eventually, Lisa covers a large yawn with the back of her hand.

"I'm sorry," she says. "I think the adrenaline is wearing off."

"That's okay. I'm in the same boat."

I bring the glasses to the kitchen sink. I rinse them out and place them in the dishwasher. It's the work of about thirty seconds, but by the time I get back to the living room, Lisa is stretched out on the futon, fast asleep. Her unconsciousness is a form of escape. I take the comforter and spread it over her.

I plunk down in the comfy chair and watch her sleep. She almost died tonight. A friend of ours died in her place. My emotions can't reconcile these things. I watch Lisa sleep and try not to think of what might have been. How many nights I could have laid down with her. How many mornings when her face would be the first thing I'd see. The things that would be built from those simple beginnings and endings. I go to the window and look out at the street. The snow has stopped. There's no trace of it on the ground. Just the long shadows of barren branches. I walk to my room, shutting off the lights as I go.

***

Somehow, I manage to sleep through the night, though I can't say my dreams were particularly pleasant. I can't remember the storylines, but they all involved some kind of chase and ended in some kind of disaster. I get out of bed feeling more worn out than I went to sleep.

It's a gray day. The leaves on the trees are either shriveled or gone entirely. It's like November has come early, with its gray and barren vista. Lisa has made coffee. Her eyes are rimmed with red, telling me she didn't sleep well herself. She makes no mention of last night's conversation. She spends the morning looking at the internet, reading stories about the mysterious double homicide in Stockholm, Wisconsin. It doesn't look like anyone has connected it with the Longson campaign or us. If the campaign *is* asked about it, they'll probably write it off as a disgruntled former campaign staffer with an iffy history stalking the campaign manager. It will get buried. Lisa agrees with me.

"It will be forgotten by tomorrow," she says.

And with Rick gone, we have no idea where the evidence is or even what it is. We're at a dead end. To add to this little pleasantness, the door buzzer sounds. I don't like the door buzzer at the best of times. This, obviously, is not the best of times. I debate answering it, then hit the intercom. It's Carol. I buzz her in.

I called Carol last night to let her know about Rick. She was stunned, naturally, and we left it at that since I didn't feel like talking. I'm wondering how she's taken it. She had a soft spot for Rick, but they only dated briefly, and it's been over for several months. After a few moments, Carol hesitantly steps in.

"Hi," she says, subdued. "Are you guys okay?"

"Hanging in there," I say.

Lisa has her business face on. "We're fine."

Carol accepts these answers. She declines my offer of a cup of coffee. "I'm on my way to lunch," she says. "I'm meeting somebody." Lovely. I'm ninety-nine percent certain her plans involve Fabio. But I don't want to get *that* debate started. Carol looks for something to say. "Rick was a really great guy."

Lisa turns toward Carol. "How long did you two date?"

Carol slips me a brief *So, you told her* look. But Lisa's tone is inviting rather the interrogating. Carol steps over to the desk.

"Just a month, month-and-a-half," she says. "We met at a fundraiser. He was funny and charming. I didn't like the fact he worked for Bill Longson, but it seemed like just a job to him."

"Did he talk much about it?" Lisa asks.

"Not really. Just said he was a glorified errand boy. Since I wasn't all that curious about his boss, I didn't ask him too much."

"I'm sorry things didn't work out," Lisa says.

"Have the police said anything so far?" Carol asks.

"No," I say. "And we doubt they will."

Lisa fills Carol in on what we've found and what we suspect. Carol is intrigued by the existence of the tape and the file and equally frustrated we don't know where these things are. She looks from one of us to the other.

"You're not giving up on the story, are you?" Carol asks.

"We don't want to," Lisa says, "but we're not sure what to do next."

Carol's eyes flash. "You can't give up. If they killed Rick, if they killed those other people, they need to swing for it." She puts a hand on Lisa's shoulder, "The two of you are smart. You'll think of something."

Lisa puts her hand over Carol's. "We'll give it a shot. It's what Rick deserves."

Carol nods. "I have to go." She halts at the door. "Joe, do you have a minute?"

That throws me off, but I agree to it. Carol says goodbye to Lisa and steps onto the landing outside the front door. I close the door behind me. I hope this isn't anything my neighbors would be interested in. My reputation is bad enough as it is.

"What's going on?" I ask.

"Thought I should give you a warning," Carol says. "Ollie and Frankie want to fire you and Lars."

My head snaps back, much the way Lars's might. "Where did you hear this?"

"Where do you think? Fabio gave me the whole story. Ollie's been telling Frankie the script is garbage, and you need to get fired."

"How does Lars figure into this?"

"He just sits there at the meetings and doesn't say anything. They think he's either checked out or he's useless. They want him gone."

That's great, Lars. Master plan backfire much? If not for the events of the last twelve or so hours, this would be at the forefront of my mind. As it is, it's a damned annoyance.

"Is Fabio on our side?" I ask.

Carol inclines her head. "I wouldn't say he's on your side necessarily. I don't think he wants to fire you because you're friends of mine and he and I are…"

"Knocking boots? Bumping uglies? Doing the Horizontal Mambo? Taking the old skin boat to—"

"Do you have to make it sound stupid?" Carol asks.

"I'm sorry if I've cast aspersions on your bedding a spoiled, rich, idiot man-child."

"I will remind you that the spoiled, rich, idiot man-child is the only thing standing between you and a pink slip. So, I wouldn't be quick to judge."

"Understood. But what am I going to do? I'm not going to write the script Ollie wants. It would be like recreating World War II in real time. Lars and I need your help. You've got to work on Fabio. Convince him that Ollie is an idiot, and he's going to sink this whole thing."

"And I can't say the same thing of Lars?"

"For once, he's the lesser of two evils."

Carol rolls her eyes. She knows I'm right, despite her distaste for encouraging anything Lars is involved in. She takes on a lecturing tone. (Oh joy and rapture.)

"I'll do what I can for you and Lars," Carol says, "but only because I like the two of…well, because I like you."

"I appreciate it."

Carol slips her purse over her shoulder and starts down the stairs. She stops and turns around. "Lisa seems pretty cool. I'd like to know more about her."

"Maybe I'll do that sometime."

"You should." She takes a breath. "I'm sorry about Rick."

"Thank you."

Carol drops down the stairs. I step back into the apartment. Lisa is sitting on the arm of the futon. Her eyes follow me as I plunk down at the breakfast bar.

"We should visit Katie," she says. "Rick's ex. It…feels like something we should do."

"For the story?"

Lisa shakes her head. "For decency."

I can't help agreeing. An uncomfortable thought occurs. "Do we tell her that her name was one of the last things Rick said?"

"It wouldn't do any good. I know they weren't together, but…there must have still been some feelings there. You know what I mean?"

"I do. Would you mind giving her a call?"

"It's what I do best," Lisa says.

She picks up the phone and calls Katie. I get myself another cup of coffee. I try not to think about Rick or what, if anything, might come next. Whatever it is, I get the feeling it won't be pleasant. Then again, I'm getting used to that.

***

Katie agrees to see us. According to Lisa, she sounds a little subdued on the phone, as if she doesn't know how she's supposed to handle Rick's death. It's early evening when we stop by. The sun is down, and the air is crisp. Katie shows us in. Her face is ashen and her eyes are red, whether from crying or lack of sleep (or both), I can't be sure. The house could use some picking up. A few dishes lay about. Paperwork is piled up on the dining room table. A few items of clothing are found here and there. Lisa and I accept Katie's offer of some tea. Katie moves slowly, distractedly. We gather at the dining room table while it steeps.

"Are you okay?" Lisa asks.

"I'm hanging in there," Katie says. "It's weird. I'm not Rick's wife. But I still feel like I lost someone. You know?"

Lisa sets her hands on her lap. "Are there any…arrangements being made for Rick?"

"Yes," Katie says, "up in Porter's Bay. I talked to his mom on the phone. She's doing everything. His dad was never a decent guy. I doubt he's even going to be there."

"Are you going to be there?" I ask.

"I thought I should be. I always got along great with his mom. She needs somebody." Katie takes in a breath through her nose. "I've only been to Porter's Bay once. Right after Rick and I got married. He showed me around." Her eyes brighten. "He even carved my name in a tree. Some overlook where he hung out in high school. Something bluff."

"Revelation Bluff," I say.

"That's right," Katie says, "And he had some place he liked to bring girls."

Lisa and I answer at the same time. "The Fields of Gold."

Katie's face clouds, realizing the circle of women Rick brought to The Fields of Gold was not exactly exclusive. "I think that was it," she says, practically mumbling. She takes a breath and focuses on us. "What happened to Rick? Really? Do you know?"

We hesitate. But Katie deserves to know the truth. We tell her the story. That Zoe Court may have had information on Senator Longson. That Zoe died and Rick came to be in possession of the information. That he tried to contact Lisa but had to go on the run before they could meet. That two gunmen apparently followed us to Rick's hiding place. (We step lightly around how Rick knew of the Hausers' summer home.) And that Rick shoved Lisa out of the way and took a bullet intended for her. When we're done, Katie sits back in her chair.

"Longson wanted him dead," she says.

I nod. "Or at least someone in Longson's campaign did."

Katie turns to Lisa. "He saved you."

Lisa's voice gets tight. "He did."

"Did he…was he able to say anything?" Katie asks.

This is Katie asking *Did he suffer?* Lisa looks down. I trace a circle on the table with my fingers.

"He mumbled a couple things," I say. "We didn't quite catch what they were."

The teakettle whistles. Katie goes into the kitchen and busies herself with getting our tea. Lisa wipes her eyes. I start to put a hand on her shoulder but stop before I get there. Katie returns with our tea.

"I'm going up to Porter's Bay tomorrow," she says. "Rick's mom asked me to bring a few of his things."

"Like what?" I ask.

"The hockey stick," Katie says. "*The* hockey stick. And his old jersey." She sips her tea. "The historical society up there is putting together a display for the visitation and the funeral. The stick, his jersey, his gold medal. The high school is even loaning the picture of Rick scoring the goal. His mom is okay with it. I don't think she knows how he felt about that stuff."

We finish our tea in silence. I'm not sure if Lisa and I should attend Rick's services, but it's not something we need to debate here. We've paid our respects to Katie, and we've intruded on enough of her time. Lisa stands up.

"We should probably get going," she says.

Katie walks us to the door. The neighborhood is quiet and dark. As we step out, Katie leans against the doorframe.

"This is going to sound weird," she says, "but I'm glad you two were there. When Rick died. I think there was a part of him that always felt alone. It's nice to know he wasn't alone in the end."

Neither Lisa nor I know what to say. Rick *was* always a square peg in a round hole. A jock who'd rather hang out with nerds. A guy who didn't value athletics whose most notable accomplishment was an athletic feat.

"He was a good guy," I say.

"He could be," Katie says.

She steps back inside and closes the door. Lisa and I don't say anything as we walk to the car. I didn't know Rick all that well, but he always seemed glad to see me, as if we were closer than we really were. I didn't know he always felt alone. Didn't know until the night he came to my apartment that he struggled to live up to his moment of glory. Maybe I should have made more of an effort to be his friend. To treat him as more than a memory. Before he actually became one.

Lisa climbs in the car. I glance back toward the house. The lights go off. The wind sends a chill through me. I get in the car and drive away.

CHAPTER TWELVE

SUMMER, AFTER SENIOR YEAR

Over the years, there have been times—if I let my mind drift onto the subject—when I've wondered if Lisa and I continuing to date that last summer was a mistake. While we still had a good time and still saw each other almost every day, it was the only time tension crept into the relationship. Try as we might, we couldn't escape the pending Big Thing around the corner. Even during our best times—evenings at the gazebo in Bennett Park, a night at the county fair, slipping away to Revelation Bluff—the idea that things were coming to an end was always around, like sand slipping through our fingers. I couldn't help comparing it to the previous carefree summer and finding this one wanting.

That summer, Lisa did take a job as a receptionist at her dad's office. She regretted it. Her father hounded her about moving plans, even though Lisa was more on top of it than anyone else. She also endured constant reminders about the expense of living in New York and how her parents wouldn't be able to help her with everything. All this felt like some attempt to control her long distance. Lisa was aware of it. I lost count of the number of times she told me she couldn't wait to get out of there. Then she would apologize, remembering that leaving her parents and Porter's Bay also meant leaving me.

For my part, I procrastinated when it came to college prep. I think some part of my subconscious believed if I dragged my feet, I could somehow slow down time and prevent the inevitable from happening. My parents had to (sometimes literally) stand over me and make sure I got registered for class, got my financial aid application submitted, made arrangements for housing for the fall, etc. My father openly wondered if he and Mom would have to attend classes with me to make sure I got there. While they were certainly frustrated, they didn't come down too hard on me. I think they understood I was dealing with enough already.

August came and the sand was nearly out of the hourglass. The days got shorter. The sun rode lower in the sky. Lisa would leave just after Labor Day. We hung out as much as we could. We didn't talk about the end coming, beyond mentioning it in passing. The playgrounds emptied out, as did the beach. Everyone prepared for the arrival of fall. Slowly, painfully, I began to join them in this preparation.

Labor Day weekend arrived, and Lisa and I got one more night together, just the two of us. Her parents and sister left to attend a volleyball camp. I again used an overnight visit to Sam's as an excuse to get out. In some ways, it was like the first night Lisa and I spent together. We made dinner, played games, watched a movie. Sometimes, I found myself imagining what it would be like if this was our life, forever, just the two of us. Eventually, I realized the thought was making me sad, so I tried to push it away.

When I woke up in Lisa's bed, I was alone, tangled in the bedsheets. I got dressed and went downstairs. Lisa was sitting on the deck, wearing her robe, sipping coffee, heedless of the neighbors. I joined her at the table. She slipped her hand into mine without looking at me.

"Are you okay?" I asked.

Lisa's eyes were inexpressively sad. "That was probably the last time we'll ever do that."

She was right. Her parents would be back that day. Both today and Monday had been set aside for family activities. Tuesday was final prep for moving. Wednesday morning, they would leave for the Cities and by the afternoon, Lisa would be on a plane to New York. Even if we found a minute, even we went back upstairs, there would still have to be a last time. Things were coming to an end. We sat there and held hands, not saying anything.

The next few days flew by. I talked to Lisa on the phone a couple times, but there wasn't a chance for us to get together. She invited me over for Tuesday night, her last night in town. Her parents would be there, so it wasn't going to be much of a date. But she needed to see me one last time. And I knew the feeling was mutual.

Lisa was still packing when I got there. Her parents were, as usual, polite but not outgoing. Lisa closed the door to her room, the only time she ever did that when her parents were present. Nothing happened, but it might have been a statement of independence on her part. We chitchatted. Lisa told me a little about her dorm and her classes. I mentioned a few things about Adams College, where I would be going to school. Mostly, though, we were silent and sad, packing up the life she'd had, ever-so-briefly, in Porter's Bay.

When we finished, it was getting late. Lisa had to be up early. It was time to say our goodbyes. We decided to take a walk around the block, just as an excuse to spend another minute or two together. It was a nice night. No humidity, a cool breeze coming in off the lake. We talked about our plans for the future, haltingly, feigning excitement. In the silences, we could feel the weight on us. We rounded the corner onto Lisa's street, and the last sands were running out of the glass. We walked up the steps to her front porch, standing together one last time.

Lisa put her arms around me. She held me tight, crying. Her body trembled, her tears warm on my neck. When she could speak, she whispered, "Are we doing the right thing?"

I wanted to tell her no. *That I couldn't imagine how my life would be any better without her in it. But that was how I felt. Lisa was too smart, too driven, too talented to stay yoked to me. I knew from the first day I met her she was destined for big things. There was no way I could stand in the way of that.*

"We are," I said, trying my damnedest to mean it. "Even if it hurts. It's the right thing."

I still regret saying that.

After what seemed like a long time (but not long enough), we parted. Lisa laid her forehead against mine.

"I love you," she said.

"I love you."

We stepped back from each other. Lisa's face was wet. Mine wasn't any better. She gathered her strength and looked for something to say, something I could take with me, some summation of our time together.

"Have a good life," was all she got out.

Something in that caused my heart to sink. It was kind of her to say, but it underscored how we would be living separate lives from here on out. This really was the end.

"You, too." My voice caught slightly as I said it.

Lisa darted into the house. I listened to the door close, echoing the finality of it all. I walked home, darkness enveloping me, my eyes blurred with tears. Everything was quiet.

It's a quiet morning at the Davis estate. Lisa is working at my desk, her manner a bit listless. Squiggy oversees the grounds from his perch on the shelf over the radiator. Lenny enjoys a morning snooze on the futon. I'm in the kitchen, cleaning up after breakfast.

Of course, things cannot remain peaceful. The front door flies open. Lisa spins out of the desk chair and bounces to her feet. I slide out of the kitchen, holding the spatula I was drying in front of me like a sword. Lars comes to a halt, holding up his hands like he's at gunpoint.

"Problem?" he asks, his eyes flicking from me to Lisa and back again.

I lower the spatula. "It's fine. You might want to make a less…flamboyant entrance in the future."

"No can do, mein Freund," he says, flipping the door shut behind him. "I gotta be me."

"Which is a shame for the rest of us," I say.

Lars lets the insult fly past him (assuming he noted it at all). I return to the kitchen and continue work on the dishes. Lars pours himself a glass of orange juice (thus dirtying another glass). He sashays to the breakfast bar, giving Lisa a deep bow and a greeting of *Madame*. She struggles with her composure, but Lars is oblivious. I turn to Lars as I wash a plate.

"Something you need?" I ask.

Lars takes a sip of his (?) juice. "I got problems. Mrs. Hanratty is going to rat me out. I thought I was done with her, but apparently, she's been recording the sounds coming from my apartment. They capture the unmistakable noises of a couple *en fuego*."

"On fire?"

"Wait, no. What's the sex one?"

"*In flagrante delicto*."

"That's it," Lars says. "Although, if you do it right, you can be *en fuego*."

I resist snapping him with the dish towel. "And so…"

"She confronted me, and I had to tell her something. I said I have a very active girlfriend who simply doesn't understand boundaries. I added that she and I are in a committed relationship and might even be headed for the altar. I don't think Mrs. Hanratty bought it."

"Why not?" I ask.

"She asked me the name of this girl. That threw me completely off. I mean, I was largely pulling this out of my keester to begin with. So, I said *Keely*. Then she asked for a last name. And I said *Smith*. It sounded good to me. At the time."

"Keely Smith. I do believe there was a singer by that name."

"Indeed," Lars says. "That's probably why the two names seemed to go so well together. At any rate, Mrs. Hanratty has heard of Keely Smith. In fact, she's a fan. She seriously doubts I'm shagging a singer who is, sadly, no longer with us." He runs a hand through his quasi-pompadour. "I'm in deep trouble here, Joe."

For once, Lars isn't blowing things out of proportion. I've had the sneaking feeling management has been looking for a reason to get rid of him (other than gross negligence when it comes to doing his job). A morals charge may be the excuse they're looking for.

"Any ideas for taking care of this?" I ask.

"Not really. I talked to Chuck about it. He suggested getting rid of Mrs. Hanratty."

Oh boy. Any suggestion from Lars's friend Chuck is usually homicidal in nature. It's Chuck's default mode. (Though I'm not certain he's ever killed someone. Frankly, finding that out one or another would require more interest in Chuck than I consider necessary.)

"You mean *getting rid of* as in…?" I ask.

"Neutralizing her, yes," Lars says. "But don't worry. I'm not going to do it."

"Ah," I say. "Thank God."

"But I need to think of something. Maybe I can muscle her."

I look to the heavens but realize the Almighty and I have the same agreement about Lars as we do about Mike. "Do I have to remind you the last person you tried to muscle literally kicked your ass and knocked you down a flight of stairs?"

Lars sniffs. "You don't have to, but I'm sure you will."

I'm not sure where to go from here. Lars paces the apartment floor, putting most of my Halloween decorations in jeopardy. Lisa brightens up, having something other than the investigation to work on.

"What do you know about Mrs. Hanratty?" she asks.

Lars strokes his goatee. "Other than her puritanical repression and general busybodiness, I don't really know anything about her."

"Maybe that's what you need to do," Lisa says. "Talk to her. Find out something about her. If you have common ground, maybe she won't push things with management."

"I see what you're saying," Lars says. "Ask her some questions. Get her to open up. Then when she least suspects it, push her out the window."

Lisa's face falls. "That's…that's not what I…"

"I don't mean actually push her out the window," Lars says. "I mean nearly push her out the window. Let her know I can't be predicted. I could strike at any time. She best keep her mouth shut or I could go nuts." He slugs the rest of his juice and sets the glass on the coffee table (but not on a coaster). "You have a brilliant mind, ma Amie. I thank you for your assistance."

Lars sashays out of the apartment, closing the door with a flourish. Lisa slowly turns toward me.

"You have a *very* interesting collection of friends," she says.

"If by *interesting*, you mean *psychotic*, I completely agree."

I finish up the dishes and hang the towel on the rack over the sink. That done, I grab a cup of coffee and take a seat at the breakfast bar. Lisa is still in the desk chair, facing me.

"You should probably go to Rick's funeral," she says.

"I should," I say. "What about you?"

"I don't know how much longer I can stay. My editor wants me back in New York. If I don't have anything to show him, I have to go."

My heart sinks. I should have known it would come to this. Lisa might have a national reputation, but that doesn't mean she has free reign to run around the country on Metro Communications' dime. If there's no story, there's no reason to say.

"We were witnesses to a murder," I say. "And an attempted murder. That's something."

"What proof do we have? The two gunmen never mentioned Longson's name. Or Madeline's. What's to say Rick's death is connected to the campaign? We have a lot of conjecture and a whole lot of nothing in the way of evidence."

"The only shot we've got is to get the tape and/or the file."

Lisa blows out a sigh. "And we have no idea where they are. We've gone through all this, and it still feels like we're nowhere close to proving anything."

Lisa is right. There have been a lot of bullets flying and a lot of people dead. And we don't have a thing to connect it to the guy we're certain is behind it all. And we've lost a friend of ours in the process.

"Get 'em," I say. "It's the last thing Rick said. He wanted us to get them. it's not looking good, is it?"

"No, it's not. I feel like I need to apologize to Rick. Especially after..."

Lisa's voice gets tight. She doesn't finish the sentence. I have an idea how she feels, but only an idea. I've had a few people save my life. But none of them gave theirs for mine. I gaze at the arch windows.

"It's weird," I say. "Even with some of the scrapes I've been in, I never let myself think there's going to be a last of something. A last Christmas I ever have. A last birthday. A last meal. My last words."

"Whether you want them to be or not."

"I know. I'd love to think I'm going to say something profound, but it'll probably be more along the lines of *Damn, this snow is almost too heavy to shovel. I wish I had the money for a snow bl—*"

Lisa smiles, wanly. "Mine will probably be something like *Get a shot of th—*"

"For Rick, it was *Get 'em.*"

"And *Katie.* And *Sti...*" Lisa trails off.

"No, he got the whole word out."

A look of intense concentration comes over Lisa's face. A few seconds later, she's pacing the living room. I assume she isn't doing an impression of Lars. I set my coffee aside.

"What's up?" I ask.

"*Stick*. What if Rick was trying to tell us something?"

"Such as?"

Lisa closes her eyes, trying to put the sequence together. "Rick broke the stick. The one he used to score the big goal. Then he repaired it by hollowing out parts of it and screwing it back together."

"I remember that."

"Then before he disappeared, he stopped at Katie's house and was digging around the basement. But he didn't take anything with him when he left."

"Yeah…" I say, drawing the word out.

"What if he was leaving something instead? What if he hid the tape in the stick?"

"Why would…" Then I catch myself. "He needed to separate himself from the evidence. In case Longson's people caught him before he could meet with you."

"Exactly. The tape was small enough to fit in the stick. He was hiding it in plain sight, like your friends with the bathroom door."

Unbelievable. Who would have thought the idiocy of Robbie, Stoner and T.J. would come in so handy? I join Lisa in the living room, fighting off my own desire to pace. (It would just make the cats nervous.)

"What about the file?" I ask. "You think that's what he meant when he said *Katie?*"

"No. If Rick left the file with Katie, she would have given it to us. It would have been."

"Or maybe Longson's people got it. They *did* break into Katie's place."

"But Katie would have told us it was missing. Hell, she might have given it to us the first time we talked to her." Lisa hops over to the desk and picks up her phone. "I need to call Katie. She's supposed to go up to Porter's Bay today. Maybe I can catch her before she leaves."

The call doesn't take long. Because Katie has, in fact, left town. In fact, she's already in Porter's Bay and has handed over the stick to the people at the historical society. (The woman must have gotten up at the crack of dawn. Didn't she realize we were about to make a major break in the case?) Lisa sets the phone down.

"We're going up there anyway," Lisa says. "The tape will be okay. I don't think Longson's people know where it is."

"And the file?"

"One disaster at a time." She clenches her fists. "I need to get this guy. Or his minions. Whoever is behind this."

"It would make a hell of a story."

Her eyes are soft. "You know what's funny? It's not even about the story anymore. Rick…I owe him."

Lisa looks toward the window. I reach for her. But I stop. It's her sorrow. I don't have a place in it. Not anymore. I turn back to the breakfast bar, leaving Lisa to her solitude.

***

"Nothing in the rearview mirror?" Lisa asks.

"Not that I can see. Then again, I'm not great at spotting a tail."

We're driving up Highway 35 in Lisa's rental car. (There's a slight chance that someone in Porter's Bay might recognize my car, so we opted for hers. Not to mention the fact my car doesn't like long drives.) We're about twenty minutes from Duluth, meaning we're about two hours from Porter's Bay. Jack pines and maples nearly barren of leaves are visible out both windows. There's a slight vacancy in the horizon, hinting at the vastness of the lake. I haven't been up this way since my dad's retirement last summer. I assume it's been even longer for Lisa. She stirs uncomfortably in the passenger seat.

"You think we're on the right track?" she asks.

"It's a lead," I say, "We have to follow it. You know that better than I do."

"I suppose."

Lisa fidgets, flipping the pages of her notebook. I glance at her.

"You okay?" I ask.

"Fine." She fumbles with the radio. "Guess it's too soon to pick up the Porter's Bay stations."

"If you're more than four feet outside the city limits, none of them come in."

"Nothing changes, I guess."

"Not really."

Lisa gazes out the window. I feel the tension coming from her. But I don't want to get into it. Thankfully, I get a call from Mike. (And how often have I been able to say *that*?) Mike speaks in hushed tones, making me wonder where exactly he's at (or if he's mistaken this for an obscene phone call).

"I've got a problem," is how he opens the call.

"Just one?"

"You want to be serious?"

"Fine," I say, "What's the issue?"

"I've got a problem with Gillian. And Moira."

"That's what I hear. Something new?"

"I'm at a B&B with Gillian. And Moira."

Huh. I've seen a few adult-themed features operate from a similar premise. "That sounds…cozy."

"It wasn't my idea," Mike says, "Either the B&B or Moira being here."

"Okay, what's going on?"

There's no air rushing or anything on the other end, so I don't think he's pacing. Remarkable that he can be calm under these (or any) circumstances. Then again, his tone doesn't exactly convey a sense of wellbeing.

"Okay, Gillian's been planning this B&B thing for a while. I'm not a fan, but, y'know, you gotta keep the girlfriend happy."

I'm with him on that one. I've never cared for a bed-and-breakfast. What some might see as a charming, intimate getaway, I see as invading some batty old person's home. Mike's objections are due less to privacy than intimacy. His line of B.S. is best viewed from a distance. A B&B is the kind of intimate setting that exposes his actual personality. That's usually the death of his relationships.

"I'm feeling you," I say.

"We get to the place. It's nice. We settle in our room. Start to take one of those naps that isn't really a nap. You get what I'm saying?"

"I do."

"Things are moving along and, suddenly, there's a knock on the door. At first, I figure it's another guest, maybe complaining about the noise. Gillian gets kind of loud, y'know? Then I realize: we're not going at it. We're still half-dressed."

"It took you a second to realize that?"

"Shut up. Anyway, I get it together enough to answer the door. And who do you think is standing there?"

"Henry Kissinger?"

Mike blows right past me. "Moira."

"What was she doing there?"

"That's what I wanted to know. She said she heard from Gillian what a great place this was, and she wanted to check it out."

"How did Gillian feel about that?"

"She was wondering where *you* were.'

"Me?" I ask.

"That was what Moira said. She completely forgot the whole *dating you* cover story. I told Gillian you were working on something and that must be why you couldn't make it. Moira went along with it, but she wasn't exactly giving us that *lovelight in her eyes* sort of look when your name came up."

"Sad when the magic goes out of a pretend relationship."

"Anyway, I snuck into Moira's room to have a chat with her. Try to get this whole thing straightened out. She told me she hates me, thinks I'm a pig and not nearly good enough for her sister. And she's kind of obsessed with me. Says she needs to save her sister from me. I tell her how much I like Gillian and that I'd do anything for her. Moira says that me sleeping with her proves what a scumbag I am."

"A lot of layers to this thing."

"You're telling me? I want to break things off with Moira, but then she'll tell Gillian what happened. I had half a thought about breaking things off with Gillian, but I don't think Moira would be interested in me if I wasn't dating her sister. It's bending my mind into a pretzel."

"You come up with any ideas?"

"Not yet. I was trying to figure it out when I was in Moira's room, but she started giving me a handy. I got kind of distracted."

"That'll happen."

Mike lets out a sigh. "I don't know what to do. We're supposed to be at this B&B for another day or so. How the hell am I going to keep Moira away? Assuming I even want to do that? And if I don't, how am I supposed to keep Gillian from finding out? The place isn't that big, and the walls aren't that thick."

Even if the walls aren't thick, Mike certainly is. (That joke plays better in Britain.) Right now, though, I don't have a suggestion to offer, and I've had nearly all of this conversation I can take. (The fact Mike is sleeping with two women, and I've had sex only once in the last nine months might factor into my bitterness.)

"Just keep your head down," I say, "On all fronts."

"I'll give you updates as they come in."

There's a roar of rushing water on Mike's end. I hold the phone away from my ear, then bring it back.

"Mike, where are you calling me from?" I ask.

"The crapper. Where else can get a guy get two minutes peace?"

"And what I heard just now was…"

"A courtesy flush."

"So, you are…"

"Sitting on the toilet. What do you normally do in the crapper?"

I fight the instinct to toss the phone out the window. "Mike, I'm going to let you go."

"You can't handle it, can you?" he says. "The thought of me sitting on my porcelain throne, pants around my ankles, master of all I survey."

"I'm hanging up now."

"It's your issue, not mine."

"Goodbye, Mike."

"I am not an animal!"

I ring off and drop the phone in the cup-holder. Thanks to our close proximity, Lisa has overheard every word of the conversation. A grin slides across her face.

"I'll say it again: *these* are your friends?"

"They're not bad people," I say. "Just…not all that smart. You still bummed I didn't tell them about you?"

"It's fading."

We stop briefly in Duluth to get coffee and something to eat. It's another ninety minutes to Porter's Bay. The day is overcast and the wind whips heavily. The gales of November are just around the corner. I wouldn't be surprised to see snowflakes in the air. We're quiet as we drive up the North Shore. Lisa looks out at the bluffs and the waves crashing against the jagged rocks. Sites she hasn't seen in a goodly number of years.

"When was the last time you were in Porter's Bay?" I ask.

"The summer we…the summer after my freshman year of college. Once Mom and Dad moved, there was no reason to come back."

"I suppose not."

Lisa turns away from the window. "It isn't because I hate the place. It's… complicated."

"It's okay."

She seems to want to explain more. But she looks out the window again. Eventually, we hear the first strains of a radio station from Porter's Bay. Daylight is waning. The lights of old stomping grounds come into view. Lisa moves her eyes from the window to the road ahead.

"Here we are again," she says.

"Bring back any memories?"

"Oh, only about a thousand."

Very little has changed in the years since Lisa's been here. Arthur's Diner is gone. A few of the businesses on Lake Drive have changed. But it's probably like being in a time machine for Lisa. Maybe it's an anti-climax. It's dark by the time I pull into the parking lot of Terzich's Grocery. Time to change into my dark suit. I reach into the backseat to get my garment bag. Lisa puts a hand on my arm, stopping me.

"I need tell you something," she says. "When my parents took me to the Cities, so I could fly to New York for the first time. The night after we split up. I was alone in the backseat. My sister stayed home that day, thank God. I laid down in the back and put my face against the backseat and cried the whole way to the Cities. My parents thought I was asleep. I put on some sunglasses, and I said my goodbyes to them. Then I got on the plane and pulled my hoodie low and I cried the whole flight to New York."

"It was that hard to leave home?"

"It was that hard to leave you." Lisa grips my arm. "That's why it was so important to stay in touch with you. Even if we couldn't be together…I just wanted you in my life. And when you stopped writing and calling…" She clears her throat. "It's nice to check in on social media. But it's not the same."

"I know." I stare at the dashboard. "It hurt too much. For a while. Lately…" My eyes shift to the window. "You ever heard the song *What a Fool Believes?*"

"The Doobie Brothers. Yeah. Why?"

"It's about a guy meeting a former girlfriend for lunch. To him, the relationship was the great love of his life. To her, it was just another fling. Nothing special." I shrug. "I guess I didn't want to be the fool."

I feel like a prize idiot. Weighing the smallness of my time with her against the bigger picture of her life and her accomplishments. It's like some high school pal of Edward R. Murrow telling him *Hey, remember that time we whipped shitties in the Cub Foods parking lot?* I run my hands along the steering wheel.

"I'm sorry," I tell her. "I'm being stupid. What we had was just a little while and it was a long time ago. What you've done with your life is incredible. I knew it would happen, too. I might have written something about it in your yearbook. I don't remember exactly—"

"Lisa, you will do great things. The world will hear from you, and it will know your name. It will know your brilliance, your huge heart, your bravery, your decency, your drive, your integrity. It will know all the things I know about you and love about you. I look forward to the world seeing that. Thank you for sharing it with me. I love you. Joe."

I have no idea the look I have on my face. Blank, probably. Shocked, certainly. After a moment, Lisa turns away from the window and grips my hand.

"Do you think you're just anybody to me?" she says.

A light snow is falling, the flakes melting as soon as they hit the windshield. Lisa keeps hold of my hand. My brain tries to form words, but I just get a light humming. Lisa finally removes her hand from mine and wipes her nose.

"You should get dressed," she says. "You need to get there."

I hesitate, then grab my garment bag and walk into the store. Lisa is visible through the windshield, wiping her face. She watches the snow.

CHAPTER THIRTEEN

FIRST YEAR OF COLLEGE AND THE SUMMER AFTER

After Lisa left for college, I had two weeks to walk around in a fog of depression and loneliness. I found myself constantly wondering what she was doing, if she was happy, if she ever thought of me. As they had all summer, my parents had to coax me along in getting my stuff packed and getting myself ready for college. I was only interested in my own misery.

I was halfway functional by the time my parents dropped me off at Adams. I met Mike during orientation, and we became fast friends. I hid the Lisa situation from him, thinking (probably correctly) that turning into a puddle of tears would end our developing friendship. So, I got into the habit of not talking about Lisa. Then I tried to get into the habit of not thinking about her.

In short order, Mike and I fell in with a group of guys who lived on our floor in the dorms: Stoner, Robbie, TJ, Wayne (though we never determined if Wayne was a student or just a guy crashing in the dorms).

We started down the primrose path to debauchery of all kinds. Slowly (very slowly), I started getting over my grief and enjoying college.

The problem was, every time I seemed to be getting on top of my misery, I'd get a letter or, worse, a phone call from Lisa. She was doing well at school. She was excited by her classes. She loved living in New York City. She was curious how I was doing and would ask me all kinds of questions about life at Adams College (as if life in a Podunk college town was on the level of the Big Apple). Hearing from her would make me happy for a few minutes, then plunge me right back into depression. Hearing from her only heightened her absence.

It took me six months to start dating again. And I use dating *in its broadest sense. Marnie was the name of the young lady I took up with. She was a sophomore and had an interesting philosophy regarding dating. "I don't want a boyfriend," she told me. "It's too weird to break up with someone and then sit next to them in class. But I didn't take a vow of chastity, either." As long as it was understood that no relationship would develop out of this, I was welcomed to come up to her dorm room on certain afternoons and evenings and hang a sock on the door. My introduction to Friends with Benefits. It was exactly what I needed, since I hadn't taken a vow of celibacy myself. At first, it felt like a betrayal of Lisa. Then I got over it. Marnie transferred to another school after that year, and I didn't hear from her again.*

I was feeling better, almost back to normal, when I returned to Porter's Bay for the summer. Even though I was a legal adult now, I wound up working the same hours in my dad's hardware store that summer:

afternoons during the week and all day on Saturday. I was a bit dismayed to hear Lisa was coming back as well. She had written to me about it, but I kept hoping she'd change her mind and stay in New York. The calls and letters still had the effect of casting me down. I wasn't sure I was ready to see her in the flesh.

Avoiding each other wasn't all that difficult. Lisa had once again taken a job in her father's office, so most of her days were occupied with work. I hung out with Andy and Sam and was careful to avoid any place we might bump into her. She hadn't called me and there was no point in writing me when we only lived across town.

I thought The Hub was a safe place since I couldn't imagine Lisa wanting to revisit it after her summer of working there. (She had studiously avoided it during our senior year.) I stopped in one morning to grab a box lunch before work. I was waiting at the counter when someone tugged on the back of my shirt.

"I was starting to think you went to summer school."

I turned and there was Lisa. She hadn't changed much in a year. I don't know what my expectations were. Maybe I thought she'd be more…cosmopolitan after a year in New York. Happily, she still looked like the Lisa I remembered, right down to the wire-frame glasses and the simple blouse she wore to her dad's office. The only difference was she was smiling, which had not been the case the last time I saw her.

"I was starting to think you had stayed in New York, after all," I said. "Y'know, how you gonna keep 'em down on the farm…?"

Lisa laughed, and we hugged. It was familiar and strange at the same time. Beyond the spontaneous hug after solving Mr. Jacobson's murder, I had never hugged her as a friend. When we parted, Lisa straightened her glasses.

"What are you up to?" she asked.

"Lunch. Forgot to pack it this morning. How about you?"

"To-go coffee. My dad refuses to buy anything but the cheap stuff for his office. My taste buds will be permanently scarred if I drink that swill all summer."

"We don't have that fancy espresso you New Yorkers enjoy, but we do all right here in the hinterlands."

Lisa rolled her eyes. "I've met people in New York who don't know enough to pronounce espresso *without an* x, *so give yourself some credit."*

We chitchatted until my turkey sandwich-and-chips and her large coffee arrived. It was as easy as it had always been. We walked out together and stood on Lake Drive. The breeze from the lake threatened Lisa's already-precarious hairdo, but she didn't seem to mind.

"We should get together," Lisa said. "I'm sorry I haven't called since I got back."

"Don't worry about it," I said. "Funny thing about a phone is that it's a two-way instrument. I haven't called you, either."

"Let's correct that, shall we? I'm not doing anything on Saturday night. You want to get together?"

"I would love that."

We exchanged one more, slightly less awkward, hug and went our separate ways. I noticed my mood for the rest of the day was more buoyant.

I picked Lisa up at her parents' house on Saturday night. (She still didn't have a car and that wasn't likely to change now that she lived in New York.) As soon as I pulled up, Lisa came out of the house as if shot from a cannon (thus saving me the chore of talking to her parents). She wore a black t-shirt and beat up jeans and had her contact lenses in. She slid into the car and tapped the roof.

"Where to, Jeeves?" she asked.

"Champagne and caviar at the beach?"

Lisa arched an eyebrow. "When you actually mean…?"

"A burger at Arthur's."

"Sounds heavenly. Let's do it."

We stopped into Arthur's and found a booth right away. We didn't see anybody that we knew. I know this is irrational, but I've always felt like the graduation and departure of me and my friends was the death knell for Arthur's. It wasn't as if we were the only people who hung out there. But after my class graduated, the place never really regained its status as the afterschool hangout. On this night, the business was noticeably smaller than it had been. In another year, it would try becoming a Fifties Throwback diner. A few years after that, it would go out of business altogether and be converted into an overflow parking lot for a nearby clinic.

This night, though, all of that was in the future and I was more concerned with the here and now. Lisa and I sat at the booth in the corner, largely ignored by everyone (including our server) and largely ignoring the food (when it did eventually arrive). We were absorbed in talking about our first years of college. Yes, we had updated each other on the occasions when we chatted or wrote, but that was mostly just an overview. Now, we were able to go into the blow-by-blow details. Lisa talked about her favorite places to hang out, how she had done all the touristy stuff in her first few months in New York, what were classes were like, what her new friends were like, etc. I gave her a few tidbits about my adventures at Adams, which were more of the bored college kids wreak havoc on unsuspecting small town *variety. She didn't ask me about my dating life, and I studiously avoided any mention of Marnie. If Lisa had the male equivalent of a Marnie in her life, she was kind enough not to mention it. I certainly wasn't going to ask.*

I wiped my mouth with a paper napkin. "I'm surprised you came back to Porter's Bay. No way to stay in New York for the summer?"

Lisa's eyes dropped to her plate. "There are a bunch of ways. But I wanted to be close to my parents." She ran a hand through her hair. "I don't know. I was so anxious to get away from them. Then when I was in New York, I had a lot of time to think. It's too easy to blame them for everything that's gone on. I had a hand in it, too. Maybe somebody has to make the first move, y'know? I thought I'd give that a shot."

"How's it working out so far?"

"It's not. I've tried taking an interest in the office. I've tried talking about sports with my dad. I've tried getting Mom to open up. Nothing is working. We're exactly like we were."

"I'm sorry."

"Maybe that's how they want it. They're comfortable writing me off as Little Miss New York and putting all their eggs in Amy's basket. They don't want to try."

"Still plenty of summer left. Maybe something will happen."

"I've been waiting all my life. I don't think a few more months will make a difference." Lisa suddenly reached across the table and took my hand. "I've missed this. Just…sitting and talking with you. Phone calls are fine, and I'm always glad to get letters from you. But they don't replace this."

It was only at that moment, sitting in that little booth at Arthur's with Lisa once again holding my hand, that I realized how much I had been walking around feeling like half of me—the best half of me—had been cut away. I squeezed her hand.

"What do you want to do next?" I asked.

"Why don't we go for a walk? I haven't looked at the lake much since I got back."

We finished up our meals, and I drove us to the lake. Lisa was happy to walk along the beach, collecting various agates and small rocks to bring back to New York. She slipped her hand into mine. I was happy—something I had not truly been for a long time.

We decided to go for a drive. Lisa told me she had only really gone between her parents' house and the office (save for the occasional trip to The Hub) since she'd come home. It had only been a year, but she wanted to look around Porter's Bay again. We drove past the high school, the fairgrounds, Bennett Park, and The Hub. Eventually, the path wound up toward the bluffs overlooking the lake. I slowed as we reached the entrance to Revelation Bluff.

"Should we stop in?" I asked. "See the old place?"

Lisa slipped me a look. "Did you plan this?"

"We're just out for a drive," I said, waving my fingertips off the steering wheel, "and we wound up here. We don't have to go in."

"No, let's go," Lisa said.

I pulled in. There was the possibility our old spot would be occupied by some new couple. It was Saturday night, so more than a few spaces were occupied. But ours was still available. I squinted toward the far end of the road.

"Is that Rick Michaels' car?" I asked.

Lisa looked past me. "I think so. I knew he was staying in Porter's Bay, going to community college."

"The Fields of Gold lives."

I pulled into our old space. We got out and walked to the front of the car. The moon hovered brightly over the lake. It was like old times. Lisa laid her head on my shoulder.

"I've thought about this place," she said, "almost every day."

"It's not much compared to New York City."

"I wouldn't say that. New York is great, but…this place has so many memories."

"Good ones, I hope."

Lisa looked up at me. "Almost all of them are about you."

I turned to her. She held my gaze. I leaned in and kissed her. She pressed herself against me and gently ran her hands up and down my back. Things swiftly got more intense. I sat on the hood of the car, Lisa straddling me while she ran her hands around my stomach and rib cage. When we came up for air, she leaned her forehead against mine.

"Do you still have the sleeping bags in back?" Lisa asked.

"Pretty sure I do."

"Good."

She took my hand and led me toward the back of the car. I laid out the sleeping bags and we crawled inside. I stared into Lisa's eyes as I slipped on top of her.

"I love you," I said.

"I love you."

Afterwards, we lay in the sleeping bags, holding each other and not saying anything. Lisa was the first to suggest we go home. We dressed and climbed back into the front seat. The drive home was quiet. I wasn't sure if it was the old, comfortable silence or if this was something different. When I pulled up in front of Lisa's house, she grabbed my face and kissed me.

"I've missed you," she said. "I really have."

When she pulled back, there was something uncertain on her face, just for a moment. Then she slipped out of the car. I watched her dash up the steps and through the front door. I drove home, feeling better than I had in a while, trying to fight a creeping unease.

I didn't hear from Lisa the next day. Because of the silence, my mood swung back and forth as the day progressed. One minute, I'd remember the night before and be almost giddy. The next minute, that creeping unease would take over. When we were dating, Lisa called me every day. We weren't exactly dating, but what had the night before been? As the afternoon went along, I couldn't take the suspense anymore. I decided to surprise Lisa at home. Along the way, I stopped at The Hub to pick up some coffee.

Lisa's sister Amy answered the door. She was a shorter, less pretty version of Lisa (too many of her dad's genes in the ol' DNA), save that her hair was clipped short, and she didn't need glasses. She called up the stairs to Lisa, not even offering me a greeting. (Not a big deal. I don't remember many—if any—conversations with Amy). I stood alone at the front door. Lisa's parents didn't appear to be home. Lisa came down the stairs. I held up the to-go coffee from The Hub.

"Thought you could use a pick-me-up," I said.

Lisa forced a smile and looked away. My heart sank. I knew her well enough, even still, to know where this conversation was going. She took the coffee and guided me to the front steps.

"That's very nice of you," she said, biting her lip.

Foolishly, I plowed forward. "I just wanted to say hi. See if you want to do something tonight. Or maybe tomorrow."

Lisa took a breath. "I don't think that would be a good idea."

"If you're busy, we could wait until—"

"It's not that," Lisa said. "Last night was wonderful. It's the best I've felt in a long time. And not just…up at Revelation Bluff. I mean, the whole night. But I think it was a mistake."

In the years that followed, many women would refer to me as a mistake. *It never hurt worse than it did at that moment. Something froze up inside me. Lisa tried to make eye contact but didn't get there. I found myself slouching onto my back foot.*

"Oh," was all I got out.

"I'm sorry," Lisa said, wiping her face.

I tried to find something to say. There was a buzzing in my brain, like white noise. Thoughts were coming but not coalescing. I tried to keep my knees from buckling.

"It's just…I thought…"

Lisa put a hand on my arm, stopping me. "It would just be like last summer. Going our separate ways when it's all over. What would be the point? It would hurt all over again."

I slipped out of Lisa's grasp. "I get that." My voice sounded far away.

She looks past me. "Maybe it was a mistake coming back here. Just…everything." She reached for me again. "I'm really sorry."

For a moment, the fog cleared. I knew what I wanted to tell her. That I loved her. That the only truth I knew was her. That the only home I had was where she was. That being with her was the only thing that made sense. That if we could clear the bullshit, we could build on that. That maybe that was where happiness lay.

But I didn't tell her any of that. I wasn't sure Lisa wanted to hear it. She would go away from here, back to New York. She'd find happiness. Just not with me.

"It's okay," I said, not looking at her.

I walked down the front steps. I was halfway to my car when Lisa called to me.

"It was great," she said. "I just…"

I half-turned toward her. "I get it."

I climbed in my car. I looked toward the house. Lisa had gone back inside. I pulled away from the curb and drove home. I didn't look back.

The visitation is held at the Cease Funeral Home on First Avenue in Porter's Bay. I swear I am not making up the name of the funeral home. It's a family business with several locations in northern Minnesota. The snow has stopped by the time we pull up. I look longingly toward Nick's Corner Bar, just a few blocks away.

"Don't suppose you're carrying flask on you?" I say.

"Gave it up for lent," Lisa says.

I fuss with the suit. I've never been a fan of this thing. I try to check my tie in the rearview mirror, but I can't get a good look. Lisa's hands take over the operation.

"Let me," she says, straightening the tie. "You look good. Very handsome."

"Thank you," I say. "Last chance to come along."

"It's weird enough being in town without running into anyone. Or explaining why I'm here."

"Understood." I wave a hand toward the alley behind the building. "See if you can park by the backdoor. Just in case I need to grab the stick and run."

"Let's hope it doesn't come to that."

I step out of the car. Traffic is nonexistent on First Avenue right now, even though it's one of the main thoroughfares in Porter's Bay. A couple people I don't recognize congregate on the front steps of the funeral home. None of them acknowledge me as I duck into the building.

There isn't much to the funeral home. It's a square cement building with a glass front door. It was probably an undistinguished office building in another life. A couple steps take me up to the lobby. The carpeting is plain, and the walls are beige. A gregarious, straw-haired man points me toward room number three, where Rick's viewing is being held.

The first thing I notice is Rick's mom, a tiny, diminished, haggard-looking woman about a decade younger than my parents, standing in the corner. Her graying hair is pulled back and her skin hangs like parchment. She looks ravaged with grief. She receives visitors as best she can. Katie stands next to her. In another corner is the urn holding Rick's remains. Around the urn is a display which includes the hockey stick, a Porter's Bay hockey jersey with the name *Michaels* on the back, and a black and white picture of Rick scoring the state championship-winning goal. The guests are scattered around the room, all having the hushed, uncomfortable conversations one has at a visitation. I recognize a few guys from high school but have no desire to chat with them. I decide to pay my respects to Rick's mom. I mumble my name and condolences. She looks up at me, her eyes glassy.

"Joe Davis," she says, her voice thin and even. "Rick mentioned you. You're a writer."

"I am," I say. "Kind of."

"Rick really liked you. Thank you for coming."

Another guest moves in. I step over to Katie, who seems subdued and uncomfortable. (That makes at least two of us.) She wears a black dress, and her hair is clipped back. We shake hands, perfunctorily.

I give her a sympathetic look. "Hanging in there?"

"It's an interesting group," Katie says. "They either don't know Rick and I are divorced or they didn't know Rick was married in the first place. I'm looking forward to getting out of here and having a martini or seven." She looks past me. "Where's Lisa?"

"She's around. She didn't feel comfortable coming in."

"I get that. Boy, do I get that."

I move on, once again crowded out by other guests. I make my way over to the display for Rick. The stick, in its repaired state, is propped on a stand. Next to it is a small card reading *Property of the United States Hockey Hall of Fame.*

Son of a bitch. I was going to ask for the stick once the visitation was over. I have to assume the Hockey Hall of Fame is not going to let some goofball writer handle their property. I'm going to have to steal it. It's just a matter of getting it out of here without anybody noticing. How the hell am I going to pull that off? It's not like I can slip it into my coat pocket. Someone stands next to me. Great. Now I have to plot *and* make uncomfortable conversation.

Imagine my surprise when I turn and see my brother Owen.

He's three years younger and two inches shorter than me. He gets the stockiness from Dad and the sandy hair and needle nose from Mom. Like me, he wears the only suit he owns, and he doesn't seem any more comfortable with it. He keeps his voice down.

"What are you doing here?" Owen asks.

"Rick was a friend of mine. What are *you* doing here?"

"We played football and baseball together in high school. He was a good guy."

I suspect it also has something to do with Owen now owning Davis Hardware and attempting to succeed my father as a pillar of the community. (I hear he's having indifferent success in that venture.) I look around the room.

"Are Mom and Dad here?" I ask.

"They stopped by earlier," Owen says. "Did you tell them you were coming?"

"No. I'm just going to slip in and out of town. Didn't want to bother them."

I know it sounds fishy the second it comes out of my mouth. I've never set foot in Porter's Bay without stopping to see Mom and Dad. And a *bother* is the last thing my mom would consider a visit from me. Owen knows this as well as I do. His suspicious look bears an uncanny resemblance to our father's. But he lets it go.

"I'll tell them you said hi," he says.

I fidget with the cuffs on my suit. "Thanks. I assume Mary is home with the kids?"

"And the cat."

My eyebrows go up. The kids, Ty and Natalie, I know about. I am, in fact, Ty's godfather. However, when I last saw Owen, his household was pet-free.

"You have a cat?" I ask.

Owen struggles not to roll his eyes. "Got it a month ago. Mary and the kids had been bothering me about getting a pet. I wanted a dog, maybe a hunting dog. Mary didn't want to deal with a big dog, and she's home with the kids most of the time. So, we got a cat. He's a little older. Six. Good around kids."

"What's his name?"

Owen barely opens his mouth as he says it. "Stampy."

The corners of my mouth go up. "Stampy?"

"It was Ty's idea. The cat came with the name Austin, but Ty wants us to call him Stampy. I guess there's a YouTuber named Stampy Longnose. You heard of him?"

"I have."

"Ty's a big fan. That's why we went with Stampy."

I can barely hide my amusement. "That's…that's very cute."

Cute is a word I've never used in any context regarding my younger brother. And if you knew my dour, humorless sibling, you'd realize it cuts him to the quick more than any other. Owen appears as if he wants to crawl into the floor. He looks at his watch (yes, he still wears a watch), probably wondering how much longer he needs to put in an appearance.

"Weird that I just saw Rick a few weeks ago," he says.

I snap him a look. "Here in Porter's Bay?"

Owen looks annoyed. "Of course. I don't have time to go anyplace else."

"Where did you see him?"

"Outside the store. He was getting into his car. I said hi. We talked for a few minutes."

"About what?"

"Nothing, really. Just about what we were up to. He was working for Bill Longson."

Owen frowns. Politically, he's like my dad, somewhere in the middle, leaning a tad to the right. But the radicalized politics of Longson's ilk has made him bedfellows with liberal pantywaists like me.

"Did Rick say what he was up to?" I ask.

"No. He was going to drive up to Revelation Bluff. Kind of weird, if you ask me. It's too cold to be up there. Especially with the wind coming in. But who knows? Rick didn't get back here much. Might have been his only chance to do it."

Interesting. I look toward the stick, trying to think of a way to get the damn thing out of here. But something else occurs to me. Various things coalesce in my mind. Rick's last words. Katie talking about when she had been here. Owen bumping into Rick a few weeks ago. Son of a bitch. I might know where to go next. But I have to get a hold of the stick first.

"Good seeing you," I tell Owen. "Excuse me. I need to talk to someone."

I start to step away. Owen grabs my arm, stopping me.

"Joe, is something going on?" he asks, concern replacing suspicion in his eyes.

I hesitate. Owen's not an idiot. It's hard to B.S. him. I don't even try. And I promise you it's not a diversionary tactic when I give him a hug. He stands there, shocked, then tentatively returns it. When we break, I pat him on the shoulder.

"I'm going to slip out of here shortly," I say. "I need you to roll with whatever happens next. And for the love of God—"

"Don't tell Mom and Dad," he says. "I get it."

I slip away from Owen and make my way across the room. I avoid making eye contact with anyone, lest I get pulled into a conversation with someone I haven't seen in years and didn't much care for in the first place. I sidle up to Katie.

"You got a minute to chat?" I say.

"I would love that," she says.

We make our way into the hall. No one seems to notice us. Katie looks tired and desperately in need of the drink she mentioned earlier. I keep my voice down.

"I need to get ahold of the stick," I say. "Is it being guarded at all?"

"The guys from the Hockey Hall of Fame have someone watching it. Is it important?"

"It might be the key to figuring out what information Rick had." I look back toward the room. "There's a backdoor in there. Maybe I can grab the stick and run if we find some way to create a distraction."

Katie glances down the hallway. "I have an idea. Just go back in and get close to the stick. Be ready to move."

"How will I know when it's time?"

"Trust me. You won't miss it."

I'll take her word on it. I walk back into the room. Katie doesn't follow me. I position myself near Rick's display, trying to look appropriately somber. A second later, an ear-splitting ring fills the entire building. People reach for their ears and look around, confused. The sandy haired gentleman appears in the doorway.

"That's the fire alarm, folks," he says, his high-pitched voice trying (and failing) to project an air of calm. "If we could please make our way to the exits."

There's a moment where everyone is giving the funeral director their undivided attention. It's my opening. I yank the stick off its stand and run for the backdoor.

I come out into a small parking lot and hustle down the alley behind the building. The rental car is visible. I struggle with the stick, trying to keep it out of sight. I run for the car, my footsteps echoing on the pavement. I hop into the passenger seat and hold up the stick.

"I got it," I tell her. "And I think I know where the file is."

It's not Lisa who answers. Instead, a clipped voice from the backseat says, "That's good. We can all find it together."

I slowly turn to look. Mr. Reynard is the backseat. His pistol is aimed at Lisa's head.

And here I thought the visitation would be the worst part of the evening.

CHAPTER FOURTEEN

INTERLUDE, SOMETIME IN MY TWENTIES

My parents always spoke highly of Lisa when we were dating. In the years that followed our breakup, though, they rarely mentioned her. I wondered sometimes if this was out of respect for me or if they were somehow veiling a long-hidden disapproval. Either way, it wasn't a subject I felt like broaching.

Whenever I visited, my mom and I had an unspoken ritual with meals. She'd have breakfast ready before I came downstairs, so there could be no debate about making breakfast for myself. Everyone ate dinner together. For lunch, she would offer to make something, I would decline. She would insist. I would acquiesce. This ritual continues to this day.

On this particular day, I was eating a BLT with just the right touch of mayo (nobody makes a sandwich better than my mother). Mom stood in the little nook where the pantry and the refrigerator were housed, sipping coffee (which, sadly, is the worst coffee known to man). We were quiet until she asked me a question out of the blue.

"Do you ever talk to Lisa?"

I don't know what prompted her to ask. It had been years since Lisa's name had come up in conversation. She hadn't yet achieved the kind of celebrity that gave the town reflected glory. And I certainly hadn't mentioned her in a long time. But I was no longer a surly teenager who would simply mutter an answer, then drop the whole subject. I set my sandwich down.

"We say hi on social media every now and again," I said. "I haven't actually talked to her, though. Why do you ask?"

"I was just curious. You two made a nice couple. I liked her a lot."

"So did I."

"You loved her."

I snapped a look at Mom. It wasn't like her to call me out on something. And I never gave her a lot of credit for being observant (at least, not until then). I turned away.

"I was seventeen," I said. "I didn't know what love was."

"Do you now?" Mom asked.

I could only think Damn, Mom is working me like a speedbag. *I shrugged and said, "Guess I don't."*

Mom sat down at the table with me. She was half-turned away, which told me that her mood was more contemplative than confiding. "You are the only one of my children I got to see fall in love."

That confused me, since I was the only one of her children that wasn't married. I set my sandwich aside. "How do you mean?"

"Kevin was living in California when he and Jordan started dating. The first time I met Jordan was the day before the wedding. And Owen…Owen is a wonderful boy, but he's very stoic. I know he loves Mary, but…"

"He's pretty good at hiding it?"

"Let's just say not expressing it. But you? You wore it on your sleeve. You couldn't have hidden it if you tried. You couldn't hide the heartbreak, either. I haven't seen either of those on your face since." She sipped her coffee. *"I just wonder sometimes."*

I didn't know what to say. Mom, though, dropped the subject and said she had to get dinner started. I wanted to know more about why she was asking. Instead, I went back to my sandwich. I never did ask why she brought the subject up. Maybe she was just bored.

Or maybe even Mom felt Lisa was the one that got away.

Right now, getting away is chief in my thoughts. I'm just not sure how to pull it off.

Lisa takes the rental car out of the alley and down First Avenue. We don't have a destination yet. Reynard remains huddled into his black coat, giving off a casually threatening vibe.

"You can give me the hockey stick," he says. "You make even the slightest move I don't like, and I will put a bullet through your girlfriend's head. You got me?"

I'm not going to mention Lisa's long-expired status as my girlfriend or that shooting the driver is likely to lead to a low-speed accident that benefits nobody. No point in calling his bluff. I hand the hockey stick to Reynard. He sets it on the seat beside him, never moving the gun.

"I'm guessing this is where Michaels hid the tape," Reynard says. "Take me to where the file is."

Lisa looks to me for directions. I keep my eyes forward.

"Revelation Bluff," I say, "In The Fields of Gold."

Lisa takes a right at Howard Street and cruises toward Lake Drive. Silence hangs over us. Lisa glances into the rearview mirror.

"You followed us up here?" she asks.

Reynard nods. "Kept an eye on your boyfriend's apartment. I thought you might lead me to the stuff Michaels stole."

I turn slightly, trying not to make any sudden moves. "And you followed us to Stockholm?"

"No, I figured that one out on my own," Reynard says. "Just my fucking luck that you two were there."

Yeah, doesn't everybody involved in that shit feel lucky? Lisa takes a left on Lake Drive, heading north out of town.

"You know what's on the tape?" she asks Reynard.

Reynard's voice remains calm and steady. "None of anybody's fucking business is exactly what's on the tape. End of story."

That ends the Q-and-A portion of our program. We now return you to our regularly scheduled silence. A few miles later, Revelation Drive comes up on our left. We go almost straight uphill right after the turn. The trees on the right screen the lake. The entrance finally comes up on the left. Lisa maneuvers the rental car down the trail through the bluff. Nothing has changed. Nobody else is here. We pass our old space. Lisa and I give it a glance. It would be nostalgic under any circumstances other than these. Finally, The Fields of Gold looms ahead. Lisa eases the car to a halt. Reynard sits up.

"That it?" he asks.

"Yep," I say. "I think it's buried somewhere in there."

"Let's look," Reynard says.

We get out of the car. Lisa and I fire up the flashlights on our phones. Reynard follows us. For the moment, we're several steps ahead of him, though we have no place to run. Lisa leans her head slightly toward me.

"You realize if we find that file, we're not walking out of here," she says.

"I know," I say. "But we're not in a position to go on strike."

We walk between the two trees that mark the entrance to the Fields of Gold. The place itself is just a rectangular patch of earth with a not particularly great view of the lake. (Although, to be fair, looking at the lake was the least of anyone's concerns when they were here.) Our footsteps crunch on the fallen leaves. An occasional twig snaps. A cold breeze ruffles the mostly bare branches. Far below, waves crash against the shore. Lisa and I come to a halt.

"What are we looking for?" she asks.

"A tree with Katie's name carved on it."

Lisa's flashlight plays over the thick collection of jack pines and says, "Swell."

We split up and each take a side of the rectangle. Lisa moves slowly, perhaps hoping an opportunity to escape will present itself. Reynard casually stands between the two trees. He seems to read our thoughts.

"Don't get any ideas about running," he says.

"The only thing beyond here is a cliff," I say. "You run out of room pretty quickly."

"Good for you," Reynard says.

Lisa stops at a tree in one corner. A single glance from her and I know she's found the tree. She pretends to ignore it and looks around the bushes. We can't let Reynard know the location of the file. The gunman lets out a disgusted breath.

"It can't be that fuckin' hard to find," he says. "Get a move on."

Lisa reaches the edge of the perimeter and moves toward me. I parallel her movement. We wind up a few feet away from each other. We drop our voices.

"The tree is right behind me," she says. "*Rick + Katie 4ever.* And there's a little heart around it. And some turned up earth under the tree. It doesn't look deep. Won't take long to find the file." She tries to keep her breathing even. "You have any brilliant ideas?"

"I have ideas. None of them could be classified as brilliant."

"So…"

"We better hope for a miracle."

Reynard calls to us. "What's the hold up? It's there or it isn't."

Lisa and I catch eyes. We're almost out of time.

Probably good that our miracle arrives.

At first, I think Reynard has turned his flashlight on us. Then the light gets brighter, and I realize it's more than just Reynard's flashlight. A pair of headlights are coming toward us. Reynard realizes it, too. He spins around.

I start to say something, but Lisa is already on my wavelength. She douses the flashlight. I follow suit. We plunge into the weeds, disappearing into the darkness.

"What the fuck?" Reynard shouts, dropping the hockey stick.

The headlights come closer. I peek through the weeds. Reynard has his gun drawn. He's aiming at the headlights coming toward us. Whoever is driving has saved our asses, but their own is in deep trouble. Reynard starts firing. The headlights veer from side to side. I wonder if the driver has been hit. But the car keeps coming. Reynard keeps firing.

Lisa nearly has her face buried in the weeds. "We've got to do something."

"I'm on it."

I feel around. My hand closes on a rock. It's a little smaller than a baseball and much heavier. I get to my feet. Reynard still has his back to me. I chuck the thing, side arm and off my back foot, just like they teach you not to do. It doesn't come as any shock when the rock sails past Reynard and strikes one of the trees. He spins around and aims at me. But Reynard has lost track of the car. He looks over his shoulder just before the car reaches him. He jumps slightly, landing on the hood. Then he rolls off and hits the ground. The car comes to a halt.

Imagine my surprise when my brother Owen jumps out.

Reynard gets up. Owen hits him with a right cross. Reynard staggers to one side but doesn't go down. He tries to bring the gun up. Owen kicks him in the hand, knocking the gun loose. He tries a takedown, but Reynard rolls through it and flips Owen away. They hop up. Reynard throws a side kick that catches Owen square in the chest. Owen sprawls out on the ground, trying to catch his breath.

I make a break for the gun, leaping over Owen's carcass. Reynard and I dive for it. He elbows me in the face, catching me below my left eye. Everything stops. I land flat on my face and roll over. Reynard stands over me, the gun aimed right at my head.

Then Reynard stiffens up. He drops to his knees and falls forward. Behind him, Lisa is holding Rick's once again broken hockey stick. I sit up.

"She shoots, she scores," I say.

Lisa hefts the half of the stick still in her hand. "Nice of you to avoid the obvious line."

Owen slowly gets up. "You guys okay?" he asks, trying to get his breath back.

"I'm fine," I say. I take the gun from Reynard, who's enjoying a nice snooze in the loam. I hold it between my thumb and forefinger, like I've just scooped up after a dog. "Nice driving," I tell Owen. "How the hell did you know to come here?"

"I followed you," Owen says. "You think I didn't know you were up to something? Especially after that bullshit fire alarm."

Since Owen is more comfortable with weaponry than I am, I hand him the gun. He puts the safety on and slips the gun into the waistband of his jeans. He looks over Reynard's unconscious form.

"We need to call the police," Owen says.

I pull out my phone. "Is there cell service up here?"

Owen frowns. "I don't think so. No."

Naturally, my nerdy brother hasn't been to Revelation Bluff in years, so he wouldn't know about the cell service. Given that he just saved our asses, I'll let it slide. Lisa pulls something out of the remaining half of the stick. I glance at it.

"The tape," I say.

"Let's see what's on it," Lisa says.

She goes to the rental car and rummages around her bag until she finds a small handheld tape recorder. She pops the tape in and presses Play. We gather around and listen.

A female voice (Zoe's, I'm assuming) comes in first. **Is it true?**

Longson's voice follows. **You stuck your nose in it. You tell me.**

Zoe: **You killed Mark Gardner. You killed a U.S. Senator.**

Longson: **No. Jeremiah Kincade killed a U.S. Senator.**

Zoe: **You gave him money. You gave his family money. You arranged the whole thing. I have proof.**

Longson: **Don't be so dramatic.** Here, Longson pauses. **You going to write about this?**

Zoe: **I have to. I…I can't just let this go.**

After a few moments, Longson's voice becomes warmer, his volume a little lower. **Do you love me, Zoe?**

Zoe: **That's—**

Longson: **Do you *love* me?**

A moment passes. Zoe's voice is soft, breaking. **You know I do.**

Longson: **Then why would you want to hurt me?**

Zoe: **I…I don't want to. I really don't.**

There's silence. Then Longson can be heard letting a breath out through his nose. **You know what, Zoe? I don't believe you.**

The next thing we hear is screaming. It seems to go on for a long time. Then a crash.

End of tape.

Lisa switches off the player. "He had Mark Gardner killed. Then Zoe found out and he killed her."

"We need to get the file," I say. "That's where Zoe put the proof."

Before we can get the file, though, Reynard reappears.

Such is our preoccupation with the tape that we don't hear him coming. Lisa lets out a little gasp. Reynard hits Owen square in the back with a flying knee. Owen crashes into Lisa, who drops the tape recorder. It lands in the leaves. I reach for it, but Reynard grabs my coat and throws me backwards. I land in the gravel, skinning up my hands.

Reynard takes the gun off Owen. He spots the tape recorder, then raises a foot to stomp it. Lisa dives at Reynard, stopping him. Owen scoops the tape recorder out of the leaves and rolls away. Reynard slips behind Lisa and puts the barrel of the gun against her jaw. He pulls her back, creating some distance.

Reynard's voice is preternaturally calm. "This is what's going to happen. You're going to give me the tape. You're going to toss it over here so that it lands at my feet. Any other move from either of you and I blow this lady's head off. Are we clear?"

I hold up my hands. Lisa moves her head slightly, trying to tell me not give in to Reynard. I silently apologize for not doing as she asks. There's no way I'm sacrificing her for the tape. Owen nods, letting Reynard know he'll play ball.

Reynard seems satisfied. "Good. Throw it to me."

Owen pops the tape out of the player. He hefts the tape in one hand. Lisa's body sags. Then she throws an elbow into Reynard's gut.

Reynard expels some air. The gun moves away from Lisa's head. She throws an elbow to Reynard's face. Something goes crunch. Reynard stumbles back, holding his nose. Lisa swings a kick toward his balls. Reynard catches Lisa's leg. She falls on her back. He aims the gun at her.

"No!" I shout, running toward them.

Before I get there, though, the tape recorder hits Reynard right in the ear.

I have to give Owen credit: all those years playing shortstop were not wasted. Reynard cries "Fuck!" and grabs his ear. The gun is lowered. Lisa boots it out of his hand. She crawls toward the gun. Reynard lurches toward it as well. I leap over Lisa and hit Reynard with a tackle, sending us into the leaves. When we hit the ground, I roll off Reynard. He reaches for the gun, but Lisa gets it first. Reynard grabs her wrist. They struggle.

I grab Reynard around the neck, hoping to pull him off Lisa. He rams the back of his head into my cheekbone, the same damn spot he hit earlier. My grip slackens, but I hold on. Reynard draws his left fist back to swing at Lisa. I move my grip to his elbow, preventing him from throwing the punch. Reynard is stretched out on the ground, stuck between me and Lisa.

Then Owen reappears, toting part of the broken hockey stick. He stands over Reynard, hoisting the stick like he's a Samurai warrior.

Until Reynard kicks him in the balls.

It's a clean shot, wingtip to testes. Owen's body curls around his noogs, and his eyes go unfocused. He drops the stick and crashes into the leaves. Timberrrr.

Reynard flicks an elbow into Lisa's face. She lets out a sharp cry and loses hold of the gun. Reynard yanks it away from her. He shakes himself loose of me and gets to his feet.

"Where is the fucking tape?" he says.

I hop up and run at Reynard, lowering my shoulder. I hit him in the midsection. We go down and roll to the edge of the brush bordering the bluffs. Reynard tries to raise the pistol, but I grab his arm. I have to keep him from getting a clear shot at me. Reynard brings up a knee, hitting me square in the ribs. My whole left side is fire. I gasp for breath. Reynard gets to his feet. He takes aim at me.

Something whistles over my head. The broken half of the hockey stick hits Reynard square in the face. He stumbles backward and disappears over the bluff. His voice echoes as he falls. Then everything is silent.

Lisa gasps and drops the hockey stick. We crawl to the edge of the bluff and look down. There's no sign of Reynard.

"What's the next thing he'd hit?" Lisa asks.

"Lake Drive," I say. "And it's a long way down."

Lisa tries to catch her breath. "I didn't mean to. I just…"

I put a hand on her shoulder. "You hit him. He fell. That was it."

Owen staggers up behind us, one hand still on his inflamed nutsack. "What happened?"

I look over the edge again. "Reynard is gone." I shake it off. "We've got to get the file."

We run to the tree and start digging. Lisa is right. The hole isn't deep. It only takes a minute or so to find what we're looking for. The file is in a plastic bag. Lisa opens it with trembling hands and pages through it. Owen and I hold our flashlights over it so Lisa can read. It's all there. Wire transfers, conversations through intermediaries, letters from Kincade to his family. It's unmistakable. Kincade was acting on orders from Bill Longson when he arranged the plane crash that killed Senator Mark Gardner. Longson can be tied to the deaths of Zoe Court and Rick Michaels. And possibly Roger Neill. Lisa lowers the file. She leans her forehead against the tree. Her voice comes out in a whisper.

"We got 'em, Rick. We got 'em."

I put a hand on her shoulder. Lisa slides into my embrace. We stay that way, and the snow once again begins to fall.

EPILOGUE

THE YEARS SINCE

Despite the nasty finish to our date, Lisa and I **did** *stay in touch. At least for a while. She called me before the summer was over, and we chatted for a bit. The subject of the one night stand was tacitly avoided. Lisa told me her summer had not gone as she hoped. She and her family were no closer, and she sensed they were relieved she was going back to New York. She was going to look for something in New York the following summer, just to avoid coming back to Porter's Bay and spending more time with her family. Part of me was saddened by that. A larger part of me was relieved.*

There was no goodbye this time when Lisa left Porter's Bay. Once she was back in New York, she continued to correspond, a little more furiously this time. Maybe she wanted my forgiveness. Maybe she wanted to keep some *connection to Porter's Bay. Maybe she was just lonely. Whatever the case, the calls and letters came frequently that fall. Maybe because of what happened the previous summer, I became more acutely aware of how downcast I was every time Lisa contacted me. I began to realize I was happier when I wasn't in contact with her. Maybe that's cowardly, and I wouldn't blame anyone who threw that accusation at me. But it got to be too easy. I returned her letters at a ratio of one for every three. I dragged my feet in returning her phone calls. I'm not sure if Lisa got frustrated and gave up or if she sensed I didn't want to be in contact with her. Whatever the case, the letters and phone calls began to dry up as the year went along. By the next summer, they had stopped entirely.*

I followed Lisa's career from a distance. I'm not sure if she did the same. The year we turned twenty-eight (coincidentally, the same year The Daily Planet *hired me), Lisa broke a story about a Hollywood honcho with a pattern of sexual abuse. It led to her being hired by Metro Communications. Shortly after that, she took down a politician who was receiving massive kickbacks from a company determined to pollute the atmosphere. A few years later, she broke the big story of her career: a major company bilking its employees' retirement accounts in order to both stay solvent and pay massive bonuses to its executives. Lisa made a few appearances on a variety of cable news networks. She probably could have found a side gig as a talking head for hire, but she didn't want that. She was a reporter, first, last and always. She was more interested in the work than in celebrity.*

One day a handful of years ago, I got a friend request from Lisa, accompanied by the message Remember me? *I replied with* As if I could forget *and accepted the request. Since then, Lisa and I correspond from time to time. We keep it light, just checking in. I find, as I have many times over the years, that glib is a great defense mechanism.*

I try not to think about Lisa very often. It brings up too many memories, too many emotions I can't really define. I always respond to her messages. Otherwise, I try to keep thoughts of her at arm's length. It's just easier that way.

At least, I think it is.

I sincerely doubt Senator Bill Longson believes in (or is even familiar with) the concept of poetic irony. After so much homicide and attempted homicide in order to avoid a campaign-killing *October Surprise*, that's exactly what he's hit with. But in typical narcissistic fashion, he doesn't believe he's done anything wrong. In an ironic twist, the irony is lost on him.

Lisa spends many hours on Zoom calls with her editors at Metro Communications. Within twenty-four hours of her first article appearing, both federal and state authorities have opened investigations into Longson's role in the deaths of Mark Gardner, Zoe Court, and Rick Michaels. Within forty-eight hours, he's been arrested. A favorable judge allows bail to be set, and Longson spends a good deal of the family fortune to pay it. Still, his mugshot is splashed all over the internet, cable news stations, and newspapers.

Longson continues to campaign, using every stop to decry the witch hunt designed to steal the election from him. If it *is* some liberal conspiracy, it's a remarkably successful one. In a matter of days, Longson's standing in the polls goes from a lead of fifteen to twenty points to a deficit of fifteen to twenty points. Other Republican candidates treat him like a leper. Even if Longson pulls off a miraculous comeback in the next few weeks and retains his senate seat, leaders of both parties (one more than the other, confessedly) are seriously discussing not seating him. Longson has dismissed this ostracism by calling his former allies *fair weather fiends* (which is as close to clever wordsmithing as he's likely to come).

Longson has his own issues with loyalty, though. He fires Madeline Hauser, who is under investigation herself, as his campaign manager. Many campaign workers follow her out the door. With no qualified politico willing to helm the sinking ship, Longson turns to a local right wing talk show host (and close friend) with no previous experience. What the campaign lacks in savvy, it now makes up for in sheer volume. While a certain percentage of voters are still doggedly devoted to the Senator, the general perception of him by the public cannot be ignored: he's a criminal under investigation.

Mr. Reynard's body is found on Lake Drive, far below Revelation Bluff. Turns out his real name is Edgar Uric, and he's got a criminal record longer than my...well, it's long. There isn't much of a paper trail connecting him to the Longson campaign. But many staffers, anxious to avoid prosecution, are willing to testify they've seen him at campaign HQ, chatting with senior campaign officials. Reynard's movements coincide with both campaign stops and the mysterious deaths of certain people in and around the campaign.

While Lisa could get a hotel room again, now that the danger has passed, she chooses to remain at my apartment as she works on the story. Eventually, things slow to a near halt. The investigations are ongoing and promise to drag out. Very little new info comes to light. Lisa makes plans to go back to New York, needing only to return here as newsworthy items pop up.

"I've got to look in on my plants," she says, packing a bag that rests on the futon.

I sit at my desk chair, fighting off a sinking feeling. "You have plants?"

"As soon as I buy them, I will. It's been on my to-do list for a while."

I turn to the windows while Lisa packs. The day is bright and sunny. Halloween is right around the corner and after that, Election Day. For once, I'm looking forward to it. I'd drive Lisa to the airport, but she has the rental car to return. Once she's done packing, she's leaving. "You'll have your place back!" she told me. I guess that's something.

My cell phone rings. I pick it up from the breakfast bar. It's Carol. She greets me in a celebratory tone.

"You're in the clear," she says.

That's cryptic enough. "In the clear for what?"

"The movie. You and Lars. You're not going to be fired."

Weird. During almost any other stretch of time, the movie would have been my top priority. But we haven't had a production meeting in the last few weeks, and I haven't given it a thought. Hearing about the movie now is like hearing news from a foreign country.

"What happened?" I ask. "I assume you Buttering the Biscuit with Fabio had something to do with this?"

Carol lets out a cluck of disgust. "Buttering the Biscuit. Nice. You kiss your mother with that mouth?"

"Now who's being disgusting?" I swivel my chair around. "What happened?"

"Ollie shot himself in the foot. He was sleeping with Frankie. And she really fell for him. From what Fabio tells me, she sleeps with a lot of guys, but it's rare for her to get attached."

"Must keep the family therapist in clover."

"Probably. Anyway, Frankie wasn't the only one Ollie was sleeping with. In fact, she wasn't the only one he was sleeping with in her room at the Piper house."

"Whoa."

Carol, who once caught a boyfriend in a similar position, is not entirely unsympathetic. "After she got done chasing Ollie and his girlfriend around the grounds with a weed-whacker, Frankie decided to break things off."

"Sounds like Ollie was lucky that's all that was broken off."

"Then Frankie decided to fire Ollie. Fabio went along with it. You and Lars are safe and still onboard."

"That is good to hear," I say. "Thanks for putting in a good word for us."

"Don't mention it. I'm looking forward to the next production meeting."

"Oh? You're going to be there?"

"Of course," Carol says. "Remember what I said about you, Lars and me being a package deal? I was serious. So is Fabio. He wants me to be part of the team as well."

All I can muster up is, "Oh. Great."

"And I've got plenty of ideas," Carol says. "Starting with the women in the script. You've got a real sausage-fest going on. The women need to be in stronger positions. And we really need to go over these sex scenes. Too explicit. Too degrading. We need to rethink the whole thing."

Something I need to make clear: I have the utmost respect for Carol. Seriously, my respect is the most *ut*. But with two financial backers and now *two* friends onboard, the last thing this clambake needs is another opinion. I try not to sound dismayed.

"That's…lovely," I say.

Carol rings off, chuckling as she does. I set the phone on the desk. Lenny and Squiggy float around my legs. Clearly, they're not happy Lisa is leaving. She pauses in her packing.

"Everything okay with the movie?" she asks.

"Depends on who you ask," I say.

The front door opens and Lars glides in. He gives Lisa a small bow, which she returns. The cats have the good sense to clear out. Lars's smug look matches the one in Carol's voice.

"Greetings and salutations, my friends," he says. "I trust your voyage into the world of political corruption is coming to an end? I want to get back to work on the movie."

"I just heard about that from Carol," I say. "Sounds like we're in business."

"I hate to say I told you so. But I *did* say that if we gave Ollie enough rope, he'd hang himself."

I'm not sure Lars's strategy involved Ollie rutting with one of the producers, then cheating on her. But I'll let him have his moment. Whatever it takes to get Ollie off the picture and common sense to move forward again.

"I guess we'll have to find a new director," I say.

Lars wags one of his long fingers. "Already taken care of. We have hired a new director, and he is me. And it is good."

Wow. We've managed to turn a minor *Ishtar* into a five-alarm *Waterworld*. Lisa covers a laugh. Even *she* can see what kind of idea this is. I try to stay upright in my chair.

"*You* are the new director?" I ask.

"I am indeed," Lars says, his self-satisfaction likely visible from space. "I put it out there for Fabio and Frankie, and they loved the idea."

I have to look on the bright side: this is *still* better than working with Ollie. Lars, at least, might be willing to compromise. There was no hope that would ever happen with Ollie. Maybe I just have to get over my misgivings.

"I offer you my congratulations," I say, "and I look forward to working with you."

Lars gives that a slight bow. "And I with you, my friend. Speaking of which, we should meet later. I want to go over the script. We need some major changes. All this stuff Ollie was after was impractical. We have to get back to what this movie is about: raw, naked sex."

I do a double-take. "Raw…"

"Naked sex. As I said. After all, what is a vampire movie without seduction? And what is seduction without copious amounts of copulating? And what is…?"

"I think I follow you," I say.

Lars spins around, ready to move to the front door. Before he gets there, Lisa holds out her hand, stopping him.

"What happened with Mrs. Hanratty?" she asks.

Lars spins back around and puts his hands in his pockets. "All is well, Ms. Lisa. I did what you suggested and talked to Mrs. Hanratty. Turns out she's a musician. When I finally confessed what I was doing, she was fascinated by it. And she wants to help."

I cock my head to one side. "Help you score porno films?"

"Yes. We've had a few sessions. She's actually quite talented. A multi-instrumentalist. Plays by ear. Enjoys porn. She checks all the boxes."

Great. Lisa seems amused. I'm tempted to remind her Lars was following *her* suggestion. But Lars found a way out of his conundrum, so I'll take this as a win.

"I'm very happy for you," I tell him. "Just a word of advice: make sure Mrs. Hanratty doesn't get the wrong idea about your relationship."

Lars seems confused. "Wrong idea? In what way?"

"You're working on…very intimate material. Someone might get…"

"Horny?" Lars asks.

"I, uh, I guess that was the word I was looking for."

"Not a concern at all. We're already doing it."

Thank God I wasn't sipping my coffee. I'd have choked on it. As it stands, I nearly choke on the bile that comes up. I try to get my breath back.

"You and she are doing…?"

"It?"

"It."

"Indeed." Lars waggles his eyebrows for added effect.

"How old is Mrs. Hanratty?"

"I prefer to think of her as *experienced* rather than *old*," Lars says, "but I would venture to call her hella experienced."

Even Lisa looks shocked, and she's been in a war zone. Lars, though, gives off a glow of contentment, so who am I to judge? (Not that I'll let that stop me.)

"Best of luck to you both," I say.

"Thank you, brother," Lars glides over to Lisa. He takes her hand and kisses it. "Pleasure to meet you, madam. Safe travels."

Lisa curtsies in return. "Thank you. Take care."

"Always."

Lars glides out the front door, flipping it shut behind him. Lisa giggles and returns to packing. I get up from the desk and stroll into the kitchen for some coffee.

"You sure you don't want anything to take with you?" I ask.

"I appreciate that, but I can't take anything on the plane. And it's not that long a drive to the airport."

Lisa's right. I'm not even sure why I'm even offering. I remind myself of my mom, offering endless things just as I'm trying to get on the road. I always thought it was because she wanted to keep me there as long as possible. Huh. I think I get it now.

My phone rings on the breakfast bar. It's Mike. This ought to be fun. Mike starts talking before I do. He sighs and says, "It's over."

I grab a seat at the breakfast bar. "You and Gillian?"

"No, me and Moira. But also, me and Gillian."

I knew we'd get here. I haven't had much chance to talk to Mike over the last few weeks. As far as I knew, he was still cavorting with both sisters. Moira confessed she wasn't really testing Mike or trying him out. She was just attracted to bad boys.

"What happened?" I ask.

"Gillian found out about me and Moira," Mike says. "She broke things off. We were at The Tav when it happened. She threw a saltshaker at me."

"Ouch. Sorry to hear that, man. What happened with you and Moira?"

Mike hesitates. "See, when Gillian broke up with me, I ran after her and tried to talk her out of it. I said she was the one I really liked and that everything with me and Moira had been a mistake. Anyway, I got really wound up and I might have…started crying."

I'm so glad Mike isn't here. He wouldn't like to see my intense amusement. "I didn't think you had it in you," I say.

"I know. I haven't cried since the last time the Vikings lost a conference championship game. And at least that was for a good reason."

"How did Gillian take it?"

"She called me a pussy and kicked me in the shin. I guess she likes bad boys, too. She confronted Moira. They had a big fight. Gillian told her about me crying. Then they had a big laugh over it. Now they're the best of friends and neither of them wants to see me again." He sighs. "It isn't a total loss. I got to sleep with twin sisters. That's legendary."

"It would be more legendary if you slept with them both at the same time."

"Hey, that's what I'm going to tell everybody. You going to rat me out?"

Great googly-moogly. Then again, who am I to stand between Mike and a great bullshit story? "Probably not. I'll take it up with my staff."

Mike sounds satisfied with that. "I'm going to The Tav later. Might as well check out the action. You want to meet me there? Maybe around eight?"

"Sounds good."

We ring off, and I toss the phone on the breakfast bar. Lisa finishes packing, zips up her bag and brings it over to the door. The cats make their way over to Lisa. She kneels down and pets them with each hand.

"I am going to miss you guys," she says.

"You're welcome to come back and see them," I say.

"I would like that." Lisa stands. "I'll probably be in the Cities at some point. Follow up on the Longson story."

"See him off to prison?"

"We can only hope."

We stand there, not saying anything. Time's up. After sixteen years apart, we've had…this. Whatever *this* is. Lisa bites the corner of her lip.

"I have to go," she says.

"I know."

Lisa slips her arms around me. Her face is tucked into the crook of my neck. We hold each other tightly. Neither of us says anything. Lisa's hand cups the back of my head. Finally, we part, slightly. She grips the front of my shirt. Her eyes don't quite meet mine.

"Please stay in touch," she says. "More than what we have been. I…I would like that."

"I'll make sure we do."

Squiggy takes the opportunity to rub up against Lisa's leg. She reaches down and gives Squiggy's ears a scratch.

"You take care of him," she says.

"I will," I say.

"I was talking to Squiggy."

"Of course."

Lisa scoops up her bag and opens the front door. She lingers in the doorway. I slip my hands in my pocket.

"Call me when you get back to New York," I say. "So I know you got home okay."

"Will do."

I look down. "This is going to sound weird, what with everything that's happened. But…" I look up. "It was really great. Seeing you again."

A broad smile crosses Lisa's face. "Maybe things will be more peaceful next time."

"I hope next time is soon."

"I would love that."

Lisa lingers for another moment then ducks down the stairway. I close the front door behind her and wander into the living room. The place looks exactly the same as it normally does. But it seems empty now.

Once upon a time, I would have been anxious to move on from any thoughts of Lisa. Now, I realize: I had never moved on from Lisa. Never got over her. The defense mechanism is no longer necessary. I guess this is what you call closure. I guess.

I step to the arch windows. The day is clouding over. Lisa crosses the street to her rental car. Just as she gets there, she looks up at my window. She gives me a little wave. I return it. She climbs into the rental car, wiping her face as she does.

A feeling rushes through me. I give it a voice, just to acknowledge it. To recognize its reality.

"I love you."

My breath fogs the window. Then fades.

THE END

Randall J. Funk is the writer of the Joe Davis Mystery series. He is also an actor, director and playwright. His plays include *The Hound of the Baskervilles*, *The Mudslinger Party*, and *Bring Me the Head of Dominic Papatola*. He teaches Composition at Arizona State University. He currently lives in St. Louis Park, MN, with his daughter Bea.